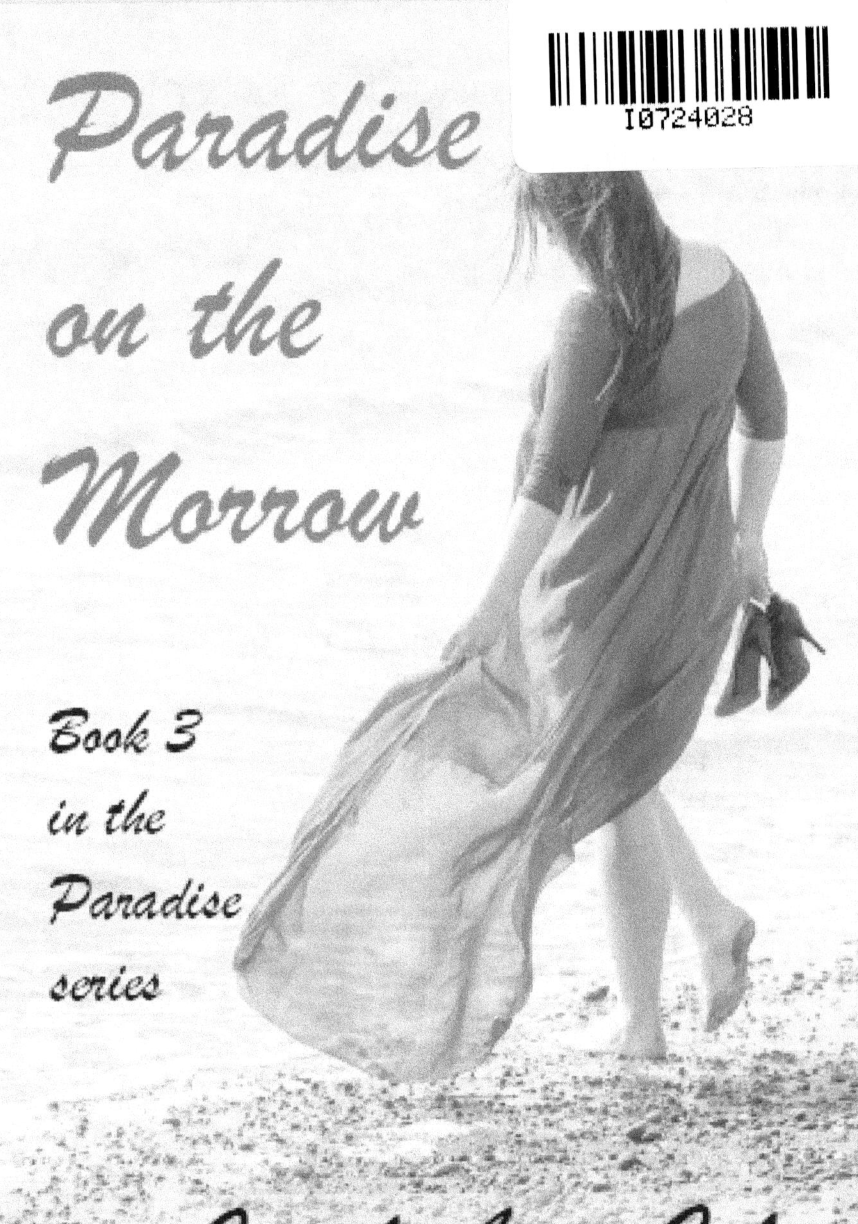

Paradise
on the
Morrow

Book 3
in the
Paradise
series

Carol Ann Cole

Cover image: Meleena Amirault
Model: Carissa Amirault

Editor: Andrew Wetmore

ISBN: 978-1-9992687-4-9
First edition July, 2020

397 Parker Mountain Road
Granville Ferry NS
B0S 1A0

moosehousepress.com
info@moosehousepress.com

We live and work in Mi'kma'ki, the ancestral and unceded territory of the Mi'kmaq People. This territory is covered by the "Treaties of Peace and Friendship" which Mi'kmaq and Wolastoqiyik (Maliseet) People first signed with the British Crown in 1725. The treaties did not deal with surrender of lands and resources but in fact recognized Mi'kmaq and Wolastoqiyik (Maliseet) title and established the rules for what was to be an ongoing relationship between nations. We are all Treaty people.

Carol Ann Cole books

The Paradise Series

Paradise
Paradise 548
Paradise on the Morrow
Paradise Private Investigator – *coming soon!*

Non-fiction

Comfort Heart - a Personal Memoir with Anjali Kapoor
Lessons Learned Upside the Head
If I Knew Then What I Know Now
From the Heart with Deanna Jones

Dedication

"Nana, do you have to go home today? Why don't you stay for one more sleep and go home on the morrow?"

The above quote is from a discussion I had with my granddaughter, Lexi Scott, when she was six years old.

This one's for you, sweetheart. I look forward to reading your first book. When I watch you journal my heart sings.

Acknowledgements

Connie Dea, you have been with me through the entire Paradise Series. You listen when I need to talk through a particular character development, you proofread, make suggestions and read a draft from front to back and back to front simply because I ask you to. You are the ebb to my flow. I absolutely would not do this without you, and I am so grateful. Thank you, dear.

Phyllis Pedicelli, I appreciate your phone call alerting me to the new publishing house in Nova Scotia! Thanks so much my 'Wilmot friend.'

Brenda Thompson, owner of Moose House Publications, thank you for trusting me and agreeing to publish my novel. I am proud to be one of your authors. Additionally, thank you for the gift of being able to work with your editor.

Andrew Wetmore, thank you for working with me as my editor. You have taught me to take a step back and allow my characters to speak for themselves. I watch them dance thanks to you. I promise to be more tolerant of my characters who stand on the sidelines even though they too want to be on the dance floor. I am grateful for all I have learned from you.

Finally, thank you to the dedicated fans and readers of The Paradise Series. You are the reason I continue to write. I appreciate you – each and every one of you.

Table of contents

Paradise on the Morrow takes place in 1987

1

Not able to get out of his own way, Thomas continued to make mistake after mistake. Dark days in Honolulu.

Thomas was the first to admit that things had to change, including having a serious dialogue with one of the two women he was in love with. From his days as a small child, Thomas had been in love with Paradise. Wikolia came into his life much later, after he moved to Hawaii.

Paradise was the stronger of the two, so initially Thomas concentrated on helping Wikolia. When she was healthy they would have 'the talk,' he told himself. Wikolia worked hard to get and keep her mental health under control and Thomas didn't want to do anything that might stall her recovery.

He made an appointment to speak with Wikolia's doctors, with whom he was on first-name terms. He hoped they could help him figure out the best way to approach her.

Wikolia's condition was volatile, but she was not violent. She moved forward yet back, like a twig on the tide. She showed signs of caring for Thomas, yet days came and passed with Wikolia having no interest in communicating with him at all.

Thomas wanted to help, but even a phone call was sometimes more than Wikolia was willing to accept. She went from needing to see him every day to not even wanting to speak with him on the phone. She definitely set the pace and, as her doctors had explained many times, Thomas had to accept this.

"Not about me," he kept telling himself.

Standing by Wikolia during her mental health struggles over the past few years might have cost Thomas his relationship with Paradise. He was wrong to have thought they could withstand anything thrown their way, given the number of years they had fought to find each other and reunite with their daughter Hope as a family. Thomas and Paradise continued to live worlds apart, and he knew it couldn't go on. He feared his heart would break if things didn't change soon. Understanding his relationship with Wikolia was one thing, but this was on an entirely different level.

Thomas visualized Paradise whenever he picked up the phone to call her. Her beguiling profile, the scent of her ocean-spray shampoo and the sound of her strong feminine voice caused the deepest fibres in his body to shake. He could picture her standing rather than sitting, with her long legs crossed at the ankle as she leaned against the closest wall. She would be looking around the room during their entire call, eyes always seeking that chair that should be moved or the picture that would look better in another room. Paradise was a master multitasker. The only thing that kept her from going to another room during their phone call was the length of the phone cord.

Arriving unannounced in Cape St Mary, in far-off Nova Scotia, to surprise 'his girls' didn't work out as Thomas had planned. Hope was definitely excited to see him, but Paradise—not so much. Thomas was thankful he sought Hope out first.

"Oh. My. God. Daddy, I am so happy to see you and I'm so surprised you're here. Wait until Mom sees you. Does she know about your surprise because if she doesn't, I don't want to be around when she sees you, Daddy!"

Hope burbled on as they walked up the road, "I'm really sorry my school wouldn't let you drive me home, but like my teacher told you, you're not on the parents' list. Don't ask me why. You'll have to ask Mom."

Thomas could see, by the little flinch she didn't quite conceal, that Hope, well, didn't have much hope about what Paradise's reaction would be.

"Honey, it's okay. I'll talk with mom and it'll be fine." He was ready to sit down with Paradise and face facts about their relationship.

"Did you bring your other kid, Daddy? Is T.J. with you? Because if he is I don't think you can stay with us. I think we have the room but that'll be one more thing you really need to talk to Mom about."

"Your brother made the first leg of the trip with me, but he's in Toronto with his grandparents. My mother is thrilled to have him bunking in with her for as long as necessary. Of course he will also spend time with Paradise's parents. I'm sure he will be just a bit spoiled when I pick him up!"

A lot had changed since the day Hope first met all of her grandparents in Toronto and inadvertently blurted out that she had a baby brother, T.J. Thomas's very Catholic mother had coiled into herself while screaming, "My son has an illegitimate child? What in the name of the Lord has my son done with his life? Holy Father in Heaven pray for him."

Eventually she came to accept T.J.'s existence, but continued to pray for Thomas and his many sins. Understanding was one thing but forgiving was almost impossible.

Thomas had been pleased that Hope asked about her brother. Not much love in the question but he would take what he could get. He reflected on the reaction from Paradise, so very different from what he had imagined on the plane.

Convincing Hope they really should continue this discussion with mommy, Thomas walked to his car outside of the schoolhouse as he watched his daughter fly down the dirt road with her long arms and legs in flight and kicking up dust. Her beautiful hair looked golden in the sunlight with the wind blowing it every which-way. Hope would stop at the police station to meet her mom and they would walk the rest of the way home together as they always did when Paradise worked at the station all day.

Thomas took the scenic route and arrived in front of the house just seconds before they did.

"Really? *Really*, Thomas? What in God's good name are you doing here without even a phone call to warn me? Don't get me started about you going to my daughter's school. How dare you!"

Thomas's response just slipped out, and it was probably not the smoothest one he could have offered. "Our daughter, Paradise. Hope is our daughter."

"Whatever you have to say, I do not want to hear it right now."

Paradise was livid with him and in that moment he realized that making this trip might be the biggest judgmental error of his life. He was certain, though, that, given the right time and place, they would discuss and resolve everything.

Thomas had wanted to be the bigger person and let Paradise go if that was what she wanted, but it still hurt like hell to look ahead and imagine his life without her. How could either of them erase so much history? He had not been ready or able to bring up something so intimate over the phone. Their future was too important to be discussed via long distance. They had to sit down, just the two of them, with no family around and no distractions, so they could talk at length and make a decision about their future together...or apart. And no surprises. Definitely no surprises.

There were days when Thomas thought about Paradise every waking second. He had days when he thought about Wikolia every waking second. To enjoy life with one to the fullest, he had to let the other go. Thomas knew this. He just hadn't and couldn't act on it.

It proved to be a long, hot summer in many ways. Thomas found a room in the village rather than bunking in with Paradise and Hope. His daughter introduced him to everyone they met and took him to every possible corner of her world in and around Cape St Mary.

Before arriving at the Cape, Thomas had only the *Encyclopedia Britannica*'s description of Cape St Mary. The text was very bland.

> Located on the western tip of the Nova Scotia peninsula in the Canadian province of Nova Scotia, Cape St Mary continues to be a well-kept secret, a treasure for the locals to enjoy without the intrusion of strangers—tourists who came once but never returned.

Something mute like that.

Hope brought the Cape, and Mavillette Beach in particular, to life. "There," she whispered. "That's where the nests are, Daddy."

"Why are we whispering? They're turtles. Do they even have ears?"

"*Dad*..."

They were lying side by side on the landward rise of a dune, peering over its edge at the flat sand just above high tide. In the dim light of pre-dawn, Thomas could see the mother turtles doing whatever they were doing to try to make their eggs safe until their young hatched.

Hope kept up a running, muttered commentary as if this were a BBC nature show.

Thomas saw that she was happy in Cape St Mary. Her honesty was refreshing and he carried her stories in his heart. He could close his eyes and hear his beautiful daughter's voice long after he returned to Honolulu.

"Dad, every single morning you can walk along Mavillette Beach and see gifts the night's tides have brought us. The sand is always new and the waves bring the rocks ashore to keep us on our toes—literally. See some of these huge rocks? They were not here before the huge storm we had last year. The waves were a mile high. Well, they weren't really a mile high but you know what I mean. That storm was incredible and I hope we never have another one like it."

She checked that the turtles weren't doing anything amazing, and then turned to mutter straight at him. "We have a great school here in the Cape and a great café, Dad. Café Central is where all the old people go for coffee and sometimes they have a whole meal! Isn't that crazy? Maybe mom could take you to the Café before you leave. Mom says you better be leaving soon. I'm not sure if you know that, but you didn't hear it from me."

Paradise left her hardest hit for his last evening in the Cape and Thomas hadn't seen it coming. "I love you with my whole heart, Thomas. You already know you're my first love and that hasn't changed. But us two living apart is becoming an issue. And now there's Lenny."

"Lenny?"

"Don't pretend you haven's seen him mooching around, trying to keep out of your sight."

"Okay," Thomas sighed. "What does Len have to do with us?"

It was Paradise's turn to sigh. "Over time he has crept into my heart. Watching the two of you dance around me makes me nervous. I want to be sure we clear the air."

She paced away from him, but he knew she wasn't done. He held still, neutral-faced, ready for when she turned and picked up the thread.

"Thomas, I'm struggling to understand how I can have feelings for Lenny when I am in love with you. It's as hard as trying to figure out how you can love me and feel whatever you feel for Wikolia at the same time."

There. She had said it. Words clogged his brain so he couldn't say any of them.

She put her hands on her hips. "For Christ's sake, is it so impossible for you to say the name Wikolia and give me some idea where your head is with all of this? This woman is keeping you in Hawaii. Not your job. Not your son. Wikolia"

The pause lengthened. Thomas knew he was failing miserably.

"You don't know how hard it is for me without you to help me, and I sometimes think…"

"What do you think? That I should return to Honolulu so I can look after *your* son?"

"It's not just T.J., but also Wikolia. I spend so much time at the hospital with her and she—"

"Okay, now you're suggesting I should return to help you cope with Wikolia? You know how I feel about that. Wikolia and T.J. are your problems, not mine, and if you can't share your feelings without constantly throwing something in my face then we are done."

Why do women always need to talk about feelings? In the end Thomas said nothing more. He didn't feel comfortable speaking about Wikolia as she lay in a hospital bed. No, that was an excuse and he knew it. The opportunity had been there yet he said nothing. He left that baggage packed away.

When it was time to leave, the boys made the flight back to Hawaii. T.J. was up for anything and travelled with no worries in his young mind.

The flight was not as easy for his dad. Thomas was anguished and unsure if he still had a future with Paradise. Just hearing her mention Lenny by name bruised his heart.

~

As Wikolia successfully put one foot in front of the other, day after day, and worked so hard to regain her mental health, Thomas couldn't deny that he had deep feelings for her, too. He had not acted on these feelings, of course, and was pretty sure Wikolia was not aware of how he felt.

Wikolia had no trouble sharing her feelings. She wanted Thomas and she fought for him. "You listen to me, Thomas. I may be locked up but I know every move you make. I know you tried to adopt my boy."

How could she know about the adoption papers? "T.J. is *our* boy," he said as smoothly as he could, "and he will always belong to us. Both of us."

"And you can kiss Paradise goodbye when I get out of here, so why don't you get busy with that right now? You were my sinsational lover for four years, Thomas, remember? I know you remember."

In the early stages of her recovery Wikolia had worn him down and won him over. He saw it coming but did nothing to ensure her health was the only topic of discussion most of the time. Thomas was being dishonest to both of the women in his life.

Had he always felt this way about Wikolia or was he simply in awe of how far she had come from her early days in a windowless, padded room? Yet in every lucid moment she made sure Thomas knew how determined she was to be with him and with T.J.

Thomas had some difficult work to do. Emotional work. "What a bloody mess," he thought, not for the first time.

2

Paradise wanted to be a nun until she didn't. She wanted to have a life with Thomas until she didn't. She wanted to work with Hawaii 2.0, in the arms division of Hawaii 5.0, where all recovered stolen guns were sorted and labelled with the intention of tracking criminals through their firearms, until she didn't. She wanted to live in Hawaii until she didn't.

Her decisions deserved to be questioned.

Moving forward, Paradise was trying to be more confident in her decision-making. She wanted to be a mother and a private investigator. Hope and her PI accreditation meant everything to her.

Days of second-guessing every decision she made were behind her. Finally Paradise felt she could see her future – even though there were some missing parts and people.

Raising her daughter in Cape St Mary for now meant a life that included Pops. He needed his great granddaughter and great-great granddaughter, even though he wasn't quite ready to admit he required help from anyone. Pops was slowing down. He knew it, but he was a very proud man.

Sergeant Curtis with the Cape police force had approved a number of PI training courses for Paradise, including advanced training at the police academy, and now she had a full time job with the force. Curtis often loaned Paradise out to the Royal Canadian Mounted Police detachments across the province. The Mounties provided policing for most Nova Scotia small towns and villages. Cape St Mary, with its own force, was an exception, and Curtis didn't want this to hold Paradise back.

Feedback was positive. A two-week stint working with her former PI partners in Ontario, Clint and Jim Taylor, meant Paradise was gaining national recognition for her work. Sergeant Curtis received accolades, some from unexpected sources, about his female PI.

He also heard the slurs.

The year was 1987 and gaining acceptance would be an uphill battle for Paradise and for her mentor. The world, or at least the world they knew, wasn't ready for a female PI. Even her name was causing jokes to float, and this had prompted Sergeant Curtis to suggest they use the nickname the Cape police force gave her when she had worked with them a number of years ago.

At that time Paradise had not yet moved to Honolulu in search of her birth parents. She didn't know what her middle initial 'd' stood for and had shared this with Curtis. He had been more concerned about the jokes being made about her first name but they clearly didn't bother her and she never did explain the reason behind her name.

Curtis listened to comments from his peers from across Atlantic Canada made during a conference when they were reviewing lead members of the force and, more specifically, who was ready for a promotion

"Hey there, Curtis," brought the first slur during the reception the evening prior to the beginning of the conference, "How's that little woman of yours doing, way down there past the Annapolis Valley?"

Curtis knew who was yapping without even turning around. He had watched this guy enter the bar looking and smelling in need of a bath. He was close to being drunk before his first drink with the team. His name tag read, 'Whose askin?' and he was quite proud of his humour. "Is she really paradise for your guys, or is that just her name? Surely to God it's not her given name. Tell us all about her, beginning with those curves. Real or modified body?"

Curtis decided he wouldn't respond during the booze-filled evening. He would see if similar comments floated up the next morning as the leader presented the conference agenda.

It took no time at all. Over that first cup of coffee, a member of the Halifax Mountie detachment sat down beside Curtis. "Will we have Paradise laid out like this agenda, Curtis? That would keep me alert, for sure. Every Goddamn time I hear her name my cock wakes up."

Immediately upon his return to the Cape, Curtis called Paradise into his office. "We have a problem."

"What is it?" Paradise was sitting on the edge of her seat. "Something at the conference? About me?"

"This is a problem you and I can solve right here, right now. Do you remember when you handled a couple of cases for us years ago and my guys made fun of your name? I know you were aware. We solved that problem by introducing your middle initial and called you Pd PI."

"Of course I remember." She slumped back in her chair. "So some of the guys at the conference had comments to make. Only related to my name, correct? Not a word, I bet, about my performance and if I was ready to move up the ranks."

"Sadly, yes, it was about your name and, frankly, your good looks." He held up a hand to cut her off before she could speak. "Like I said, I have a solution for you to consider. In fact, before I left Halifax I called that printer in Digby we use. Alex came through for me, and I picked up a small gift from me to you on my way through. So here you are." Curtis pushed a small box across his desk.

Paradise knew she had a steep climb if she wanted to be successful as a PI. A tear escaped her eye and she turned as if to glance out the window while she brushed it away, hoping Curtis hadn't noticed. She would face obstacles far more difficult to address than her name, but it was a start.

She opened the box and saw the business cards: Pd Private Investigator in bold letters.

Paradise looked up and gave Curtis a nod and the hint of a smile. She was grateful to have a boss who understood and was prepared to guide her going forward.

Paradise didn't want to get too personal with Curtis. There was a good reason her name was Paradise d'Entremont, a reason she had not shared with him. One day maybe she would tell Curtis about the blood-stained note attached to the blanket she was wrapped in just seconds after her birth. Today wasn't that day.

If Paradise could get her personal life in order by making the hard decisions right in front of her, then her boss would be able to rest a bit easier. She knew Curtis worried that she would just pack her bags and take off, maybe go back to Hawaii. She didn't think she would, but every time he brought the matter up she found it impossible to give him a straight answer. She was sure he thought she was teasing him, maybe holding out for special treatment. But it wasn't that at all. She was sure of that, although she couldn't even say to herself clearly what it was.

~

Madeline, who died giving birth to Paradise, had been friends with Elise since they grew up together in the Cape. They bonded at school when they realized they both shopped for clothes at the local Frenchy's store. When their classmates said, "I need to ask mother for some money for new jeans," they had smiled at each other. In both of their worlds there was no money and there was no mother.

Now a village matriarch, Elise shared stories about Madeline with Paradise whenever they were able to be together. Paradise always wanted to learn more, because the stories made her beloved mother more real. She was certain her mother had had a hand in Elise coming to her.

Not all the stories Elise shared were sad and Paradise was always able to smile as she listened to what she privately called "Maddy and Elise's Excellent Adventures".

"Paradise, dear, did I tell you about the time your mom and I took the train all the way up the line to Greenwood to do a bit of shopping, planning to return by train later that same day? We set off quick, before anybody could tell us we couldn't go. Honest to God we almost peed our pants when the train left the station to deliver us home."

"Why? What happened?"

"We arrived in Greenwood, no problem, and went our separate ways for some individual shopping. I wanted to look at fabric and

Madeline wanted a summer coat. She had never had a new one and we had heard there was a great sale on coats on that particular day."

After taking a slug of milky tea to draw out the moment, Elise painted the picture. "Now, girl, you just imagine us coming towards each other on that main street in Greenwood. Me with a huge bag of fabric and your mom with a brand new white coat. She had worn it out of the store and I saw her dump her old ratty coat into a trash bin. Now I began to worry. You see, I had spent more than I planned to and I was counting on her, being a careful shopper and all, not to find anything to buy so she would have money for the tickets home. But she had that pretty white coat."

"Did she have to take it back?"

"We couldn't! Everything we bought was on sale, no returns! My lord, we had long faces. We pooled what we had left and it wasn't enough. Now we had longer faces. Then your mother's eyes got wide. I said, 'What is it?', but she just turned and ran back up the street to that trash bin. She hauled out her old coat and it was like she was wrestling with it. By the time I caught up to her, her face was shining. 'I remembered the rip in the pocket,' she said, 'so I said a prayer and dug in there.' She showed me two twenty-five cent pieces that were down in the lining. Now we had money for our fare home and eight whole cents left over!"

Elise rocked back and forth with laughter. "Paradise, we laughed all the way home and both felt like a million dollars. Tomorrow would bring us back to reality soon enough but we embraced that train ride home with all we had."

Paradise considered Elise a cherished friend. As difficult as it was to hear about her mother, since all stories led to her death, she always had more questions to ask. Elise always made time for her just as she had for Madeline.

Paradise could often feel her mother's presence. As she learned more and more about her mother and how her young life ended so abruptly, Paradise felt stronger. She would get her public and her personal life together: she owed it to her mom. Madeline had gone into labour alone on the cold linoleum floor in the bedroom after

Pops and his son, her beloved husband, Cole, had gone out to sea for the day. She gave her life so her daughter, Paradise, could live.

3

At the young age of eighty-four Pops told all who would listen that he had never felt better. His home at 548 Cape St Mary Road was the perfect family home for Hope, her mom, and him. Their home faced the ocean, looking out at beautiful Mavillette Beach. Pops was some glad he had listened to the crew rebuilding his house when they insisted his home must face the ocean. Paradise and Hope seemed to love it, and that was good enough for Pops. He continued to remind Paradise the home belonged to the three of them. It was not just his home anymore.

Pops would be forever grateful to Aurel and his crew for building his new home after 548 had to be pretty much torn down to the façade. Even the word 'façade' had been new to him. Lots of learning had come his way since family came to town.

Pops took his boat out now and then, when he and Hope felt like some of what they liked to call 'alone time'. They loved being anywhere together.

Hope had asked about her mom's parents and when Pops felt she was ready he told her the story. It wasn't easy to tell, of course, and it took half a dozen boat trips and navigating shoals of questions from Hope for him to share almost everything with her. Hope had a great mind for detail and Pops didn't mind answering all of her questions. Every single one of 'em.

So far Pops had been able to keep the most heart breaking detail from Hope by being a bit vague. "I screamed as my beloved Cole dove for the side of this boat, Hope. But as God is my witness, I saw he changed his mind and tried to turn around and come back to me."

On this particular day Hope asked Pops about the day Cole died, and Pops decided it was time to tell her everything. It was the only detail he had left out so far. Pops knew it would upset Hope and he tried very hard to not relive the details himself unless absolutely necessary. The 'sad' hurt too much. It still broke his heart and he didn't like to cry in front of Hope. He had done that a few times but it wasn't a comfortable emotion for him to share—at least his old mind kept telling him that.

Like so many other things, though, Pops was working on it. He said he was learnin' at least one new thing every single day, thanks to his roommates. It was Hope who had first called them roommates.

The saddest memory of Pops' life was the story of that day he and Cole went to work. They silently set out on their fishing boat. Suddenly Cole, heart-broken from giving Paradise up for adoption, seemed to be confused, perhaps not even aware of where they were. Pops had never seen Cole act this way.

For an instant it looked like he was going to jump over the side of the boat. First he went to Pops and told him he loved him and was sorry for what he was about to do. He turned and ran towards the other side of the boat, but then Pops saw him hesitate.

His grandson changed his mind. Pops could see it in his eyes as Cole twisted his upper torso so he could turn and look at Pops.

Then he slipped. He did not jump. Pops saw it in his eyes.

My beloved grandson did not commit suicide.

Years later, when Pops first heard the word, he realized 'depression' was the look in Cole's eyes during their last days together. They were both depressed. They didn't understand this was a mental illness and therefore they didn't ask for help. They made the mistaken decision that no one could help them.

As Pops would often explain, "We just thought we were sad, that's all. We were both wearing a whole heart full of sad."

When Pops finished sharing his story with Hope, they both cried. It wasn't hard to cry in front of her that particular day.

Hope reached out and gave Pops the biggest hug ever. This confirmed to Pops that he'd done the right thing. Hope was a young thirteen-year-old, but she needed to know. She always liked to have all the facts, as she would often remind Pops as well as her mother. Hope liked to say she 'worked better' with the facts.

As they walked along the wharf and up the hill to their home Hope startled Pops by taking his hand and squeezing it. She said, "Some days you're like a dad to me, Pops."

They walked on a few steps, then she added, "An old dad but still a dad." Pops wondered if what she said wasn't about him, but about Thomas. He needed to sit Paradise down and find out what was going on. In the moment, though, he was just happy to be holding Hope's hand. She liked to swing their arms when they were holding hands and she always found a way to make them both laugh at something silly.

As they shared a laugh the night air was filled with happiness. Hope's laughter echoed along the road and neighbours smiled with them.

4

"Guess what...I've got a boyfriend," Wikolia whispered to Cory, the security guard at the patients' entrance of the mental health facility in Hawaii where she lived. "I know you won't believe me, but it's true."

"Of course you have. We've met him many times," Cory replied with a smile. He had been watching for her. Everyone liked Wikolia, but lately she was breaking the rules and this worried the security team. They didn't want to tattle on her, but she was taking more and more liberties with her day pass. Maybe it was time to tell Thomas what was going on. Cory had already reported Wikolia to his boss but maybe he should give her an update.

If anything happened to Wikolia, the security team would be responsible, especially if they had kept to themselves what they were seeing. Returning to the facility at the agreed time was right up there among the rules to never break.

"Thomas is a great boyfriend, young lady. Now, you're late, so let's get you back inside these doors. Don't be late again or your day pass might be revoked. That smile of yours won't be as big if something goes wrong. You've worked very hard to earn day pass privileges and we would hate to see them taken away from you." The guard wasn't sure Wikolia was paying attention to anything he was saying. He felt responsible and wanted to get through to her. "No one with day privileges can be late returning all the time. Do you understand me, Wikolia?"

With a look that would never be mistaken for a smile Wikolia replied, "Oh I understand you perfectly, sir. But trust me: you do not understand me." She was acting as confident as possible.

Her health continued to be an issue and Wikolia understood that. Anger crowded her days and almost anything could bring on a screaming episode louder than the previous one. It normally took two attendants to restrain her. God, how she hated restraints and she couldn't be rid of them soon enough.

Every time she returned to her room after a visit with Donald Junior she found herself stewing over her new reality. Maybe she would run away one of these days.

Wikolia had a delicious secret and she was playing with fire. Her only worry was that she might get caught. Wikolia knew that staff had discussed her full release several times. It seemed set backs here and there were keeping her within the hospital walls. At least she had her day passes to look forward to.

Doing her own banking once again made her happy. Wikolia rushed to the bank every time she was given a day pass. The first day she opened her account and deposited a $10.00 bill. The next visit she took most of it out.

This is how she met her boyfriend. He was her big secret. Wikolia understood that Donald Junior had what he described to her as 'special needs' so she needed to be the adult when they were together. He trusted her with his secret and that made her happy.

~

Donald Junior looked after customers at the bank. Customers who knew Donald Junior or his father went to him to make small cash deposits. If customers needed to make small withdrawals he could handle that, too, but Donald Junior found counting money to give to someone very difficult. He often got mixed up and had to start over and he knew several customers had complained.

"Wikolia, I have to tell you something. I'm pretty sure my dad owns this bank. He told me I would have a job here as long as I wanted one. Did you know you were almost my first real customer?"

"That makes me very proud, Donald."

"One more thing, Wikolia. I have two fifteen-minute breaks a day plus my lunch hour and that is forty-five minutes long. Come and have lunch with me sometime. Do you want to do that?"

Wikolia sure did feel special around Donald Junior. She felt very free with no one watching her. In 'the big house', as she called it, she was observed all the time. On more than one occasion Wikolia forgot she was supposed to be the adult in the room when she was with Donald Junior. She knew she should know better. She was far more mature than her boyfriend, but in the heat of certain moments she didn't care.

Before long, Wikolia and Donald Junior were meeting during his lunch break at least once a week when she had a day pass. Except now they didn't meet at his desk inside the bank. They met out back. They figured it was important to make sure they were far away from prying eyes.

One day they became girlfriend and boyfriend. Everything they did was a secret and they both understood they were not supposed to tell anyone. Not one single soul. They would have to share their secret in a few months, though.

Wikolia was in love. Even more than the love she felt for Thomas, and Wikolia wouldn't have thought that was possible.

It wasn't long before Donald Junior was in trouble with his dad and with his immediate boss. He returned late from his lunch break often and seemed to think this was a liberty he was allowed.

Donald Junior's father was frustrated with his son. As he listened to his son's floor supervisor he also felt some guilt for having initially insisted his bank would hire Donald Junior or else. Now it was up to Donald Senior to do the right thing. "Fire him. Special needs' be damned. Just fire him. Maybe this will teach him a lesson...we won't like having him at home all the time though. He makes his mother crazy when he follows her around day and night. I try to talk with my son, but I have no idea what to talk with him about."

5

Sunday dinner with my parents. Bombshell time!

Donald dressed appropriately, suit and tie, as he did every Sunday for dinner with his parents. He looked around as he entered the formal dining room that he had come to hate. This was a home full of dark oak, dark floors and dark memories.

Some bad things had happened to Donald in this room. He hated Sundays. "Hi, Mother. Hi, Father."

No response.

"I have some news. Some exciting news." Donald was anxious and nervous but eager to continue.

"Not now, Donald, your father is carving the roast. You know he likes us to enjoy this moment with him, and in silence, of course."

"But I—"

"Your mother said not now, Donald."

Maybe I won't tell them my secret at all, Donald thought.

Sunday roast was best served with baked potatoes and gravy made exactly the way Donald Senior liked it, steamed vegetables to Donald Senior's liking as well, and wine. Lots of wine. Milk for Donald Junior, of course, even though technically he was an adult. He often asked if he could have wine, but not today. They always said no, anyway.

"How was your morning on the golf course, dear? I hope you didn't encounter rain."

Donald knew why his mother was the one who could break the silence, but couldn't contain himself. "Wait. Why can you ask a question, mother, when I'm the one with some exciting news? I want to tell you my news."

"Be quiet, son. Your mother and I are talking. The golf game itself was fair to middlin', however my own game was excellent, if I must say so myself."

"I'm sure it was, dear."

"I have a girlfriend." Donald's words landed in the middle of the meal like a mouse in the soup. "I have a girlfriend and we meet every time she can get out."

"Don't speak nonsense, Donald. You wouldn't know what to do with a girlfriend."

His mother remained silent but she did look worried about what he might say next. Donald was angry that his parents went on talking as if he wasn't in the room, just like every Sunday dinner.

"Mom, I tried to tell you about Wikolia but you told me you didn't want details, remember?"

Father put down his fork. "What kind of a name is that, Wikila? Sounds like what a horse would say. Does she look like a horse?"

Donald tried to keep from crying. "Her name is Wikolia and she's my girlfriend. She was born here in Honolulu and both of her parents were born here, too. They didn't move here like we did just because your job made us move."

"I am the President of my bank, and I suggest you go back to eating your dinner with your head down and allow me to speak with your mother. Is that understood, or should you and I have one of our walks outside?"

"Yes, I know you're speaking with mom because during our Sunday dinner is the only time you speak to her."

A slap across the face was Donald's reward.

"Perhaps you've had enough to eat for today, Donald," his mother said without looking at him. "Would you like to go to your room?" His mother always tried to come to his rescue, but she knew how far she could go.

"No! I don't want to go to my room. I want to tell you about my girlfriend." Donald ducked away so his father's hand wouldn't find his face a second time.

"I have already told you I didn't want details. You're not able to have a girlfriend, son, because your mind didn't grow up. Remember, we have talked about this. Your stories are all fantasy, son. Your mind is still a child-mind. Do you remember me explaining that to you and helping you spell your special word, child-mind?"

Donald could see his mother was getting nervous. He knew his dad could be bad to his mom. He had heard it all from his bedroom so many times. His mind wasn't as young as they thought. But he couldn't stop.

"I bet you'll want to know this not-so-little detail. Wikolia and I are going to get a baby,"

Silverware clattered on plates.

"All this time that I've been working at your bank, Wikolia has been coming to see me. We go out back to eat our lunch and now a baby is growing in her belly. Isn't that incredible?"

"Go to your room," his father shouted.

"I guess you know Wikolia lets me stick my pecker down-there," Donald added in a last defiant burst. Then he ran to his room, slammed the door and cried.

Donald Senior turned to his wife. "How could you let this happen? I told you taking our idiot son to my bank would result in nothing but trouble. I hope you're happy now."

With that, Donald Senior threw his napkin in his wife's face. He pulled out a cigar and stomped off toward the study. Then he stopped and wheeled on her. "You get to the bottom of this. If there is a girlfriend I want her dealt with. If there is a baby I want that dealt with, too."

"Of course, darling," she murmured to his retreating back. "I will look after everything." She knew she was safe as long as he stayed in his precious study.

After she had cleared the table and done the dishes in silence, she went off to her son's room. She tapped lightly once, then opened the door and went in.

Donald was done crying. He was staring red-eyed at nothing. "I have a learning disability. I'm a real person. You told me that a hundred times. I hate him."

Gathering him in her arms she began stroking his back. "There, there. I'll look after everything. Why don't you tell me all about your girlfriend, starting with where she lives? I think I would like to meet this Wikola."

"Wikolia."

"Wikolia. Could you take me to her home one day very soon?"

6

A few days after T.J. turned two years old, Thomas filed for full custody of his son. It took longer to complete the paperwork than it did to make T.J.'s new status legal. It felt right, but it didn't feel like a win.

Thomas had spent months thinking and wondering if it was wrong for him to file for full custody. In the end he knew he had to think of T.J. ahead of anyone else. When Wikolia's mental health issues were under control, T.J. would be back in her life. Thomas would make sure of it.

T.J. knew his daddy and his nanny well. Sadly, he did not know his mother. As much as Thomas tried to include Wikolia in their conversations, the mind of a two-year-old moves on to other things very quickly.

T.J. had turned into a darling little boy and was glued to Daddy's side whenever possible. If Daddy was home, T.J. was playing nearby or sitting on his lap. He looked more and more like Thomas every day and seemed to be growing up far too quickly.

At a small birthday party for his son, Thomas found himself saying, "Where have two years gone?"

But along with the lightness his son brought to his world, Thomas couldn't help but acknowledge the darkness as well. Would T.J. ever get to know his mother?

There continued to be no discussion about Wikolia leaving the hospital, and Thomas worried she wouldn't be able to look after both herself and her son if and when she was released. She hadn't seen T.J. in months and she asked about him less and less as time passed. She had stopped fighting for her son. Thomas found that profoundly sad and he often didn't know how she, or they together, would move forward.

Wikolia had become an angry, childlike shadow of herself, had lost a lot of weight and complained she was vomiting all the time. And something new seemed to crop up daily for her to complain about. Wikolia had recently asked Thomas if he knew she had a boyfriend. He tried to get her to tell him more about this man, but she was quick to say, "It's a secret because my boyfriend would get in trouble with his dad and I would lose my day pass."

Thomas was shocked at the level of detail in Wikolia's story.

Often Thomas came to visit Wikolia in the early morning after his night shift at 2.0, the arms division of Hawaii 5.0, and before going home to T.J. Had he missed some signs? Was his exhaustion catching up with him? He was working the same twelve hour night shift that Paradise had worked before her 'escape' to Canada. She had seemed to manage to do everything while on shift and again when she returned home. Thomas had the official contract with 2.0 and knew he was spending more hours at work than Paradise had. He made a mental note to recheck his schedule.

Right now, though, he had questions for the doctors. After spending an hour with Wikolia he picked up another coffee and one for Doctor Legault and headed for the conference room. They always met in the same dull, dreary and poorly-lit room. Sometimes Doctor Legault came alone and other times he brought his entire mental health army with him. Thomas had requested the good doctor come alone on this particular morning.

"Are you still hands on with Wikolia's care? Do you have her current medical assessment notes with you? I need some answers."

"Settle down, Thomas. This isn't like you. What has you so agitated? I just saw Wikolia and did a quick evaluation because she seemed upset—something about you not believing she has a boyfriend. Did you see her before you came here?"

"Christ-on-a-stick, what kind of a man do you think I am? Of course I saw Wikolia before our meeting. I always visit her here before doing anything else. So tell me, was this the first time you have heard about the boyfriend?"

"Of course not. Wikolia talks about you all the time. I know you're her boyfriend. I think she has referred to you that way all along. Sit down. We will get nothing resolved with you walking back and forth like that."

With an effort, Thomas stood still. "I need some answers and if I have to take Wikolia elsewhere to get those answers I'll do exactly that. I'm tempted to take her home today, and that's on you."

He lowered himself into a chair and leaned toward the doctor, speaking in a lower tone but sounding slightly strangled. "The Wikolia I saw this morning was child-like and happy when she shared her secret with me. Her secret is that she has a new boyfriend. When she is not talking about him, whoever he is, she becomes angry, argumentative, and lost. She has lost an awful lot of weight and I hope you can speak to what you have done or are doing about that. She says that she is vomiting all the time and no one will help her. This is a fucking mess, Doctor Legault. You don't even realize that the boyfriend Wikolia is talking about is not me. Tell me how that's possible. I don't know who I can trust these days." With that Thomas began to weep.

Doctor Legault let a pause extend until Thomas had gotten himself back under control. Then he spoke. "Thomas, Hawaii's Mental Health facility is among the best in the world and you know that. That's why you brought her to HMH. Wikolia has been with us longer than most and, if anything, I believe she receives more attention, not less. She is well cared for and well loved."

The doctor stood, adjusting his white jacket. "I will not have you disrespect a staff that does nothing short of their best for every patient we care for. I have made notes that include all of your concerns and I will take some time today to assess the changes in Wikolia's health myself. Go home, get some sleep and let me know when you can come in for another chat. Meet me here. I'll have your answers."

At the door Doctor Legault added, "We're not the enemy here, Thomas."

Alone, Thomas sat hunched over the big table. He lowered his head to rest on his arms and had a nap almost despite himself. He woke up wondering how his meeting with Doctor Legault had played out. Was he really as unprofessional as he remembered? He would soon find out...

Tucked under his left arm was a handwritten note:

I shut the lights off and raised the room temperature for you. Have a long and necessary nap and then go home. We will resolve this, I promise you. Just remember I'm on your side.

But if you speak to me again as you did today I will leave the room. Do not do that again Thomas.

Doctor L.

7

Looking up the word 'hypocrite' in his tattered office dictionary, Sergeant Curtis was certain he would find his own name. 'A person who pretends to have higher standards than they really have.'

Firing his dictionary to the other end of his office at the Cape police station he said, "Close enough."

"Everything okay, boss?" Gary, the office clerk, was a local high school student working through a co-op assignment. He entered his office offering a second cup of coffee that might soothe whatever was eating away at Curtis. "Long night, sir?"

Curtis didn't even look up and that was not like him.

Gary returned to his cubicle and flagged down one of the constables on shift. "What's eating away at the boss, do you know?"

Out of the loop regarding anything about Sergeant Curtis, Constable Roop offered to find out. "Leave it with me, young lad. I'll give 'er a go."

Gary watched the constable square his shoulders and march into the sergeant's office. He had a sinking feeling.

"Hey, boss, how are the wife and kids?" Roop said.

"What in hell is that supposed to mean?" Clearly Sergeant Curtis was in a bad mood.

"It's just that the young fella said you're a bit ugly today so I thought I would cheer you up."

And now both Gary and Constable Roop were in the middle of it.

"You're doing a piss-poor job of it. Get out of here and find something to do. Preferably something out of the office. Maybe out of the county."

Roop beat a retreat, grabbed his jacket from the back of his chair, and threw Gary a dirty look as he headed for the door. Despite the look, Gary wished he was going with him.

Curtis stared at the photo on his desk of his wife and two kids. What was he doing thinking about Paradise while he was looking at a picture of his wife? I wish I could look at my wife the way I want to be able to look at Paradise.

It's not her, though, he reminded himself. She doesn't even know. But it was hard not to blame her for his terrible mood.

Curtis looked up to see who he could yell at in the office, and there she was, walking toward him. She gave a jaunty wave and he couldn't help waving back, like a high school kid.

"Sergeant Curtis, did I ever tell you I can lip read?"

He found his hand halfway toward covering his mouth, and forced it down to the desk. "You can?"

"Just a few key words, but one of them is my name." She flopped elegantly into the chair on the visitor side of his desk. "I think I just saw my name on your lips." Curtis felt himself blushing. He tried to mask it with a scowl. Out the corner of his eye he could see the photo of his wife looking up at him.

"Did I do something wrong, boss?"

Looking at Paradise for longer than he should have, Curtis realized he didn't have an answer. 'I'm in love with you, Paradise,' didn't seem quite right. This was as close as he had been to telling her the truth.

Curtis could remember the very day, it seemed a million years ago, when Pops asked for a favour. "Curtis, got a second? I'd like to talk with you about Paradise." That's how this all began. "I'm hoping you can help her with a bit of PI work. She's just getting started, as you know, and if she gets a bit of work here I'm hoping she'll never leave us."

"Consider it done," Curtis had replied. And even in that moment he was fantasizing about his newest recruit.

He could hardly tell her that. "Trust me, Paradise, you don't want to know."

"All right."

"It's personal." Saying that didn't help at all. He saw her eyes narrow in speculation. "So what you can do is leave me alone please and thank you. Now get out of my office and perhaps out of the building if you have outside work to do."

"Exactly what I came to see you about."

"It was?"

She produced a couple of sheets of paper and slid them onto his desk. "If you approve me going up to Halifax to meet with the chief coroner, I would be out of your hair for days."

Curtis stared at the pages without seeing them. He knew he had to either come clean with his wife, which would undoubtedly break up his marriage, or come clean with Paradise and see if she had the same feelings for him. And how likely was that?

She was rattling on. "It's about the death of Morning Glory. That stripper, you remember? I want to understand better what they found in the postmortem. Plus, it would be good experience for me."

"Yes. Good experience." After a moment of paralysis, Curtis found a pen and scribbled his signature on the request. "Turn in a claim for expenses when you come back."

Paradise flowed to her feet. "Thank you, boss. I will report in when I get back."

He watched her sashay down the hall. Gary was watching her, too, his mouth slightly open. There was nothing overt about it, nothing he could put his finger on (he blushed again at the image), but she walked like she was naked inside her clothes.

Now she was out of the office for a few days. Getting her out of his heart would be a different matter.

8

In the pathology department, buried several levels below the main floor of the largest hospital in Halifax, Chief Coroner Sydney Scott reread the hand-written note she'd received from some private investigator. "Pd PI", as shown on her business card, wanted to meet with the lead pathologist who conducted the autopsy on Miss Margaret Ville. Some called her Morning Glory.

Miss Ville's cause of death was recorded as 'unknown.' This was totally unacceptable to Pd PI and she listed in her letter several reasons why she couldn't and wouldn't accept such a report. She expressed shock and sadness that anyone, especially a pathologist who should know better, would treat a body in such a disrespectful way.

"Full disclosure," Pd PI wrote. "I knew this woman in another life and will not let this report stand as is. I hope you'll help me get the answers I need. Her sister is in the local jail and I will see if she has any answers that might help us. And then I will come to you."

How a PI had been able to access the pathology report was among the many questions Doctor Scott would need answers to. She wasn't looking forward to the day she would have to explain to this Pd PI person that the pathologist in question wasn't even a pathologist. Sandy Stone was 'old school', but as his boss she wasn't feeling good about throwing him under the bus. Someone had hired him and someone had let him under-perform for a very long time.

Doctor Scott herself had many questions. The day she first read the report, she could hardly believe that one of her own could be so unprofessional.

She had pushed the report to the corner of her desk, on top of the stack of reports she really needed to question Sandy about, until she would have the time to call him in for a little chat. She hadn't thought it possible that she might forget about this particular report.

Big mistake on her part.

Work got in the way, and when nobody could answer Doctor Scott's initial questions to her satisfaction, she neglected to follow up. Another mistake. With a sigh, she flipped the folder open and stared at the mess within. The autopsy read like a cut-and-paste from some show-girl poster, laced with vulgar language.

Sandy Stone had been on the job for years before Doctor Scott's appointment. She inherited him the way she inherited some of the obsolete-but-too-good-to-dispose-of equipment her staff insisted on using. When she had looked into his personnel file, she was shocked to discover that Sandy Stone was not even a doctor, that he was hired despite having no medical credentials.

There didn't seem to be much she could do about Stone, except prevent others like him from getting on staff during her tenure, Any new medical examiner had to be a physician. She had been naive to think that that would make the Stone problem magically go away.

Stone had identified the body, signed the death certificate, and notified the next of kin, Mary Ville. Some called her Dawn. He knew the sisters pretty well. He knew them better by their stage names, "Morning Glory" and "Dawn." Dawn was the younger of the two, although they both looked to be under age. He figured that wasn't his problem.

Stone just happened to be at the local strip joint the day Morning Glory fell to the floor. "Almost looked like it was part of her act," he had told his co-workers. "She fell off of the pole like a limp rag."

The next day he got her on the slab. "She didn't look like the same girl. Really looked underage."

Stone knew her sister was in jail and he wondered if she had something to do with the high drama on stage. What Stone did know for sure, and he said it often enough, was, "Morning Glory and Dawn were the best damn stripper act you would ever see, I don't care which joint you visit."

Doctor Scott suspected that, since he was planning to retire, Stone had decided to have a bit of fun with the suits who would be reading his autopsy report.

His notes indicated the autopsy had been performed, but there were no records of the findings, not even rough notes. Instead, there were notes that managed to be vivid and useless at the same time: 'She died on stage', 'she had a body born for stripping', and finally 'Morning Glory left us with my $100.00 bill stuffed in her panties.' The description of the corpse was a travesty: 'Double D's up top, legs longer than 'em all, face of an angel and rhythm like no other.'

Having asked her Assistant to make an appointment for Mr. Stone to be in her office first thing in the morning, Doctor Scott learned for the first time he couldn't be found.

Stone had signed off on his report and quietly retired. He seemed to be sticking it to the department as he left, snubbing his nose at everyone. Why else would Stone behave this way when he knew he would be harming the very department he had called home for so many years? He should have retired with thanks to whomever had given him the job with no qualifications all those years ago.

Doctor Scott sent a memo asking for everything they could dig up on Sandy Stone. Pronto. Too little, too late, and she knew it, but she would ask anyway. She owed it to the deceased. Stone had infuriated her and she wouldn't let him get away with this.

Embarrassed for her department and disappointed in her own performance Doctor Scott reflected on her time on the job. When she had first arrived she should have spent more time getting to know each member of her staff – including their qualifications. "I'm better than this," she whispered.

She hoped this Pd PI would work with her, not against her. It might be a lot to ask, but Doctor Scott had always been brutally honest and that wouldn't change now. Owning her mistakes with this case would have to come first.

She pressed as firmly as possible on the bright red 'Assistant' call button on her phone—as if that would make the sound reach her assistant faster. "Connie I have a unique opportunity for you. Come to my office immediately, or even faster." She tried to be less aggressive than she felt in the moment. After all, Connie had done nothing wrong.

"There was a whole lot of jagged-emotion in that message, boss. What can I help you with?"

"I have left a report from Sandy Stone on the edge of my desk for far too long. Does that give you a bit of direction regarding how I'm feeling?"

Connie opened her mouth to respond, but Doctor Scott continued. "For starters, I need you to take this business card and call the PI for me. I can't even tell what her name is from this card. Can you?"

Connie looked at the card and frowned at her boss. "Are we sure this person is a PI? Who do I ask for when I call? Is his or her name just the letter 'P'?"

"I don't have any answers, Connie. That's why I'm asking for your help." With a smile she added, "That's why I have an assistant, I believe. Let's assume that we're talking about a female. I want this PI, whoever she is, to know we have her card and her message, we know about the death and botched autopsy and we would welcome her visit in my office at any time. No, that's not urgent enough. Say we'd like her here soon as possible."

Connie raced back to her office. When Doctor Scott was focused on something and asked for help, Connie knew there was trouble ahead. She dialed the PI's number before sitting down at her messy desk. It was one thing for Doctor Scott to misplace or forget about a file but it would never do for her assistant to do the same.

She was surprised when the call went to an answering machine. If this PI could afford an answering device of any kind her business must be doing well. She was even more surprised with the quick and unprofessional message.

"Talk to me. At the sound of the tone you're on your own."

Connie wished she had written her message out prior to dialing the number, but it was too late now. "This message is for a private investigator with the initial P. Or maybe this says the name is Pd, but if you are this person you will know what and whom I'm rambling on about. Doctor Scott would like you to come to her office at the first possible date. Give me a call back to confirm, or you'll get me in trouble—just kidding, My boss says you can come in any day any time as long as you let us know ahead of time. Bye for now."

Sitting at her desk now Connie was thankful her boss wasn't around to hear that long and less than professional message. She was hoping the PI would call back quickly so she could give the news to Doctor Scott.

9

Lenny saw her waiting at 'their spot' along Mavillette beach. The hour was early, the beach was empty and he was carrying two very hot cups of coffee. This was their daily ritual and he loved it.

"Did I tell you Lenny Calhoun isn't my real name?" Lenny's birth name was dead to him. Family members would be safer thinking he was dead as well. Everyone in his immediate family had been murdered. He'd had a ringside seat to the show and nightmares to ensure he would never forget that day.

Paradise had asked Lenny to tell her about his life after he left 2.0 and eventually arrived in Cape St Mary.

"Hold on to your hat, Paradise. I'm gonna spill the beans and tell you a few things about me."

"It's about time," said Paradise, but she was smiling as she said it so Lenny figured he might actually get through this.

"First of all, you know why I left 2.0 and showed up here pretty much on your doorstep."

"That much I know and I think you're stalling. Out with it, my friend." "Friends, yes, and don't remind me that's all we are and all we'll ever be."

"I won't if you tell your story."

"Everything I did was a big thing for me when I left 2.0. Everything. I opened my first bank account and deposited all of my paychecks. As you know I lived within the walls of the warehouse twenty-four-seven so I had spent none of my money. Not one penny."

"Lenny, how did you first get your job at 2.0? I remember Jalen telling us they didn't advertise. They know the type of person they want to attract and go after them. That seemed strange to me, but clearly it works. How did it work for you?"

"I had some help there, but I might not get everything in during this one walk." Lenny was looking for another smile and he got it, so he went on. "You know I had a rough life growing up and you also know I was part of a gang for a while and did all kinds of stuff. When the Government was finished with me, after they had used me up, someone knew someone who knew someone. That's how they explained it to me."

Paradise jumped in. "And we both know Jalen has a soft spot for people he feels got a nasty start at life."

"Now you're telling me something I didn't know. Someone reached out and the job was mine. Commander Lexis did seem to know more about me than I ever told him. I remember him explaining that it wasn't a job interview that first day because I already had the job. He just wanted to talk and since I'm not much of a talker that meeting ended pretty much before it began."

"Keep talking, mister, I'm almost finished my coffee and I'm cold so walk a bit faster and talk a bit faster, too."

"I rented a tiny hovel on the beach. One day when I went to the bank to get a few dollars I was stunned to see the size of my bank balance. I knew I would eventually be compensated for the work I did while undercover tracking criminals for the government. The check was huge. You wouldn't believe me if I told you, so let's not go there. But it's important to me that you know I have my own money."

"You're rich," said Paradise. "I get it. Tell me more."

"First I moved to my first-ever apartment. Then I bought a map of Nova Scotia. I heard you mention the Cape often enough. You have been my singular focus, I swear, since the day I first met you."

Paradise looked at Lenny, but said nothing.

"What else can I tell you? I don't drink. I had my share of booze before I turned sixteen. Before the government released me from my contract I had to agree to see some doctors. Shrinks.".

"They don't like to be called that, by the way."

"I learned that quick," Lenny said. "They told me I was bipolar. I had never heard that word before. They told me what it meant and I said I thought that was bullshit. They told me I would receive no reference for any job if I didn't agree to see a doctor who would report back to the government. I agreed and got the reference I was after. I still think all of that is bullshit."

"Language, Lenny. You know I don't like that."

"Sorry, friend. I grew to like one of my doctors and he helped me realize that my extreme anger, my mood swings and the terrible things I felt inside were all treatable. I thought that's just how life was."

He made a gesture with both hands like a flasher opening his raincoat. "I'm medicated to this very day. Bet you didn't know that."

"I'm so sorry for all you've been through, Lenny, but I will say the medication works for you. That's just a personal opinion. We were on twelve-hour shifts together and I never saw any bad stuff. Do you feel well now?"

Paradise touched Lenny's arm. "Promise me you won't ever stop taking your medication without seeing a doctor first. I'm positive we have shrinks, as you call them, here, and I would be willing to find a good one for you if you like. In fact, I'll look it up just in case."

Lenny walked with his head down and seemed lost in thought. Paradise gave him the space.

Finally, without looking up, he said, "It's hard for me to do simple things. I learned early to never look anyone in the eye. I could shoot a man in the eye but I couldn't look him in the eye. 'Lay low,' that was my motto. Until you, Paradise. Everything changed when you arrived in the kitchen looking for a cup of coffee around 6 am after your first night shift at 2.0." He stopped and took her arm, turning her toward him. "I know you have to get Hope off to school. I won't keep you. I will tell you one final thing, though."

Paradise could feel the strength of his hand on her upper arm. She would not be able to shake him off easily...even if she wanted to.

"I'm in love with you, Paradise. I know you have a boyfriend, but seeing as you live here and he lives in Hawaii, I think you're kidding yourself about who you truly care for."

Sudden anger made it easier to get her arm free than she had thought it would be. "Easy, boy. I'm in love with Thomas and you know it. I have always made my intentions perfectly clear."

Paradise turned to head home, but his hand clamped on her arm again like it was welded to her.

"See how I can screw up so easily, Paradise? I'm sorry. Please let me explain." Len knew he should have saved his 'I love you' for another day but he'd been waiting for so long to say it.

He released her arm and Paradise slowly raised her hand like a stop sign. Then she turned and marched off toward her house.

Lenny watched her go. He knew when she gave him the hand she was done with him, for now.

10

After years of freedom, Lenny was once again looking over his shoulder. Like riding a bike, he thought. You never forget how to check all-things-happening behind you, in front of you, and all around. He had been so sure his past life was where it belonged forever – in his past.

Lenny didn't know how much time he had left on what he referred to as his life-clock. Something was nagging away at him, and he couldn't quite put his finger on it. But he knew it was there and that it was coming after him. Could someone from his ugly past have found him? He had not yet accepted that he might have made a mistake by refusing to enter the Witness Protection Program when they offered it to him in Hawaii.

He began to think of those he loved. For the first time in his life Lenny had loved ones to protect. The more he thought about it the more he was certain his haunted past-life had come to collect. He had to ensure the only person it collected from was Lenny Calhoon.

Then, sure enough, it happened...in real time. No longer just a nagging thought.

Yesterday when he wandered over to the Café for a fast coffee, Lenny was almost accosted by that old man, Pops, whom he had come to love. Pops got filled with anger and outright hatred if Lenny or anyone else did something bad to someone, anyone, in the tiny village Pops called home.

Pops was all riled up and wasn't making any sense. It put Lenny on edge.

"I need to know what's going on with you, young man, and I need to know right now. Do you hear me, Lenny? What's going on in your life that would bring strangers to our beautiful Cape St Mary? If you've brought harm to my little family I'll kill you with my bare hands."

Pops looked like he might stroke out on the spot. He stood back as if he was afraid of Lenny. Tears were falling freely from his weathered old face. This broke Lenny's heart.

"Slow down, Pops. Talk to me. What's got you all wound up?" Lenny tried to reach in and hug his old friend but Pops stepped back as he pulled out his handkerchief to wipe his brow. He was sweating profusely and looked like he was about to collapse. Lenny could see Pops was frightened.

"Tell me what's going on, because I have no idea what you're talking about." This time he was able to reach out and hug Pops. He whispered, "You're scaring me, Pops. Have I done something wrong?"

"I'm the one asking the questions," Pops replied. But it seemed the hug might have worked, because Pops settled down a bit. Not much, but a bit. He sat back down at his table, and Lenny sat opposite him and waited.

Pops drained his coffee cup and passed it over. "Grab me a refill and meet me over at that table out of the way. The one in the corner. I'm going to go and save the table."

This time Pops had lowered his voice and sounded a bit more under control. "And a biscuit or anything sweet, son. I need something sweet 'cuz I don't feel so good."

As Lenny arrived at the corner table with two steaming cups of coffee and two of the biggest chocolate chunk cookies he could find, his mind was stuck on Pops saying something about strangers coming to the Cape. Looking for him. Dear Lord in Heaven. It couldn't be.

Lenny didn't plan it this way. He moved to the Cape because he knew Paradise was living there, or somewhere nearby. She was the only person he knew in the area. Or so he had thought.

What were the chances the first and only time Lenny was ordered to hit a woman would be the one night that would haunt and follow him for the rest of his life? He hated to admit that he didn't even know the young woman's name back then. Yet years after he followed his boss's orders to 'get rid of' a specific tiny woman, it seemed she was alive and well in Cape St Mary.

To Lenny, this couldn't be possible. The hit hadn't even taken place in the Cape. It happened in Toronto, way off in Ontario, and Lenny was 100% sure he had killed the woman. At least he was

99.99% sure she was dead when he left. And even if she lived she would have been brain dead. He saw her brains all over the floor and that was from his first kick. There had been many kicks after he took her down with the first one.

Lenny recognized Wilmot first, and time passed before he realized that his wife, Marie, was the same woman he had brutalized in her little home while Meat took care of Wilmot. The fact these two people still lived was a miracle. The fact they were living in the Cape and were related to Paradise broke his heart.

Among the many things Lenny was learning from Paradise was the strength of prayer. Lord knows he was praying now. He was praying that neither Wilmot nor Marie would recognize him.

11

Wilmot and Marie spent their morning as they often did. Up early. Quick breakfast. Tidy the cottage for their return. Quick walk on the beach. Into the car...

They both loved driving in and out of different communities to study the many French Shore churches. Since moving to the Cape they had devoured the inside and outside of every church in sight and were delighted when they first learned they shared this particular interest. They had so much in common and life together was just beginning.

Wilmot could tell Marie had something on her mind but clearly didn't want to talk about it.

Marie could tell Wilmot had something on his mind but clearly didn't want to talk about it.

If they spoke of it, everything would change. If it became a reality, Paradise would be distraught and might never trust a man again. Both Wilmot and Marie loved Paradise and didn't want to do anything that would upset her world. She had done so much for them.

Wilmot didn't think Marie could relive the experience.

Marie knew she couldn't relive the experience.

Dancing around it had become a full-time occupation and they both knew it had to stop. Life is short and past experience made them want to live life to the fullest. They would start by sharing their worst possible fears with each other.

Next, Wilmot and Marie would speak with Paradise. They worried she might be in danger.

12

Thomas took the day off so he could meet with Wikolia's doctors. He didn't seem to ever have a day off from her health care, but Thomas figured Wikolia wasn't given a day off either, so he had little to complain about.

Recently he had thought they were getting closer and it was making her more and more relaxed when they were together during his visits. He was hopeful the doctors had a bit of good news for a change.

Then he received a call well in to his night shift. They had called an emergency meeting for 9 am and he needed to attend. Nothing about "Can you get the time off?" so Thomas knew something was up.

When he walked into the conference room Thomas was startled to see not only Wikolia's lead doctor Carl Legault, who was pacing nervously back and forth, but the head of Security, Sheryl Farmington. Thomas knew Farmington just in passing. He assumed something was very wrong and immediately focused on her. There were three other people around the conference table, people he had never seen before.

"Christ, do not tell me Wikolia's missing. What is it?"

"She's not missing," Doctor Legault said quietly. Sit down, Thomas."

A sense of urgency permeated the room and Thomas quickly sat down and shut up.

"There's been an incident with Wikolia," the doctor said. "I am going to ask you to let me speak without interruption. This is the most serious situation we have had here in the facility." The doctor had Thomas's attention now.

"During the past several weeks Wikolia has complained of vaginal bleeding and abdominal cramps. We saw no sign of blood but took her concern seriously and kept a close eye on her. We asked her to show us the blood the next time this happened but each time she called out saying there was blood we saw no evidence. Not to say we didn't believe Wikolia. We just couldn't seem to get on top of her concern. There was no proof."

Thomas couldn't sit still any longer. "An incident? There's been an incident with Wikolia and this is what you start with? Is she still bleeding and have you discovered what's wrong?"

"Thomas, sit down. Now. I asked you to let me speak. You'll have your answers if you let me give them."

"Okay I'm sitting and I'm going to be quiet, so talk. I'm going crazy trying to figure out what has happened. What is your head of security doing here?" With that Thomas sat back down.

"You will hear from Sheryl in due course. Please give me a chance. This is difficult for all of us."

Thomas poured himself a glass of water from the carafe on the table, willing his hand not to shake. If this was truly difficult for everyone something was very wrong.

"When Security made their rounds last night, they found Wikolia lying on the floor in a pool of blood. She was unconscious. We rushed her to emergency at our main hospital and they then transferred her to the ICU on their third floor."

Doctor Legault rose and walked around the table to Thomas. He touched his shoulder and took his time to choose his next words.

"Wikolia has not yet regained consciousness and her condition is worsening. And there is more. Wikolia miscarried a child."

A loud silence filled the room. Thomas started to say eight different things and could not manage any of them. Doctor Legault returned to his seat. "We assume this was not your child, so you will understand why the head of security is here."

Thomas thought he could peg the other people at the table now. They would be PR staff and folks who managed the hospital's liability insurance. They were not there to help him or Wikolia, but to contain them.

Legault said, "We will now require staff DNA tests, and we're attempting to determine when Wikolia became pregnant. We believe she was in the early stages of her pregnancy. Perhaps six weeks to two months, but we can't be sure at this stage."

"Was she raped?" Thomas knew no one could answer that question, but he had to ask it.

Sheryl spoke for the first time. "I promise you we will retrace every step Wikolia took leading up to both her pregnancy and her miscarriage. No stone will be left unturned and we will find the answers to all of your questions. And if I could repeat Doctor Legault's words, we are so very sorry this has happened."

"How big of you to do your job, Sheryl." The words were out before Thomas could shut his mouth, but he saw they bounced off her. This was not her first crisis meeting.

He tried again. "Can I see her? Can I spend a few minutes with Wikolia even though she's unconscious? I could talk to her about T.J. Maybe I could jolt her into waking up." Most of all Thomas wanted a chance to thank Wikolia for Thomas Junior. If Wikolia up and died, he would make sure T.J. never forgot his mother, and he would also make sure her family got to know T.J., whether they wanted to or not.

"Of course you can see her," the doctor said. "I have a car waiting to take us over to the ICU." He stood, polite as a host at a difficult dinner party.

The suits around the table had not moved, but Thomas could sense them releasing long-held breaths: so far, so good.

It was not lost on Thomas that he should be contacting Wikolia's family. And that he had absolutely no idea how to do it.

13

"Lenny, what does this mean to you?"

"What does what mean?

"This. *This.*" Paradise repeated with an exaggerated swing of their locked hands.

They were walking along Mavillette beach, sipping their early morning coffees, as they did most days. But the hand-holding was new.

Paradise stopped, forcing Lenny to stop, too. She looked at him with concern, affection and wonder. She had grown to love this man. Not in the same way she loved Thomas and she knew the words had to be said.

"Lenny I do love you, but—"

"Paradise, can we forget the 'but' and just have you admit that you're as in love with me as I am with you?"

Lenny stepped closer. Paradise moved to widen the space between them. "Why in God's name would you think I'm in love with you? I love you as I love a friend, a family member, a co-worker, which is what we were. What we are still. If we were to return to Hawaii today and if we went directly to work we would both be in the 2.0 warehouse."

"Jesus, Paradise, these early morning walks are what's keeping me going. I can't get inside that thick head of yours to understand what you're thinking. But I do know you never miss this daily walk with me unless work takes you out of town. There's nothing going on between us? You don't actually believe that, do you?"

Paradise gestured back the way they had come. "It's getting late."

"Tell me what you're thinking, because I have no idea where we go from here."

Silence spread around them like something had spilled. Lenny fought against it.

"I'll say it all, then. I love you. I want to be with you. I want you in my bed so I can kiss you all over. I want to make slow passionate love with you and fall asleep with you in my arms."

Lenny saw the look of shock on the only face he had ever loved. It broke his heart.

With more force than necessary, Paradise yanked her hand away from Lenny. She strode away, walking briskly to put some distance between them. She couldn't find words to say to this man.

My God, she loved Thomas and she wanted Thomas to do all of those things to her.

She didn't look back, but when she reached what they called their 'parting spot', Lenny was there. He had trailed after her all the way up the beach like a beaten dog.

But there was nothing she could say.

Finally, Lenny turned left to his room in the local boarding house and Paradise turned right to her magnificent home on the hill that she shared with her daughter and Pops.

Knowing they would have to talk about this eventually, Paradise gathered her thoughts but kept them to herself—for now. The next few mornings she pretended, even to herself, that she wasn't feeling well so she could avoid meeting Lenny. He could bloody well drink both coffees!

Several days later a message came through Pops that Lenny wanted to talk to her. Paradise knew what he wanted to talk about so she sent a message back with a date and time. She tried to make it sound business-like, but it was anything but.

~

Seven minutes on the clock.

Paradise sat staring at the antique clock on the wall and decided she would let Lenny continue rambling on about anything and everything. However, if he chose to not come clean by the top of the hour – seven minutes from now – she would have to ask some very difficult questions.

Tick-tock. Tick-tock.

Time's up.

"Lenny, I can't let you go on any longer. When you asked to see me I assumed you wanted to talk about the other day on the beach.

Yet, here you are, talking about nothing at all. So out with it. What's on that complicated mind of yours? I'm worried. Pops is worried too about someone coming to the Cape asking questions about you. What's that all about?"

"It's nothing," Lenny said, not meeting her eyes. "Lotta nothing."

"Pops said he was talking with you about your life before you came here, and you kept dodging his questions. And then you took off. That's not like the Lenny I know."

Lenny got up from the table, not to leave but to refill his coffee cup. She could see he was buying time to try to figure out how he should say whatever it was that was eating at him.

Finally he turned around and leaned on the counter. "Oh, Paradise, what a mess I've made of things. I'll tell you what I can, but, honey, there are things in my past life that you're better off not knowing."

Paradise could see this was difficult for him but she was at a loss to fill in the blanks.

"You're the only person in the Cape who knows I was offered the Witness Protection Program."

"Then why are you here, not off starting your new life?"

"We talked about all of this."

"No, that's not quite true, Lenny. We did not talk about 'all of this'. I have absolutely no idea where you are going. Spit it out or I'll be the one to walk out."

Trying to lighten the moment, Lenny said, "Since we're in your home it would be tough for you to leave, so I guess I better speak up."

Paradise tried to keep a neutral face. She looked at Lenny, waiting for his big reveal. She could see in his eyes that it would be profound.

"Paradise, when you met me I was living at 2.0 full time. I hadn't seen the light of day for over a year. I told you that. It must have made you wonder what I had done or what lurked in my past that might force me to stay hidden away for months on end. The strangers who came to talk with me once a month had to interest you at some level. I told you I would be leaving and entering the witness protection program."

She stirred uncomfortably in her seat. "But you never said why. I half-thought you were spinning me a story."

"It's what happened. But you left before I did, and that was a shock to me. I thought you were going to visit Pops here and then make a stop in Toronto so Hope could meet her grandparents. *You never said you were never coming back.*"

Paradise raised a hand. "I want you to tell your story right now. Don't try to sidetrack into my story."

He nodded. Took refuge for a moment in a sip of coffee. Then Lenny met her eyes. "Little by little I fell in love with you while we worked side by side. I knew your heart belonged to Thomas, but I've never taken life's easy path. I figured maybe, with time, I could win you to me. So I turned down the witness protection program, left 2.0, and came here. I worked for Pops until you showed up."

"You know that freaks me out, right? You went out of your way to get my own great grandfather on your side so you —"

This time it was Lenny holding up a hand. "You can hear the story or you can beat me up for this and that. Which do you want?"

He waited to make sure she was going to hold still, which she could just barely manage. "No one knew me here. No one in my past life could trace me to this small village. Or so I thought."

Silence.

He put down his cup and clasped his hands in front of his chest. "Paradise, someone is looking for me. They asked Pops about me. He didn't know much about the man asking the questions but it frightened him, and that breaks my heart. Might be the first thing in my entire life that has broken my heart."

"My God, Lenny, has trouble followed you here?" Her voice was shaky. "Have you put people I love in danger? My brother Wilmot and his wife? Pops?"

"I hope not."

She stood up to face him. "The 'people I love' includes you, you big idiot. Please tell me what is going on and what you are going to do about it."

"I don't know yet exactly who is after me. I'm going to find out, though."

"How?" Tears were starting to roll down her cheeks.

"I'm going to leave the Cape for a few days to draw whoever it is after me. These people here are like family to me now. I won't let anything happen to any of them. For the first time in my life I can say I have friends, and I'll be damned if anyone is going to take that away from me."

Lenny crossed the room, drew Paradise to him, and pulled her onto his lap as he sat in what had been her chair. He kissed her forehead, then whispered, "The less you know about my plans, the better. If anyone asks where have I have gone, who am I with, when am I coming back, you can honestly say I told you nothing. One day I just left, okay?"

"Does it have to be that drastic?" Paradise still knew nothing, really. He had divulged nothing at all. "You have to run away?"

"I'm not running away. I'll be drawing whoever is hunting me down away from you and everyone around you."

"It's a dumb plan." She gave her head a shake. "When will you leave?"

"I don't know when I'll leave and I don't know when I'll return, and that's how it has to be." Lenny stood up, holding her until she found her feet. Then he faced her, holding her hands in his. "I'll take my chances you'll be waiting for me when I get back. A fella has to dream."

He took her face in his hands and kissed her cheek as if she was made of porcelain and might shatter.

Paradise thought it was the sweetest cheek-kiss she had ever received. She knew that kiss came with a promise and no promise at all.

~

Lenny left knowing he had told Paradise two lies. He did know when he would be leaving and he didn't know if he would ever be back.

Walking with a purpose like never before he returned to his rooming house and packed up his few belongings. Then he waited until dark. He was pretty sure he could get out of town without any come-from-aways tracking him.

Finally it was time. He slipped out of the side door and along the least-lit path, leaving the Cape and everything he had grown to love. As he slipped along with practised stealth, he prayed silently to Paradise's God: "If I get out of this alive, dear God, I promise you this..."

Lenny didn't know how to finish his own sentence.

14

Hope lived in perpetual motion. Nothing slowed her down. She almost pounced on Paradise as she came through the door after her school day. Books and clothes dropped on the floor directly inside the front door behind her.

"Oh. My. God. What a day I've had, mom. I have so much to tell you I hardly know where to start. I got an A in a math test. I came second in a speech competition. I won a dance competition after school. I failed a grammar test. I think Matthew likes me. You know who he is right? Does life get better?"

Paradise attempted to weigh in but hadn't said a word before Hope continued. The 'failed grammar test' comment was not lost on her, but Paradise quietly filed that away for their dinner table discussion. This would be a stand-alone topic and Hope would be much more calm when the discussion began.

"What's a good name for my business?"

"Wait, Hope. You have a business?"

"I will as soon as I think of the right name for it. Barbara's mother owns a printing business up the line and she's going to print my business cards but I need to decide what to put on the cards first."

"Slow down, Hope. What kind of a business are you starting dear? And w—?"

"Oh I'll just do anything I can and then I'll figure out what I like the best."

"I understand, but what has prompted this now? Today? And why are you in such a rush to have a business name and business cards?" Paradise added, "We'll get to your failed test later."

"Believe it or not, mom, I'm earning money right now. As I stand here talking to you I'm earning my own money." Scratching her head, Hope corrected herself. "That might not be true. Let me get a drink and if you have time let's sit in the window and I'll tell you everything."

Novel idea, Paradise thought.

She silently walked over to the window seat and arranged the blankets and pillows as her daughter liked everything to be when they sat down together. It was not lost on Paradise that one day her daughter might not want to sit and chat with her mother so easily.

"So, here's the thing, mom. Mrs. Foss has hired me to plan, arrange, and execute a birthday party for the twins. I wouldn't have used the word 'execute' but that's her business word for everything so I figure I need a business of my own to deal with all of her thinking and her words."

Paradise had so many comments and observations ready to burst out of her that it was a miracle she didn't say a word.

"We've already talked about everything. All the details and stuff about the party, I mean. So I need a business to get started."

"When does Mrs. Foss want the party to be, honey? They don't come to their beach house every weekend."

"I don't know when."

"How old will the twins be this year?"

"Not sure."

"What kind of a budget is Mrs. Foss prepared to give you for this party?"

"No idea."

"Do the twins know any other children in the area, or will you be planning a family-only birthday party for them?"

"Okay, mother, I get it. I don't have all the answers."

"Sweetie, you don't have any answers. But that's okay. Why don't I help you make a list of questions, and maybe a few suggestions you could make to Mrs. Foss the next time you speak with her?"

Not getting any response, Paradise continued, "How does that sound, Hope? Would this help get you started?"

"Mom. Mom. Mom. You think a list is the answer for everything. And you could be right, but what about the name for my business? Can we please start there? I really want my own business cards."

"Okay, let's start there. I think you should use your own name in the name of your business. How does that sound?"

"So it would be Hope-something?"

"Well we can begin with that. Hope-Full?"

"I see what you're talking about. Let me think, mom."

"Sure. But I'm going to write down anything and everything I can think of while you're thinking."

"I'll think later, so say it all out loud, mom."

Paradise nodded, accepting Hope's challenge.

"A Life Full of Hope.

"High Hope.

"Hope-Full.

"A Cause for Hope.

"Hopefully."

Hope was on her feet now. "Mom, do you really feel these are all good names for my business?"

"Of course not, Hope. Sit down. This is a teachable moment. I learned this when I was first at the Private Investigator training academy. When we tried to solve a case we would go to the blackboard and write down everything we could think of. Then, when we were totally exhausted and had not a single thought left in our heads we went back to the first thought we had listed and we'd read each one aloud and discuss it. We rubbed out almost everything we had written, and sometimes we learned nothing from the exercise. But every once in a while something bubbled up and we had our answer."

"Did it surprise you?"

"The first couple of times, yes. But then I started to trust the exercise. Applying this model to your need for a business name might take us somewhere. Our list isn't complete yet, I know. But it's a beginning, don't you think?"

"Sure."

Paradise knew the moment wasn't lost, but that the exercise was finished for the day. Those one-word answers were usually a slamming of the door on whatever was taking place.

Hope surprised her mom, though. "I like the first name you suggested, but you were on such a roll I didn't want to stop you." She laughed as she spread her arms wide and proclaimed, "'A Life Full of Hope.' That's it! Thanks, mom."

She started to bounce away, but then turned back as if worried Paradise might be sad for her rejected ideas. "I'll think about the others again though, just in case I'm wrong about the name I think I like the best."

Mission accomplished for today.

15

Running to answer the phone before the caller hung up, Hope was out of breath as she dove onto the sofa with the receiver in hand and the long cord wrapped around her body.

"Hope here."

"I thought you were going to call me hours ago."

"I was. I just this second finished a long talk with my mother. It was more of her telling me everything she knows rather than having a discussion."

"I've told you a million times, Hope, I would trade mothers with you in a second. Your mother is 'with it' and you're just jealous."

"Are you freaking kidding me? You think I would ever in a million years be jealous of my mother?" Hope replied, laughing. "Anyway, your mother is dead, last I heard."

"How kind and gentle of you, Hope. I think I've just about had enough of your whining and your 'woe is me' nattering day in and day out. Does your mother even know about us? Please tell me she does."

"Hang on," Hope was on her feet making sure no one was around who might be listening. "What does this have to do with you and me and a relationship? And, there is no 'us', so stop saying that. How did we go from talking about my mother to talking about your sex life. Not mine. Not ours. Yours."

"God, Hope, how many times have we had this conversation about us and our relationship? Are you even maturing at all?"

Hope wondered how far she should take this and she wanted to get the discussion back to her mother and not about relationships. "Wasn't it you who told me to pick my battles, especially where my mother is concerned? Well, I make sure they're the ones I can win before I pick 'em." Hope wasn't sure she should go on. "My mother might be lame but she isn't stupid. I told you I would tell her about us, as you put it, when I'm damn good and ready. Is that clear enough?"

"Do you still have the expensive-looking Dior sunglasses I gave you? I bet you had to explain those to your mother?"

"Nice change of subject. I see what you did there. Actually, one of the Foss twins loves the sunglasses so she's keeping them safe for me," Hope knew that was definitely not the correct answer.

"I think you mean she's keeping them hidden, Hope."

"*Safe*. I said she's keeping them safe."

"It's only half past eight. Do you want to get together right now? We need to talk about this."

"Talk about what? What is 'this', anyway? I bet you really want to teach me something new about sex. I just turned sixteen, you know. Kind of young for sex. At least that's what I think. Especially sex with you because, like, how old are you anyway?"

"I'm nineteen. I told you that already. Is it my age or is it because you have a girlfriend not a boyfriend?"

"We are not 'girlfriends' and I told you that the night I met you. Oh. My. God, do you not remember anything I tell you?"

Francis had been thinking of breaking up with Hope anyway. She wanted to be sure Hope understood that if she didn't smarten up soon Francis would bring the hammer down! This wasn't a real relationship, but she wasn't about to admit that to Hope.

"*Nineteen*, really?"

"Hope, let's call it an end to our relationship. Today might be a good day to do that, don't you think?"

"Sure."

Francis should have known better. Hope was famous for her one-word responses to the tough questions. She was just lucky Hope didn't know her real age. She was aware twenty-four was perhaps a bit too old to be lusting after a sixteen-year-old, but it had been fun while it lasted.

She hung up the phone thoughtfully. As Francis looked up the number for a friend who might willingly take Hope's place she wondered what the chances were that she would be one of the teachers in Hope's school next year. "'Young lady, see me after class.' That would be so fine," Francis said out loud as she poured herself another drink.

At Hope's end of the line, she was smiling and continuing the discussion on her own. "Oh. My. God. I've got it! I've got the perfect name for my business. *HopeHere*. Done!"

Hope went in search of her mother. She wanted to share her name for her business and how she simply stumbled upon it when she answered the phone saying, "Hope here."

Not sure she would tell her mother about the sex thing just yet, though. She met Francis one day in town when she was pissed off with her mother. Thinking back, it's possible Francis played on that a bit, because she agreed with everything negative that Hope had to say about her mom. Their discussion made Hope feel very grown up at the time.

She went home with Francis that day and she almost stayed overnight. She certainly went a little further on the sex front than she had planned to, although a lot less than Francis seemed to want. And she barely caught her ride back to the Cape.

16

For more years than he could remember Thomas had been a lapsed Catholic. Most of the time he couldn't let his mind go there. He knew his mother prayed for him and for his family, but that might not be enough. Not today.

As he drove to the hospital Thomas prayed to Paradise's God to help Wikolia regain consciousness and come back to him. She had to, for him and for T.J.

A quick phone call to Mae, the nanny, meant T.J. might beat his dad to the hospital. Thomas was certain hearing T.J.'s voice would help Wikolia come back to them, if she could hear him. It was a long shot, but he had few other options.

Calling Wikolia's family was important. Thomas knew he would have to dig through all of Wikolia's things to see if he could find numbers for her mother and siblings. That would have to happen later today, or tomorrow if she made it out of the ICU at some point today. Maybe her family could get to the hospital within a day or two, but Thomas didn't know where any of them lived.

Calling Paradise didn't even occur to Thomas. He would question his thinking later. He couldn't recall the last time Paradise had called him other than to return his messages. Not that he was keeping score, but there were days when Thomas felt keeping this relationship alive was a priority for him but not for Paradise.

The second he arrived at the hospital, Thomas was able to scoop his son out of Mae's arms. "You got here in record time, Mae, I really appreciate it. Park your car and meet us in ICU." Mae was a huge part of their lives and Thomas could see the questions and the fear in her eyes. He would tell her everything later.

"Let's go, son. Come with me."

Thomas and T.J. were off and running through the hospital, following a nurse who led the way to the ICU. Holding his son tight to his chest, Thomas whispered, "Are you excited to see Mommy?"

T.J. was excited. To him, the moment must be like they were going to jump in the pool or get in the car for a drive or at least have an ice cream. But this was a trip to the Intensive Care Unit, and Thomas suddenly became aware of how confusing this visit might be for the boy. He hoped he wasn't making a mistake.

They entered mommy's room and Thomas came to a full stop. The body in the bed, tubed up and bandaged, looked like the survivor of a car crash.

He turned abruptly so T.J. would not get a look at the scary body and returned to the nurses' station to ask for Wikolia's room again. He was certain he must have heard the wrong room number.

"I'm so sorry, Mr. Adams, but you were in the right room. Wikolia's condition is critical. The machines and the pressure bandages are helping to keep her alive. I could go in with you, if you like."

T.J. began to get a pre-cry look on his face.

"One more thing, sir, I'm not sure this is the proper place for a young boy. Can I take him for you?"

Doctor Legault stepped in. "T.J., perhaps you could visit with me."

T.J. knew Doctor Legault and made no fuss at all as the doctor unburdened Thomas. "Let's go for a hunt, T.J., and see if we can find that nanny of yours."

"Thank you," Thomas said, aiming it equally at the doctor and the nurse. Both gave Thomas a slight nod. It was not the time for a smile.

"That way?" T.J. said, pointing down a random hallway.

"Off we go," Doctor Legault replied. "This may take a few minutes, so, Thomas, you can go and have a sit with Wikolia. I'll be back after T.J. finds the nanny for me."

In Wikolia's room, Thomas moved quietly as if he was sneaking up on the bad guys. He sat on the edge of the bed, took her hand in his, and leaned forward to whisper in her ear. "Wikolia, my love. I'm here and so is our son. If you can wake up for me, I'll bring him to you. How does that sound?"

He realized tears were dripping from his face onto hers. Thomas sat back and spoke in a louder tone that was still library-quiet. "Can you do that? Can you wake up for me? You could tell me all about that secret you have been so excited to share. No judgment here, Wikolia. I promise you that."

The sound of machines filled the room. Thomas tried to figure out how to send reviving energy from his hand to Wikolia's, but he really wasn't up on that new-agey stuff. He settled for focusing on her face, hoping the weight of attention might get through to her. It was next to impossible to accept that this woman, wrapped in bandages from head to toe, was Wikolia. Life had not been kind to her.

After a timeless time, Thomas realized Doctor Legault was standing beside him. Without looking away from Wikolia, he said, "She squeezed my hand a couple of times. You probably won't believe me but it *did* happen."

With a hand on Thomas's shoulder, Doctor Legault spoke quietly. "Step outside with me for a few minutes, Thomas. Let's have a discussion in a quiet corner. I know just the place where we won't be interrupted."

Placing a kiss on Wikolia's cheek, Thomas spoke as if they were having a regular discussion. "I'll be right back. Don't go anywhere."

"First of all, Thomas, it would be remarkable if Wikolia was actually able to squeeze your hand. If you felt something, it was probably an involuntary muscle movement. In her current state, Wikolia is unable to squeeze anything."

Thomas knew, without a doubt, that she had squeezed his hand, yet Doctor Legault seemed insistent this could not have happened. Thomas wasn't ready to give up on her but he agreed to listen. The doctor kept saying 'in her present state' and when he had the chance he would ask what that actually means.

"Thomas, it appears we didn't do a good job in explaining the sequence of events involving Wikolia when you came in earlier today. So pardon me if what I am about to say seems cruel and blunt. It's necessary that you understand."

Both men filled their coffee cups in silence and sat facing each other. Then the doctor leaned forward. "Wikolia is not breathing on her own. The machines you saw are keeping her alive, but really that's a poor choice of words. She is no longer alive."

Thomas was terrified, but remained tight-lipped. He had to bite his lip to keep his mouth shut. He would get answers to any remaining questions he had as soon as Doctor Legault gave him a chance.

"In addition to her miscarriage and extreme blood loss, I'm afraid Wikolia has suffered a major stroke. I checked her vitals again this morning and everything I have just said has been confirmed."

Thomas opened his mouth, then closed it again as the doctor pressed on. "You probably want to point fingers, and I understand that. I see it all the time. You can do that another day, and we will listen to every word you need to say. But today, this very moment, the woman who was once your partner lies brain dead. It's time for you to say goodbye and tell her she can rest. I will help you Thomas. You know that."

Thomas felt his thoughts bouncing, dodging to avoid what the doctor was saying. He wondered if Legault had taken a course on Presenting Hard Truths, or if this was a skill he had developed through having to have this miserable conversation with countless families. He wondered if the doctor had a standard entry for each file: "Broke the news to the next of kin." He wondered why he felt like grabbing Legault and shaking him like a doll until he agreed to make Wikolia better.

~

He heard himself saying, "Is she dead, then? Are you telling me to give up on her? I can't do that. There has to be a chance she will come back to us. No?"

"No."

They sat in silence. The doctor looked like he was trying to digest an unfortunate meal. Thomas didn't want to think about what he looked like himself.

Part of his mind raged, looking for a lever to pull, and action to take. Hospital security would have to come clean about when and how it had been possible for Wikolia to become pregnant. That would be a good project to aim his anger at. But not today.

"Thomas, you stay here for as long as you want. When you return to Wikolia's side, you stay with her for as long as you want. You have some tough decisions to make and I'll be here to help you. I'm going to give you a bit of space now, so you don't have to worry about being sociable."

After Doctor Legault left the room, Thomas wiped his tears. He sat for a few minutes, just listening to his thoughts churn, before he returned to Wikolia.

He decided not to bring T.J. back into the room to see his mother one last time. Even Thomas hadn't recognized her earlier, so what could T.J. possibly make of what he would see? He was content to be with Mae while daddy spent a few quiet moments with his mommy.

Thomas looked at Wikolia's unchanging, almost unfamiliar, face; listened to the machines; considered her stillness.

"I'm going to say goodbye shortly, my love." He was surprised he still had tears to shed. "I'm certain you've tried your best to come back to us. Now I want you to rest. Rest knowing you are loved."

He patted her hand gently, then moved over to the window and staring unseeing at the rest of the world, where Wikolia was not brain-dead. "It's odd, but I take a bit of comfort in knowing you had a boyfriend, because I believe he made you happy."

A little later, seeming to have changed his mind Thomas said, "I'm going to take T.J. home now, my love, but I'll be back tomorrow. If you can come back to us, I know you will. Please try to come back to us."

Tomorrow was followed by another tomorrow and another. Thomas was so used to the beeps and bings of the monitors that he barely heard them any more. The nurses coming and going threw small smiles his way, but said almost nothing.

On the sixth day, as Thomas sat his vigil, Doctor Legault entered the room.

"What are you thinking today, Thomas? Has time brought you any clarity about Wikolia's future? Drop into my office after your visit, if you like."

Thomas spoke, not to him, but to the body in the bed."Wikolia, I know now you are not able to come back to us. I hope I have not made you suffer even more these last few days as I have struggled to understand how we got here. I want to tell you I have learned your secret. You were going to tell me that you and your boyfriend were expecting a baby. Such exciting news. I know it made you very happy."

Thomas had to take a break to control his emotions but he wanted to finish what he had to say.

"Your baby is with you now, and you will be together in heaven. I will keep T.J. safe for you until we all meet again, my love." His voice was the faintest of whispers.

"We're all okay here, and I will make sure your family and friends are made aware. I know I keep repeating myself but you can rest now."

Doctor Legault whispered, "She doesn't need all the details, Thomas. You're good, and now we must let her rest. I think she's ready, whenever you are. I'll wait for you in my office until day's end."

Hours later, Thomas entered the doctor's office, two large coffees in hand. They sipped quietly for a moment or two, then Thomas drew breath. "Does it have to be today? It's only been a week. Not today. Maybe later in the week? Is that okay, Doc?"

"Anything's possible, Thomas, but the hospital needs Wikolia's room for the next patient needing ICU care and treatment."

Doctor Legault took a pause to see if Thomas wanted to speak. Silence.

"I can make arrangements for Wikolia to be moved to a long term care facility, if you wish. I must make sure you understand that once we move her, control is out of our hands. It's out of your hands. Machines can keep her heart beating indefinitely. Her condition will not improve. Her brain is dead, Thomas."

Brain dead. It sounded to Thomas like a playground insult.

"You have said goodbye to Wikolia every day for the past week. I can't make the decision for you. I won't make it for you. However, today is the day we decide if she is to be moved to long term care...or do we turn off the machines."

"Give me an hour with her. Just one more hour, then please join us. I want to be there to witness for myself if her heart stops beating the second you turn the machines off. I'll be praying for a miracle."

There would be no miracle.

17

Lenny had been on the run for nearly a week.

He hitch-hiked up the line to Saulnierville and walked from there to the Dominion Atlantic Railway station. Next, he jumped a train heading Yarmouth-way, telling anyone within earshot that he was headed for the ferry to Maine. He was not.

During a brief train stop in a dimly lit village just prior to Yarmouth Lenny silently jumped off and into the night.

Without fanfare or anyone catching up with him, Lenny boarded the Halifax bound train headed in the other direction. Not wanting to take any chances, he got off the train in Bridgetown and boarded a bus at the last minute with no ticket in hand. So far so good.

Last stop before Halifax and not really knowing how much further he had to travel to get to the city, Lenny got off the bus and hoped he hadn't made a mistake.

Wandering into what was surely a back-alley pit stop offering more than coffee, Lenny sat on the only empty stool at the counter and struck up a conversation with a man on the stool beside him. As luck would have it the nighttime trucker was headed to Halifax and was happy to have company heading into the city, so offered to give Lenny a ride. Lenny figured they both had secrets, so riding along with his new friend might work out.

"Name's Len," Lenny extended his hand to the man who had just offered him a ride. So far they had talked while eating as they stared straight ahead at the cook and waitress on the other side of the counter. He figured they could size each other up before heading out.

An easy observation would be the size of the hand he was shaking and man he was facing; big, bald and built like a wrestler on a winning streak. Lenny figured this man could crush him easily, but for some reason he was certain he could trust him.

"Nice to meet ya', young man. What's takin' you to the city?"

Not lost on Lenny that no name had been offered. He hoped that wasn't an indication of what was to come. In Lenny's world if a man wouldn't share his name with you it was best to walk away. He didn't.

"If a man's looking for a place to crash for the night, any suggestions?"

"Assumin' you know the city, I'll drop you off on Barrington Street near a rooming house I may or may not stay at on a drive-through myself. The owners are good people. Their only language is cash up front."

Lenny could see Buddy thinking hard before he spoke again. "How are ya' fixed for hardware?"

"Got one but could use another."

Sure enough, his nighttime trucker friend introduced him to a man who knew someone who knew someone who had a gun for sale. Lenny had his own gun, of course, but thought having a second piece might be a wise decision.

He closed his eyes for a minute as the big rig rolled towards the city. Someone was closing in on him. Possibly more than one person. Lenny knew he was ready. His life depended on it. He had eaten lots of frustration while he was on the run this time.

Lenny wasn't an old man but he figured he was too old to be on the run. If he escaped with his life this time he would turn his life around. Of course, he thought he had done that when he found Paradise in Cape St Mary.

Halifax seemed a suitable distance from the Cape. Lenny rented a tiny room on Barrington Street and prepared to draw his followers out of the shadows. He knew he had lost them a couple of times, but he could also sense they were probing their way through Halifax to see where he had gone to ground.

If everything went according to plan, Lenny could be back in the Cape in a few days at the most. Undoubtedly this time Paradise would insist on knowing a hell of a lot more about his past-life and would want all sorts of details. She had been so trusting and they were just beginning to make progress in their relationship. The name 'Thomas' was never far from her lips, though, and it was a slap in Lenny's face every time she mentioned him. That was just one of the things Lenny figured he could talk to Paradise about once this was all behind him.

Lenny had to give himself a shake. Spending any time thinking about Paradise could get him killed.

He forced himself to return to the task at hand. After several weeks of scouting the area and formulating a plan, Lenny was not 100% ready, but close enough.

On a rainy Monday morning, with foghorns blasting, Lenny sorted his guns under his trench coat so they wouldn't show during his walk to Point Pleasant Park. Guns would do all the talking at this upcoming meeting and he wanted a safe place away from the innocent Halifax folks who came to the Park to walk their dogs and lose their worries for an hour or two in good weather and bad. Having walked through the Park daily for the last several days Lenny was able to quickly move deep into the Park to his point of advantage for this meeting.

Today was the perfect day to kill someone to save your own life and possibly the lives of others including your loved ones. For a nanosecond, once again, he thought about Paradise. Quickly back to the present...

You couldn't see two feet in front of your face and it seemed the fog was even thicker than when he had walked to the Park a couple of hours ago. Lenny figured if he stayed on high alert he would see his followers come into view before they saw him.

It didn't take long.

There were three of them.

All on the hunt: questing, heads turning from side to side, guns drawn.

Just as he figured, there would be no talking at this meeting.

Even with the advantage of seeing them first, Lenny knew he couldn't get three shots off before one of them saw him and reacted. He had been in a situation like this before. He remembered how he got out of that one alive, and he knew what he had to do.

The hair of a second – that's all it would take.

That's all it took.

In the distance, but still in Point Pleasant Park, a local runner thought he heard a gunshot followed by more shots. He picked up his pace and kept running while he quickly visualized the nearest pay phone. Something very bad had just taken place in Point Pleasant Park.

18

Knowing *he* had recently packed up and left the Cape, Marie found it easier to voice her fear of this man and her worry that he might come back. She still couldn't say his name. She asked Wilmot if he knew the man she feared had left the Cape.

Wilmot replied with the words that would open Pandora's box. "I know."

"My God, Wilmot." Marie was already in tears. "How long have you known?" She couldn't bear to relive one second of the nightmare, yet she couldn't park the images. "Why have you never mentioned it?"

"Don't jump to conclusions, sweetheart. I just figured it out. As God is my witness, I just figured it out. Day before yesterday when I had coffee with Pops he kept talking about a stranger in the Cape asking all kinds of questions."

Wilmot took time to gather Marie in his arms. She was shaking as she wrapped her arms around her husband.

"Was this stranger looking for someone in particular?" She tried and failed to keep her voice level.

"Marie, we'll tackle this together. I swear to my sister's God. We need to talk to Paradise too, and soon."

Wilmot knew they had to say his name. They had to make it real. Marie knew it as well. But they couldn't do it. Not yet.

"So, you think someone came here already knowing this was the same man who attempted to beat me to death? Is that what Pops told you? My God, Wilmot, does Pops know?" Marie was near hysterics.

"No, Pops knows nothing that definite. But this guy asked things, said things. He could describe our drifter perfectly. Said something about how he was in the witness protection program. And if that's true, everything about him could be fake. I'm not sure where to begin. Even his name could be fake."

"You and Pops think we should believe some guy who waltzes into town and says all these nasty things about the man we think is in love with Paradise? That's not fair to either of them, and, believe me, I'm not trying to protect the drifter."

She didn't want to believe it was true. "It can't be him, Wilmot. It just can't be. What are the chances?"

How would they ever tell Paradise her life might be in danger? Everyone around this man could be in danger, especially once he figured out Wilmot and Marie knew who he really was. He would want to protect his true identity at any cost.

"Lenny Calhoon almost killed me. I'll say his name out loud and I'll also say Lenny Calhoon is an attempted murderer. You know I'm not exaggerating, Wilmot."

19

Pops wondered if he was too old to be asking for a woman's hand in marriage. He wondered if she would say no or...if she would say yes.

Where would they live if they did get married? Pops had a beautiful home with an incredible view of the ocean, but he had already decided if Eugenie agreed to marry him they would find their own place to live. It was time for Paradise and Hope to truly take over the home he wanted so desperately to pass on to them.

Maybe he could move in with Eugenie. He had never even been to her home, so he knew he shouldn't be planning to move in just yet.

Pops walked at a faster pace now. He had tried to make this walk yesterday, but his feet wouldn't let him catch up with his heart. His heart had known he wanted this for a long time.

He should have thought everything through before walking over to her house. It was too late now.

The door opened before he had a chance to knock. "Well, hello there, Pops," Eugenie said. "Why on earth are you knocking on my door? Come on in."

She seemed nervous as she fluttered into the front hall. "It isn't much, I know, but I would love to show you my little apartment. I have the first floor and a lovely young family live upstairs. Our landlady is a fine woman. I love her. Did you know I've lived here since I left the convent?"

Pops didn't think she would ever stop talking. She seemed wound up like a spinning top. He didn't want to go a step further if she was on her way out, and anyway he was too nervous to ask her right now. This wasn't going as he had planned it out last night.

"Well um...Eugenie I um...want to ask you a question, but I can see you're going out. It can wait for another time. You seemed in such a hurry when you opened the door."

"I did? How does one open the door and appear to be in a rush? What has gotten into you today, Pops? All I did was open my door."

Pops saw how she must see him. He was going on eighty-five and she was just a young whipper-snapper. They had talked about age once, and after he freely stated his age, Eugenie had said she would never tell anyone hers. He could see she was young, though. For sure she was way younger than him.

Pops decided to tell a little lie. "What is wrong with me today? I even forgot what I came over here to ask you, so why don't you go on your way and I'll head back home. I'm sure I'll remember soon enough and I'll ask you another time."

Eugenie watched him stump away back down the road. She didn't think Pops forgot what he wanted to ask her at all. The man had lost his nerve. Plain and simple. Lost his nerve.

Eugenie felt a pang of sympathy for him. After living most of her life in a convent, faithful only to her Lord, Eugenie was a constant bundle of nerves when a man like Pops was near. They just seemed so solidly, fascinatingly male.

Had he come to propose, and then changed his mind? What if he had asked the question and she had said yes? She barely knew anything about, well, sex. Would they actually have sex, whatever that meant, if they did get married? What a cruel joke if he asked and she said yes and they did all the things you did to get married and then when they were together...nothing happened.

Eugenie tried to tell herself she had nothing to be nervous about. Marriage may not even be what Pops had in mind.

She went down the path to the road and turned in the opposite direction from the way Pops had gone, even though she was now heading away from her destination.

Why is sex the first thing I always think of? Convent wisdom was that it was men who always had sex on their brains.

Would Pops still want to marry me if he knew I'm a virgin? Imagine a virgin at my age. Would he even believe me?

20

No matter how hard you try, things don't always work out as planned.

Elise, Hope and her mom had plans to go to Halifax together. It was supposed to be a business and a personal trip.

Paradise packed an overnight bag while Hope reminded her of the facts at high volume. "You bloody well promised us, Mom. You said you'd ask Curtis if you could bring us with you and we could stay in the city for a few days after you finished your work."

Using a much softer voice, Paradise began, "Welcome to the real world, honey. I didn't forget. Of course I didn't forget. We've been planning this for months. But my boss called me into his office this morning and said I was to be on the road before day's end. It's business, Hope. Sergeant Curtis wasn't asking. He was telling me to go."

Paradise stopped to gather her thoughts before going on. She didn't want to fight with her daughter before leaving for the city.

Hope took advantage of the silence. "So in the real world you can break promises."

"Stop it, Hope. *You stop this right now*. You're a smart young lady and you know how hard I work at my job. I have to work hard. I have responsibilities and you do, too. It's Monday and you have school all week, unless you're keeping something from me. You're not on a school break are you?" Paradise thought she would attempt to lighten the conversation, but no such luck.

"Not funny." Hope stomped out of Paradise's room and slammed her own bedroom door behind her.

Pops quickly came to the rescue. "You get yourself packed up and on the road, Paradise. I'll look after Hope, don't you worry. Not my place, but she was out of line with some of the things she threw at you. I won't overstep I promise. But I'll give our girl a bit of a talking to." Pops smiled as he gave Paradise a big hug and sent her on her way.

Paradise tried to give Hope a hug and an 'I love you,' before setting out, but Hope was having none of it. She wanted to sulk so Paradise left her to it.

"I'm some proud of you, girl," Pops called after her as Paradise lugged her suitcase to the car parked at the curb. She threw her stuff in the back seat, gave a cursory wave, and took off with just a touch of spinning wheels to share her feelings with Hope.

Paradise was thankful her boss let her take one of the police cruisers rather than drive her father's tank. Curtis had said with a laugh that he couldn't afford to put gas in the Cadillac anyway.

Driving time to Halifax would be close to four hours, so Paradise had lots of quiet *think* time.

Her daughter was growing up. At fourteen Hope was just two years younger than Paradise had been when she entered the convent. Thinking back, Paradise was certain she was more mature at fourteen, but comparing their lives wasn't fair and she knew better.

Her think time was better spent concentrating on two other young ladies. Getting Dawn out of jail and meeting with Doctor Sydney Scott to discuss the autopsy as it had been written for Morning Glory were the two things she hoped to accomplish before heading back to the Cape. Paradise would use stage names for the girls initially because, sadly, that's how they were registered.

The first time she met the girls Paradise was a brand new private investigator. She was on contract with the local police force while Morning Glory and Dawn were in town to 'dance' at the shaky old strip club in Digby. The sisters ended up in the local jail overnight and had been charged with murder. Murder!

Once the charges were dropped and the girls were released, Paradise invited them to share her tiny apartment. They had nowhere else to go and no money.

Paradise soon confirmed both girls were underage. She had about twenty-four hours to convince them the life they had chosen was beneath them. They were smart and could earn an honest living.

She drove the girls to the Halifax airport. When she dropped them off, they promised her they were going to change their lives immediately. They even promised to stop introducing themselves as Morning Glory and Dawn.

Sure.

~

Arriving in Halifax, Paradise knew she was cutting it close if she wanted to see Dawn that day. 'Visiting hours' at the jail would be over in 40 minutes, so she drove straight there before checking in to her hotel.

Parking fees were high in Halifax compared to no charge at all to park anywhere at the Cape. Looking around after she parked and locked her car Paradise thought she would never again live in a big city – anywhere.

Paradise could have saved her money. Dawn had been released from jail and was deemed to be of 'no fixed address.' Given that Dawn was most likely still under age, Paradise wondered why anyone would release a young girl when she had nowhere to go. Again, she didn't think that would happen in a small town.

Dawn's chosen profession probably had something to do with her having been released. It was not lost on Paradise that Dawn had most likely left with a bit of an attitude as well.

21

Getting any amount of sleep in such a noisy city was next to impossible. Paradise was up and out of the hotel early, looking for a good coffee shop close to the office of the Chief Coroner.

It was still pitch black outside – nighttime wasn't yet safely tucked away, but Paradise had a list to review before meeting Doctor Scott. She was anxious to meet the doctor and had researched her as much as she could before travelling to Halifax. The woman was extremely accomplished and Paradise knew she could learn from her.

With her first coffee now in hand Paradise found a booth facing the street. She loved to watch a city wake up. And there were other diversions...

Out of the corner of an eye and with both ears Paradise watched and listened to a commotion at the back of the coffee shop. Even at this early hour she had not managed to find that quiet corner she had searched for. Maybe such places don't exist outside of the Cape.

"Wake up and get out of here, young lady. You can't sleep in a public place. This is the very last time I will allow it."

"Shut up. Just shut up and get me a coffee." Mary was trying to straighten her sweatshirt as she spoke. During the night she seemed to have gotten tangled in her own clothes. Not lost on Mary was that she looked terrible. She felt even worse.

"I'm serious. Leave now or I swear I'll report you to the police and it won't be the first time as you know."

Probably the manager, Paradise thought. She tried to go back to her list, but then froze and listened even harder. She couldn't believe her good luck.

"I'll leave if you'll give me a coffee. A large freaking coffee." The voice was young and it was familiar.

"Really? I didn't hear a 'please' anywhere in there, so you get nothing. Now get the hell out of my coffee shop."

Paradise was up and out of her seat before Mary Ville recognized her long-lost friend. "The young lady is with me. Please give her whatever she wants and I'll be happy to pay."

Paradise turned and added, "Hello, Mary."

"It's Dawn, as if you didn't already know." The girl didn't meet her eyes. "There are lots of things you don't know so just get out of my face and leave me alone."

"I know you've suffered a terrible loss, Mary, so you can cut the tough act. I'm sorry about your sister. Now, let's get you some breakfast so we can sit down and talk."

22

Assuming the woman she wanted to see would be alone in the pathology department at this God-awful-early hour, Paradise made her way through the tangle of corridors in search of the offices of the Chief Coroner and staff.

The mystery novels she had read as a child all described the pathology department as being in the basement. Paradise was most definitely in the basement of the hospital.

Spotting a closed door, Paradise made the mistake of assuming she would find a number of offices beyond it. Wrong. She bumped the door open with her butt and backed in so she wouldn't spill the two large coffees she was holding, and was startled to hear a voice. And it wasn't just any voice.

"May I help you, young lady?"

"Coffee? It's black and I assumed you might take your coffee black. I do as well." Paradise was nervous and talking too much, but couldn't seem to make herself stop. "I'm Paradise, by the way."

"You're Pd PI, as I see on this card you sent me."

"Please call me Paradise. And please believe me when I say I don't normally go around opening doors to private offices."

She put the cups on a counter, avoiding the stacks of file folders there, removed the lids, and passed one very hot coffee to the lady standing in front of her.

"All good to know. I'm Dr. Sydney Scott, Chief Coroner. Please call me Sydney." Dr. Scott extended her non-coffee hand. "Why don't you give me your coat and take a seat in my humble but tiny office."

Choosing a chair was not too difficult, as there was exactly one that was not behind the desk. Paradise sat as Sydney took a grateful swig of coffee.

"Thanks for this. I can't figure out how my coffee pot here or the brand new one I have at home works, and nowhere was open when I came in a few hours ago."

"My God, woman, you're worse than I am. I start my day early but never as early as that."

"Busy, busy," Sydney said mildly, with a little gesture at the file folder mountains.

Paradise knew she needed to get down to business. "I'm here about Margaret Ville's death. Stage name was Morning Glory, I'm ashamed to say. The official pathology report was —"

"Not worth calling a report. I know that."

"It sucks if you ask me and I know you're not asking me."

Sydney interrupted a second time. "It was put on my desk some time ago. I take full responsibility. I could explain who wrote the report but— "

"We've already established this isn't even worthy of being called a report."

"Paradise, please." Sydney paused for effect but didn't have the chance to continue. Clearly the PI was pissed.

"I'll tell you this, when this piece of shit arrived on my desk at the Cape St Mary Police Department office I was stunned."

"Speaking of that, I need to understand how you, a PI at the other end of the province, managed to have a copy in the first place. This is a confidential report for the Chief Coroner's eyes only."

"I'll fill you in on that later, but first can you explain how these harsh, bitter, personal and totally unprofessional words ended up on this piece of paper? This came out of your office, Sydney."

"Being honest isn't always the best policy, I find. Especially if you work in a man's world. To be frank, I've been looking forward to meeting another woman in the business and I'm trying to be honest with you. But you have to shut up and let me finish without interruption."

"Consider me shut up." That lasted two seconds. "But so far I've learned nothing. Not a damn thing. I know my voice is getting loud and if I were you I would have told me more than a few comments ago to use my inside voice. I say that to my daughter all the time."

Paradise stopped long enough to catch her breath. "I'm trying here, but help me understand."

Sydney explained in detail how the botched report sat on her desk for so long and how the author had retired and dropped out of sight. "We have not been able to locate him and believe me we've tried."

With Paradise still silent she went on. "Because no one claimed the body we were able to complete an official autopsy. Paradise, your friend died of a drug overdose. She might have received her last hit just before going on stage and I suspect the dosage was too strong for her tiny body. She didn't weigh 100 pounds."

Sydney leaned over her desk to hand a thin folder to Paradise. "Details of the combination of drugs found in her system are in the official coroner's report. This copy is for you."

Paradise flipped the folder open, but then closed it again as Sydney continued.

"There's more. I must tell you. Given the location of many of the injection sites on her body, I don't believe Miss Ville administered the last few injections herself."

"Are you saying what I think you're saying? Someone murdered this poor girl?

"That's right, I believe someone murdered Margaret Ville. The police have been notified accordingly. Did you know she had a sister who was also a stripper?"

Paradise gave a small sad smile and creased her forehead. Yes, she knew. "With the backlog on your desk, I'm guessing you've been too busy to find Mary? Or even try?"

"That's not really my job, you know. But I went to the strip club myself to see if I could meet with Dawn. I called in a special officer because I believe her to be underage. Do you have that information?"

"She could still be underage, yes. And please don't call her Dawn. Her name is Mary. Mary Ville."

"My department is trying to clean up the child pornography plastered all over our city. In the main window of the establishment where the sister act danced I found a life size poster of Dawn, sorry, I mean Mary, looking 100% underage with the words written between her well splayed legs, 'Watching this pretty baby perform for you will…' I won't complete the filthy quote." Sydney shook her head in disgust.

As Paradise sat back and listened she admitted to herself that she was growing comfortable with Sydney. She hadn't worked with women until now. Not one single one! It was time for her let's-see-a-bit-of-teamwork attitude to enter the fray.

"Depending on when you were at the strip club you might not have found Mary there anyway. She spent time in the jail here."

"Paradise, I have to ask. How did you know she was here in Halifax and in the jail?"

"That's another bit of information I had before I left home. I'll share all of that with you Sydney I promise. Let's just get through all of this first and then perhaps we can work together to get justice for Margaret."

Paradise wanted to make a good impression and that surprised her. She waited for a response to her admission of wanting to work together. Looking at the bottom of her coffee cup she stood for a few seconds to put it in the glass container in the corner pretending to be a garbage can.

"This is me shutting up, Paradise. Please continue." Sydney was actually smiling for the first time.

For a brief second, Paradise smiled in return. "I went straight to the jail when I arrived yesterday and was informed Mary had been released."

"Surely they gave you an address for her, with her being so young. No one had visited her?"

"No address and no one collected her. I suspect they needed the jail cell. But there's more. This morning I went into a greasy spoon on Barrington Street and you'll never guess who I found there making a bit of a fuss."

"Not Da—, er, I mean Mary? You found her?"

"I wasn't looking, but yes I found her. Again, details on that event later. It's almost a story too good to be true." Paradise made a note of this because she had promised they could work on a number of things at a later date. She might forget some of the important details if she didn't have reference notes when she returned to the Cape.

"Long story short for now. Mary Ville is fast asleep in my hotel room while I'm here with you. I know she won't steal the bed sheets because she would have nowhere to take them. And I will speak with her about the night Margaret died, of course."

"Paradise I believe we need someone like you working right here in the city with our police force."

"You what?"

"Nobody on the force seems to care for these girls. Nobody seems to be able to find them until they turn up in a gutter. You seem to have the heart for finding them."

Paradise sat back in her chair. "I just wanted to find out what happened. I wasn't job hunting."

"The best jobs find you when you aren't looking for them." Doctor Scott sat back, not wanting to push too hard. "Give it some thought and I'll fill in the blanks when I see you tomorrow. Chew on it overnight when Mary isn't keeping you busy."

"I'll try to give your kind words some thought." Paradise said with a smile as she stood and extended her hand.

Paradise picked up the pace as she rushed back to the hotel to try to get some answers from Mary. If her luck was holding, Dawn would still be sleeping.

23

Before inserting the key into her hotel room door, Paradise knocked to give Mary a bit of an 'It's me. I'm back' warning.

"Coming, coming. Hold on."

Paradise was greeted by a towel-clad Mary. One towel around her hair and one around her wispy and under-nourished body.

Paradise was shocked to see how thin Mary's tiny body really was and how it seemed the skin was stretched as much as possible to barely cover her bones. Literally not an ounce of fat on this girl, thought Paradise.

"Oh, I wasn't expecting you back so soon."

"Mary, have you eaten?"

"Did you find out anything about my sister's death?"

"Have you eaten?"

"Did my sister die of a drug overdose?"

"Mary, let me in and please get dressed while I collect my thoughts. We need to talk, but not standing here in the doorway."

Paradise called room service and ordered the pasta special with chicken and lots of bread. She also ordered four servings, rather than two, of whatever they had on tap for dessert. An early supper for two.

She was almost 100% sure Mary hadn't eaten for days, other than the breakfast she enjoyed yesterday morning, compliments of Paradise. On the brighter side, this might indicate Mary had had a solid night's sleep. Paradise hoped that was the case.

"My goodness, girl, fresh-faced. You look fifteen years old," Paradise said as Mary came out of the bathroom.

"I know. It's a curse, believe me," Mary replied with the smallest of smiles. "I washed my clothes in the bathroom sink and that's why I'm still wearing the t-shirt you loaned me last night. I'm hoping that's okay with you."

There was a knock on the door. Mary jumped off the bed, stumbled into the bathroom and slammed the door as if her life was in danger.

"Relax, Mary," Paradise shouted. "It's room service. I've ordered us food. Lots of food."

Several hours later, after taking time to eat and enjoy every morsel of food, and for some girl talk, Paradise and Mary had talked through a plan that might allow Mary to finish school and meet some people her own age. A life changing plan, if Mary stuck with it.

"Mary, if I make the commitment to help you, I have to be absolutely certain you're willing to make the effort to finish school and live a somewhat normal life. We have lots of room in our home in Cape St Mary." Paradise paused to make sure she still had her guest's attention. She did.

"I do have a very impressionable teenager and, so help me God, if you teach her to strip I'll lock you up myself." While Paradise was talking with somewhat of a smile she was dead serious about protecting Hope.

"Paradise, I don't know what I can do other than take my clothes off for money. I think I was thirteen the first day my dad pushed me on stage at his favourite 'Gentlemen's Club'. If there is anything else that I can do, I don't know what that is." Mary started to cry so made an excuse and went into the bathroom.

When Mary returned a switch had gone off in her head and she was in her 'Dawn' persona. Paradise was stunned by how she could instantly put up a shield and become so rough and rude about everything. No respect for Paradise at all.

"I don't know what the fuck you're trying to do here, Paradise, but why haven't we talked about my sister? You promised to get answers for me. You're avoiding any talk about my poor dead sister and pretending to be concerned about my schooling. I am who I am so you can just start talking and skip the Cape St Mary bullshit."

"Stop it, young lady. You just went into the bathroom so I wouldn't see you cry and now you come back a tough-assed bitch? That doesn't work for me. Sit down, take this water, and catch your breath. And, as you would say, shut up and listen."

Mary hung her head and offered nothing further.

"I don't have the details we are both looking for, Mary. Not today. However, I give you my word that I will have news tomorrow when I see you following my morning session with Doctor Scott." Paradise moved to sit on the bed right beside Mary. "Doctor Scott is working on your sister's file this evening and I will have a completed copy when I pick you up." Mary leaned into Paradise - she needed to feel her arms around her.

"The police have her file, and they will find out what happened and who did this to your sister. I will keep in touch with those working directly on the case and because you will be with us in the Cape you will know seconds after I know." Paradise chose to ignore the bad-assed Mary who had spewed venom at her.

They talked a bit more, mostly going over the same news again and again, and finally agreed they should call it a night. Mary's cot was made up and she seemed tired out and beyond sad. Paradise didn't want to push her any further.

"You'll have the room to yourself again tomorrow morning, and then I'll pick you up and we'll head to the Cape. Assuming you won't be going out, I'll call you from Doctor Scott's office and you can meet me in the lobby. I will pay the bill on my way out tomorrow morning so there's nothing for you to do. Just leave the key in the room. How does that sound?"

"I hope I don't disappoint you," Mary said looking directly at Paradise and still crying openly.

"I hope you don't either, Mary, but I have confidence in you, so let's not end on that note. We've talked about a million things so let's say good night and with lights out we can both say a silent prayer for your sister. You can talk to her, you know."

"Please don't go there. I don't believe in that God shit."

"Got it. Good night, Mary."

"Good night, Paradise."

~

Mary tossed and turned all night. Just before dawn, she very quietly got up and went into the bathroom. She was in the washroom for what seemed like a long time. Paradise considered calling out, but decided she would give her some privacy.

In her heart of hearts Paradise knew what was about to happen. Eventually, the door opened and Mary tip-toed to her bed.

Paradise could see Mary but again decided to remain silent. She didn't like the fact that Mary was dressed in her still-wet clothes and was clearly trying to be extra quiet.

Paradise watched in silence as Mary reached for her wallet on the dresser. She took all of the cash and, although Paradise didn't see it happen, her credit cards as well.

As Mary slipped out of the room and into the night, Paradise was reminded of one of her favourite quotes. 'Fool me once, shame on you. Fool me twice, shame on me.'

Mary had fooled her twice.

Deciding she would get up regardless of the early hour, Paradise reminded herself she had done all she could for Mary. The rest was up to her. She would swing by the hotel before hitting the highway that would take her home just in case Mary was waiting for her after all.

"Good luck to you, Mary, and I wish only good things for you. You know where I am if ever you decide to let me help you. Be well," Paradise whispered as she jumped into the shower.

With that, Paradise turned her thoughts to her time with Doctor Scott and whether or not she should arrive with coffee again today.

24

Paradise assumed Doctor Scott had been kidding when she suggested a move to the city would be a good idea if she were interested in forensics. When their discussion continued the next day in the coroner's office, it was all business. Doctor Scott even pressed the button on a small recording device, and stated the date and time as if she was going to interrogate a witness.

"Paradise, I'm giving you a copy of the rewritten and professional autopsy report for Margaret." She suited her actions to her words. "There are no stage names in this report."

Sydney paused to sip her coffee before proceeding. "We've brought homicide in, obviously, and they're at the club where Margaret was working this morning. They were on site yesterday during the lunch hour, which we believe aligns with the time of the alleged shooting. Miss Ville fell to the floor only seconds after the alleged shot was heard."

Doctor Scott continued as she turned the page and pointed to a section, reading upside down as Paradise scanned the text right-side up. "Death was from a drug overdose and it was not self-administered. The injection site is not one Margaret could have reached to self-inject the heroin." The Doctor paused to ensure Paradise was on the same page. She was.

'This particular lunch crowd doesn't like talking with the police. No surprise there. No one we spoke with heard the shots, and they claim to have no idea why their 'lunch time stripper' dropped to the floor. We believe there may have been a pop-like sound in the music or someone suggested a gunshot had been heard and everyone assumed this was factual information."

"So they didn't hear or see anything."

"I guess they feel they're safer that way. Homicide has a few names to follow up on, and I'll keep you in the loop. You have my word."

Paradise said, "Can we talk about Margaret's younger sister, Mary?"

Doctor Scott closed the file and picked up another one. "Not much to talk about, but sure. Where do we begin?"

Paradise hesitated, wondering how much to share of her last conversation with Mary.

Doctor Scott let the pause lengthen, then hefted the file. "Mary has quite a long police record, I'm afraid. I asked for her file thinking it would be short, maybe one or two arrests including the one that put her in a cell most recently."

Paradise seemed to be lost in thought and remained silent so Doctor Scott continued. "My plan when I asked for her file was to have it expunged. I was shocked to see how thick it is. My God, this young woman has had a life, all documented in dry police prose since that very first murder charge."

"I took charge of the girls back then," Paradise said, "when we got that sorted out and they were released."

Doctor Scott wasn't sure this was a teachable moment but she didn't want to lose her thought. "Do you know how your peers at the police station at the Cape completed and closed the file?"

"No. Should I have followed up on that?"

"They wrote, 'Strippers arrested and charged with murder while shopping at a used clothing store in Digby, Nova Scotia. Strippers released into the care of Pd PI.' That's the end of the report, I'm afraid."

Paradise looked shocked. "Are you telling me my guys didn't even say the murder charges were dropped? God help them, because my sergeant will kick them all around the office."

Paradise was due to call Curtis before starting her drive home, but decided not to mention this little bit of news until she was at the station. She really really wanted to be the one to drop this bomb.

"Good. I knew I could leave that one in your capable hands. Let's get back to Mary. I'm not sure that file can be wiped, either, given the number of arrests. Charges of petty theft, assault, assault on a police officer, carrying a firearm while under age, a stolen firearm..."

Paradise nodded. "Mary and her sister lived through a life of crime with their parents. They were abused for years."

"Well, while I hoped I could help Mary, she's of age now, just, and is going to have to make some hard decisions herself. I'm sorry if this disappoints you but it isn't my place to have dug as deep as I have so it's the end of the road for me as far as Mary goes."

"I truly appreciate how far you've gone. I appreciate you."

It took all of Doctor Scott's self-control to keep her from catching Paradise up in a bear hug. Instead she drew a breath and said, "Let me take you to our Halifax Club for lunch – my treat. It will be the only meal you'll have today, I'm sure, so I won't take no for an answer. Anyway, we have more to discuss don't we?"

Paradise sniffed a little inelegantly. "We do?"

"I'm interested in you and your career in this male-dominated field. It's so nice to meet another woman in the line of duty."

"Believe me, in my line of work there isn't another woman. I hope that will change soon." Paradise spoke quietly this time. "We do have some things in common."

"Including, I hope, a good lunch."

~

An hour later the ladies took their reserved seats at the Halifax Club. At some point between the office and the club Doctor Scott had first-named into "Sydney."

Paradise was less than impressed, but she was prepared to give the Club a chance. The white linen tablecloths with matching napkins, not to mention the air of snobbery that emanated from the man who greeted them at the door, were not part of the world she knew. The man gave Paradise a second look because of the pants she was wearing. That's what she figured, anyway. He was on a first name basis with Sydney, though, so clearly this place couldn't be all bad.

"Now let's get some food into you, young lady. You're a wee bit of a thing and I don't like the idea of you skipping any meals."

"I will say that, on occasion, if I'm working on a time sensitive case I might forget to eat. I drink lots of coffee all day, and there are times when I know I am replacing a much needed meal with yet another coffee. There, I confessed all my sins." Paradise smiled at her luncheon date.

"Lots of excuses buried in your words, but I think you know that without being told." Doctor Scott inspected the basket of bread rolls, picked one and tossed it across the table to Paradise, who barely caught it.

"Paradise, I tried your way and became very ill. I lost almost a year off the job because of it – end of that story. Please eat!"

Sydney took her napkin and with a snap of her wrist she opened it and placed it carefully on her lap over her rather expensive suit. "Now, let's talk about your career. Where do you see yourself in ten years?"

"Huh?" Paradise hadn't heard that line before.

"I'm serious."

"Uh, in ten years I might see myself still being a PI but with lots and lots of continued education in my field. I love expanding my mind and, now that you mention it, I think I'll see what I can learn about forensic police work." With a smile she added, "How does that sound?"

"Great plan, I would say. Continuing your education can only widen your field of clients. I can help you along the way, and I don't make that offer lightly."

She put her elbows on the table and steepled her hands together. "Now: a Forensic Intelligence Unit links evidence recovered from different crime scenes. Within this unit you might find a Special Crimes Operation that does tasks like evidence recovery following burglaries or even anti-terrorism work. I would be delighted to guide you into forensics and I wouldn't even insist you move to the city. Not right away."

Before Paradise could say anything, Sydney had straightened herself up into the sort of posture the Halifax Club expected. "Here comes our lunch, so let all of that simmer for a few days. Then let's talk about how I can help you."

Lunch for Sydney was freshly-marinated, flame-grilled sliced chicken with pineapple dressing, followed by coffee and apple cobbler. Paradise truly wanted to order a deluxe burger, but felt it would be too heavy in her stomach during her long drive to the Cape. Instead, she ordered the grilled salmon fillet with mixed greens and diced tomatoes, followed by coffee and a decadent chocolate brownie for dessert.

It seemed Sydney dined at the Halifax Club often since the waiter knew she ordered her meals with no side dishes. Absolutely none.

They talked at length about city life and country life. Sydney pointed out, with whispers and subtle fork gestures, some of the big wheels of Halifax who were eating at nearby tables.

When the bill arrived Sydney signed it and had a question for the waiter. "Can you pack up a few of your wonderful chocolate chip cookies, and a couple of whatever drinks you might have in a can, and add that charge to my account? My young friend here has to drive to the other end of the province before she sleeps. I want to make sure she arrives home safe and sound."

"Of course, Doctor Scott."

Paradise was impressed with the way Sydney took charge so easily.

She was also impressed with the huge chocolate chip cookies. She devoured three as she drove and then found there were three more in the bag. Maybe she would save one for Pops and one for Hope.

Maybe she wouldn't.

25

Always great to be home, Paradise thought the next morning as Hope ran into her bedroom using anything but her inside voice. When Hope was excited she had only one volume – loud! *What has gotten my girl all fired up at this early morning hour?*

Paradise didn't have to wait long for an answer. She wasn't sure what she had expected but it wasn't this…

"Oh. My. God. Mom, you have to call dad. Call him right now. I'm pretty sure it's an emergency."

"Would you mind if I pour myself a cup of coffee first?"

"No! Dad called last night and it was clear he needed to speak with you. He didn't have much to say to either Pops or me but we could both tell he was some upset, as Pops likes to say."

At that point, Pops himself walked in, Hope turned on him in mock-outrage. "Pops, how did I not hear you coming up those stairs with all the noise you normally make?"

Pops took it in stride and held out two offerings to Paradise. "Don't get used to this, but I brought you a coffee. And the phone with enough cord to go around this house at least twice."

Pops was smiling but Paradise could see he was upset about something. "What is it, Pops? What's going on?"

Pops placed the phone on the bed, gave Hope a tap on the shoulder and pointed to the stairs. "Hope is right. You need to call Thomas immediately."

"But what—?"

Pops started shooing Hope toward the door. "I'll let him fill you in."

From the doorway, Hope said, "Pops, you know more about my father's emergency than I do. I'm his kid. Why won't anyone tell me anything ever?"

"I'll tell you about the emergency, and it is an emergency, once your mother gets your dad on the line."

"I damn well knew he told you," Hope sulked.

"Language, Hope," Paradise said.

"That's what your father asked me to do," Pops said. "It's not about you today, honey, so get that chip off your shoulder and come with me. I'll not ask again."

Paradise waved a silent thank you as Pops shut her bedroom door. His continued back-and-forth with Hope receded like a sound effect in a radio play, and finally there was quiet.

Assuming the urgency was either work, T.J. or Wikolia, Paradise tried to gather her thoughts and prepare for what could be a long phone call. What could be so urgent?

Thomas could be a bit dramatic about nothing at all. Paradise wondered if his change in personality was because he was a single dad trying to make it to the Mental Health facility every damn day plus run their little business.

Maybe the time would come that Thomas wouldn't have to do everything on his own. Paradise had been thinking about returning to Hawaii so they could work together again. But she knew such a decision would affect many others. How could she uproot Hope from this wonderful little village, and what about Pops? He was far too old to be on his own.

Paradise wondered if Thomas would be interested in her news regarding a possible job for her in Halifax after he shared his 'emergency.' She had an offer in her pocket for a position with extensive training to kick-start her. She was keen to learn so much more than her resume showed today. None other than the Chief Medical Examiner for Nova Scotia would outline and supervise her training.

~

In Honolulu, Thomas had just put T.J. to bed. The boy had started having nightmares right after his mommy died, even though he hadn't seen Wikolia for much of his young life. He was too young to understand dying and death, and Thomas had shared none of it with him. What T.J. did know was that Daddy was upset.

The phone rang just as Thomas had sat down to catch his breath. He was waiting for calls from Paradise and from Wikolia's mother or any one of her siblings. He had left more messages than he could remember and still his phone wasn't ringing. Until now.

26

"Hello?"

"Thomas, what is so urgent that you had to draw both Hope and Pops into it? I hope you're not exaggerating."

"Hi, Paradise. I was hoping you would be a bit less critical of me today." Thomas drew in a big breath before he continued. He needed to settle his nerves.

"We've talked about this before, my love."

"I'm glad it's you calling. It's about Wikolia, and I'm not sure I could talk with her family tonight. I have to tell you something about Wikolia."

"Of course you do. How many times do I have to tell you, Wikolia is your problem given the million miles between us, Thomas." Paradise took a deep breath and then jumped back in. "I figured this would be something about our business, T.J. or Wikolia. And of the three it's almost always about Wikolia. You can't disagree with me on that, so don't even try." She knew she had said too much.

"I can't disagree with you on anything at the moment. Please let me find the right words and be quiet until then."

"But—"

"Just shut up, Paradise. Shut the hell up."

There was a cold silence on the line. Thomas knew he should apologize for his language, but he felt like he was drowning and Paradise wouldn't lift a finger to help him. "I need to talk with you, not listen to you without being able to contribute to the conversation." Thomas was close to tears.

"I'm so sorry, my love. Take your time. I'm right here."

Her kind words brought sobs from Thomas and it was so difficult to get the words out. "She's gone, Paradise. Wikolia is gone. Dead, I mean. Wikolia is dead."

"Thomas, you're scaring me. She can't be dead. What are you telling me?"

Paradise was pacing her bedroom floor, trying to dress, with the bloody phone cord wrapped around her nightgown. "Tell me she's just missing from the hospital or something." Paradise knew this wasn't her finest hour.

"I wish that was it. She's dead."

"Oh. My. God. I'm trying to say that the way our daughter does but I can't do it." Nothing from Thomas, and Paradise knew she shouldn't be trying to lighten the moment at a time like this.

After almost a minute of dead air, she said, "Can you tell me what happened? I have all day to talk with you if that's what you want. Do you need me to come to you? I bet I can catch a flight tomorrow."

Paradise waited for a reply. None came. "Would you let me help you, Thomas, or would that be the wrong thing to do?"

"You're helping me right now more than I can tell you." His voice was shaky. "You sound like the Paradise I dropped off at the airport all those years ago. I know you're building your own life, Paradise, but, God, I miss you. I miss us."

"Wait, Thomas, please. How did this conversation get turned around? We need to talk about Wikolia. Please give me a few details."

"Don't pretend you're that interested. Remember how this call began? You were nasty and that doesn't look good on you." Thomas knew he had said enough.

More dead air. Then, "Wikolia was alive until she wasn't and now I'm trying to find her family because they will want to know. I hope they will want to meet T.J., too. It's important our son know his Hawaiian grandparents."

Paradise knew she deserved to have Thomas tell her to shut up. Would he ever be able to forgive her?

"I told her I was sorry. Sorry that I hadn't treated her better when we first began dating. Yes, I went back that far. I needed to beat myself up and be done with it. I apologized for the way I acted towards her when you first came to Hawaii. I confessed that I love you more than I loved her. But I did love her. I kissed her and walked away. I have never done anything so difficult."

Paradise waited to make sure he was done, then said quietly, "Thank you for telling me all of this. I couldn't be more sorry for my behaviour earlier." She realized that Thomas had taken it to heart when she told him she didn't want to hear about Wikolia. So when she died, he didn't dare call her until almost a week later. *Serves me right*, Paradise thought.

"Thomas, from the bottom of my heart I am so very sorry for your loss. Of course you loved Wikolia. You had a child together and you made wonderful memories together. You will make sure T.J. remembers his mommy and, if you let me, I will help you do that. Hope will want to help as well."

Silence at the other end of the line. Then, finally: "I don't know, Paradise."

"I know it's too soon to make any major decisions, but perhaps in time you and T.J. could come here to the Cape and live with us? We could build the business out of our home, and you know how big this home is, right?"

"Please don't take what I'm about to say the wrong way."

She dug her fingernails into the palm of her hand. "Go ahead. Say it."

"Words. You're saying all the right words, honey, but they seem to be a bit too late. You never even hinted at T.J. coming with me if I moved to the Cape. It's hard to believe you, if I'm being honest."

"I deserve that. I always assumed Wikolia would regain her good health and T.J. would of course live with his mother. And, yes, selfishly I did want you all to myself. Just the three of us, like we used to be. Now everything has changed. T.J. doesn't have his mother. But he's young enough to heal and we can help him. Please let me help. Hope will be gutted to know T.J. has lost his mother. She will want to talk with you soon."

"Tell Hope I'll call her in a few days. I'm heading out one more time to see if I can learn something about Wikolia's family. I owe her that much. T.J. loves his nanny so he will be in good hands if the trip turns out to be a week or two."

"It sounds like you have a plan, and I know I deserve to be left out of it."

"I should go. Thanks for returning my call."

"Is there more, Thomas? That sounded like you wanted to say something else. Please, tell me everything."

"Actually, there is something else I might as well get off my chest. Last I heard, you and Lenny were dating. I'm sure that's taking up a lot of your time. But next time we talk I want to hear where things stand between the two of you."

"No no no. Thomas, let's not hang up this way, please. Lenny is gone. There is no relationship and we have never been together in a 'dating' way. God, Thomas, are you even still there?"

But Thomas had hung up the second he finished speaking.

Paradise silently walked down the stairs and into the arms of Pops and Hope. All three were grieving, each in their own way.

Pops had never met Wikolia.

Hope loved Wikolia.

Paradise, if she was honest, resented the woman who had once held Thomas in her arms.

27

Hope was trying to write a letter but couldn't get past 'Dear Daddy.' Her tears were staining the page as she reflected on all the stupid things she had on her mind while Wikolia was dying.

A name for my business.
Mom going to the city without me.
My last under-paying babysitting gig. (Not for Mrs Foss, though. She always paid me way higher than my rates.)
My last way-too-short haircut.

"You seem to be lost in thought, Hope. Homework at this late hour when you should be in bed?"

Paradise sat at her daughter's desk and saw her tears. She didn't have to ask why Hope was crying. They had both been crying on and off all day, and even Pops was crying right along with them.

"Oh, Mom, I can't stop thinking about all the stupid things I had on my mind while Wikolia was dying."

"I hear you there, darling. I never did want to meet Wikolia when I first learned about her and now I'm sorry I didn't insist on meeting her. What a hypocrite that makes me."

"And you've had way longer than I have to learn how to act towards all different kinds of people." Hope saw the regret in her mom's face. Regret for so many things related to Wikolia. "Okay, that's a joke, mom, in case you didn't notice."

Hope wiped her eyes and put her arms around her mother. They sat quietly for a few minutes before Paradise spoke again.

"I did get the jab, Hope, but I don't feel like kidding today. Good try, but let's put our humour away for another day."

"Sure." Hope was certain her one word answer would at least coax a small smile from her Mom. She was right.

"I have an idea that might make both of us feel a little better, Hope. Let's crawl into your bed and you can tell me some of the things you love about Wikolia and when you fall asleep I'll go to my room. We can continue this every night until you run out of stories to share. How does that sound?"

Hope was already diving under the covers. She moved over to leave room for her mom to crawl in with her. Hope had so many wonderful memories to share and couldn't wait to get started.

"Come on, mom. As Pops likes to say, let's get at 'er. "

"I'm all ears."

Not lost on Paradise was the big yawn already coming from her daughter. It was hard to miss even though Hope tried to cover it up. "Honestly, mom, I'm not one bit tired."

"Tell me a story, then."

"My favourite memory of Wikolia will always be her hugs. I don't know how she did it but she hugged louder than anyone I've ever met. She made all kinds of noises while she was hugging me or daddy and they all worked. It's hard to explain but it's like her body was talking to mine."

Later, as Paradise tucked her daughter in and returned to her own bedroom she focused on the fact that she loved the way Thomas hugged her. *I wonder if my Thomas was in the arms of Wikolia when he learned how to really hug a woman.*

Paradise fell asleep in the arms of a profound sadness.

28

After four hours of driving in high winds and enough rain to cover the view in the rear view mirror, Paradise was glad they wouldn't be making the return trip to the Cape for at least a week. Roads were going to be a mess until the rain drained away. Paradise had not seen such a huge storm since she had returned to Cape St. Mary.

"Are you okay, honey?"

"Yes, mom. Why? Are we going to have to turn around?"

"No, I mean the sadness we've been draped in. Are you doing okay?"

"Sure."

Paradise could live with that. She didn't feel like talking either, but was concerned about Hope. So much sad for such a young lady.

They barely made it to their departure gate at the Halifax International Airport. Finding parking at the terminal was a problem and used up precious time they didn't have to spare.

"Okay, kiddo, let's grab our backpacks and run like the devil is right behind us." Paradise and Hope were travelling light.

"Ladies and gentlemen, we are now boarding Flight 123 to Toronto, Ontario with a connection to Honolulu, Hawaii. Please have your boarding pass ready to show your ticket agent."

They didn't say much as they worked their way through the gates and passages and ramps to the plane, found their seats and buckled up. Hope was nervous and Paradise remained silent, letting her girl speak first.

"Mom, I remember stuff now from when we flew here. The flight takes like a million hours, right?"

"Close enough, honey. The flight crew will give us the specifics once we take off. First we have to get to Toronto. We have time to sleep, eat, chat and whatever else comes our way."

"Wouldn't it be cool if the captain is our neighbour, Mrs. Foss? I meant to go over to their cottage before we left but I forgot and then I didn't have time."

"Mrs. Foss is at the Cape this week, Hope. I had a little chat with her last night and she is going to check in on Pops—without him realizing that's what she's doing, of course. You know how Pops hates to be reminded of his age."

"I sure do. Made that mistake once—only once."

Mother and daughter slept for more than half of the flight from Toronto to Honolulu. They had been so concerned about how they would fill the time!

They woke up when yet another meal was being served and Paradise tried to collect her thoughts. This was really happening.

"Are you awake, mom?"

"I am, honey. Did you sleep at all?"

"No. I've been thinking about something I want to ask you about but I don't want you to be mad at me."

"Hope, when have I ever been upset with you for asking me anything?"

"I know, mom, but this is kind of different. Like, it's really different."

"Ask your question and you have my promise I will not overreact."

Hope laid her head back and closed her eyes. She was getting her questions together in her head before saying anything.

"Honey, don't leave it too long or we'll be landing and then I'll need to focus on our car rental and then driving in downtown Honolulu—"

"Have you ever liked a girl?

"Okay, if that's your question I don't know why you would worry about my reaction. You know I have lots of female friends including some I like very much. Relationships are important, Hope, and as you grow up you will have lots of friends, both male and female."

"I bet you know what I really meant. Don't treat me like a child."

"Why don't you tell me about a girl that you like. Can you do that?"

"Or we could just forget that I brought it up."

"No, we will not forget about it, Hope. Your feelings and your questions are important to both of us. I honestly don't know where you're going with this, honey, so spit it out."

"Remember that day we were having a rip-roaring fight and I ran out of the house and didn't tell you that my plan was to hitch a ride to Digby?"

"What I *will* be upset with is if you tell me you were hitch-hiking, young lady. You know better than that. We'll talk about rules of safety when you're out on your own, including transportation from one location to another."

"Well, it wasn't really hitching a ride because the guy who stopped to pick me up is the older brother of a friend of mine who goes to my school. I wasn't going to get in, honest to God, mom, but when he told me who he was I thought it would be okay."

"We're getting side-tracked Hope. Like I said we will talk about rules of safety separately. Get back to this girl you like, please."

"Her name is 'Francis with-an-i.' That's how she introduces herself, then she explains that she likes the male version of her name rather than the female spelling, Frances."

"And you like her?"

"Well, I didn't like her right off the bat. Joey's brother dropped me off at a soda shop and there were no free tables so she motioned for me to sit with her if I wanted to, so I did. She even paid for my Coke. Imagine, mom, she didn't even know me and she bought my Coke without even thinking about it. We talked for hours then she said she had to go home and feed her cat and she lived right next door to the shop and did I want to go home with her for a while. She's old so I wasn't worried about anything illegal happening."

"Define 'old', please."

"She's not as old as you and Dad, but she has some skin that looks a bit saggy."

"Hang on. Is this old girl with saggy skin the girl you like? And where specifically on her body did you see her saggy skin?"

"So, we went to her tiny apartment. She called it an apartment but honestly it's one room with a bathroom. Her bed and her sofa are the same thing. She's new here but she didn't want to tell me where she works or anything personal about herself. I guess I did all the talking. Mom, I'm afraid I talked about how angry I was with you—I don't even remember why I was mad. Francis-with-an-i only wanted to talk about my 'bad home life'. I never called it that, I swear."

"I'm not hearing how and why the saggy skin was on display, Hope."

"She fed her cat and then she brought me another Coke from her tiny fridge. It was too cute. Her fridge I mean. But all of a sudden she kissed me. Right smack on the lips. And she kissed me again and again and again. I can see you're either shocked or pissed with me, mom, but I just have to talk about this with someone. No, I have to talk about it with my mother. Please tell me you understand."

"Hope, this may come as a surprise to you, but I was once sixteen years old myself. Get to the saggy skin part please."

"Oh that. It wasn't anything, really. She said wasn't it getting hot and before I could say well no it's not hot to me, she took her sweater off. I near died, Mom. She just had her bra on! Well, she had her pants on but I'm talking about the top of her. Compared to mine her skin was saggy so I didn't want to take my top off and embarrass her with my great body. I'm kidding, mom."

"Hope, did Francis-with-an-i ask you to do anything you didn't want to do? I'm not upset with you, so you can be honest. I might be upset with your new girl friend, but that will be another story."

"We kept kissing and she tried to get me to take my top off and when I wouldn't she kept trying to get her hands under my top and that's when I decided I would—"

"Would take your top off?"

Hope was blushing fiercely. "I did finally take my top off. We kissed again, then she stood up and pulled me up and she kissed me again. Here comes the good part, mom, and I'm being sarcastic. She wanted me to take my pants off! Can you imagine me doing that?"

"Honey, this is the girl you like and you have feelings for? Is that what you're trying to tell me?"

"Would that be all right?"

"I would need to be sure this person, who is much older than you and probably knows a lot more about being intimate with another person, did not make you do anything you didn't want to do. One of my jobs is to protect you. That's what I will do regardless of how much you might like her."

"Honestly? I like her and I had a good time. I felt older and grown up. I felt like I was doing something good, yet it was a little bit bad. When we were kissing my whole body shook a bit and I quivered between my legs a bit. It's hard to explain."

"You've explained it perfectly," Paradise said with a straight face.

"She wanted me to take my pants off and I said no and I told her if she took her pants off I was leaving. She zipped her pants back up and that was that. When I had to leave to catch my ride, Francis-with-an-i wouldn't walk back with me. She laughed and said she didn't want anyone to see her with the same kid she left with hours earlier. Mom, pardon my language but that pissed me off. I was good enough to go home with her but not good enough to be seen with her later. I don't know where she was going with that but I got out of there."

"And she didn't want you to do anything more than kiss? Are you telling me everything?"

"She said something else. I took it as a threat until I told my friend and she explained it. She said, 'One day I'm going to kiss you down here.' I ran out the door when she tried to put her hand between my legs."

"And that's all?"

"I haven't seen her again, if that's what you're asking. My problem with her, and it's made me like her less and less until I just don't understand how my feelings are working, is that she calls every single day. I'm sure you've watched me run to answer the phone and then take the phone as far away from you as I can so you can't hear the call."

"What is she saying to you every day?"

"She always wants to know if I have told you about 'us'. I have said more than once that there isn't any 'us' but she doesn't buy it."

"Hope, experimenting with kisses is part of growing up. Girls experiment by kissing boys and some do kiss girls, so you're not the first. I think when we are back home in Cape St Mary, if you still have feelings for Francis-with-an-i, I would like you to invite her to our home. She can have a meal with us if you like. Or she could just come over for a walk on Mavillette beach."

Hope seemed to be imaging that visit, and how much of a disaster it might be. Paradise stroked her hair and gave her a little pat on the shoulder. "Now, unless you still have more to say, let's put this discussion away for today. We will talk about her and your feelings for her another time. Deal?"

"So you're not mad."

"Not one bit, honey. Promise."

"And look what's coming, mom. We are both saved by another meal."

Paradise and Hope ate in silence. Paradise had not seen the conversation coming and she knew she needed to do a better job monitoring where her daughter was going, how she was getting there and who she was with. Thinking back to when she was 16 and alone and pregnant, Paradise was truly disgusted with herself for letting this get ahead of her.

"When we land, Hope, we have no checked luggage so we should be in and out of the terminal quickly. I have rented a car for us—"

"*What?* Why isn't Daddy picking us up? What am I missing now?" Hope was pouting and Paradise had no time for that.

"Stop interrupting, Hope. Do that and you will have all of your answers. Can you listen until I'm finished?"

"Sorry, mother," came the terse reply.

Hope slouched in her seat with her head down and arms crossed. Clearly acting like a teenager, Paradise thought. Thank God she had at least left her baseball cap at home.

"Your dad has gone to look for Wikolia's family. When we talked he hadn't been able to find her mother or any of her siblings. I believe we will find T.J. with the nanny. Do you know her name, honey? Thomas has always called her 'the nanny' and I've never asked anything about her."

"Oh. My. God. He doesn't know we're coming does he, mom! This is a mistake. I know it's a mistake. Have you forgotten dad doesn't like surprises?"

"I have not, but let's think 'going forward', shall we? I have tried to reach Thomas but haven't been able to catch him at home since our plan came together. So we get to surprise him whether or not any of us like the idea. We'll pick up our rental and drive straight to the condo. With any luck, we will find Thomas and T.J. at home."

"And if they're not home? Then what?"

"T.J. might be at home with his nanny, and before you say, 'But what if?' let me finish. If no one is there we have a hotel room with our name on it."

"What does that mean?"

"Hope, it means your mother has thought of everything. Seriously, stop worrying. We've got this."

As Paradise navigated her way through Honolulu, Hope spoke of memories of places as they drove by. She had far more history in the city than her mother. "Remember the romantic dinner cruise dad arranged for you? He talked to me about it for days before it actually happened. Then, for some strange reason, he invited me to come along. It wasn't as romantic as he had planned, right, Mom?"

"You are so right, Hope, but it's a great memory anyway."

Paradise recalled the night she had first arrived and learned Hope was in Honolulu with Thomas. It seemed a lifetime ago.

Good memories. So many warm thoughts of those early days.

Approaching the condo, Paradise recognized their car. Funny how she called it 'their car' even though she had been away for so long. "He's home, honey. Daddy's home. I see his car."

Hope was the one who finally saw an empty parking spot. "There's one. Right there mom. See it?"

She was out of the car before Paradise had properly parked in what she hoped could be called 'visitor parking' for a week or two. The parking spot was small and it took her a few minutes to wedge the rental into it.

As she hauled both backpacks out of the trunk, Paradise heard Hope yell with excitement, "I'm home."

She froze for a second, realizing she was about to come face to face with the man she had loved her entire life. She said a prayer, hoping Thomas hadn't given up on her.

29

T.J. had absolutely no idea who these people could be. Why did his nanny allow strangers to come inside?

"Not good to talk to strangers," he said in a whisper. "Daddy told me."

What T.J. did know was that these two women were making a rather silly fuss over him. They sent his nanny home. He couldn't believe she left him alone with them.

"Stranger danger!" T.J. ran into the bathroom and almost got the door completely shut before Hope pushed her foot in the way, only to have T.J. try to close it anyway.

"Oh. My. God," Hope said directly to T.J.

"Not my name."

"Oh I know that. Your name is T.J. Right?"

"Stop yelling. I don't know you."

"Am I yelling?"

"You are yelling," Paradise said, "because you're excited and that always brings your outside voice, yes?"

T.J. couldn't follow the conversation. He knew he only heard yelling when he was outside with nanny or his daddy. He really hated yelling and he didn't like the two women in his home who were breaking the house rules...No yelling. "I want my daddy to come home."

"How much have you grown T.J.?" Hope couldn't believe how big her brother had become.

"I know, he's so big," said Paradise.

"Mom, I bet T.J. weighs 25 pounds at least."

"Is that right, honey? Do you weigh that much?"

"How old are you now T.J.? Two? Two and a half?"

"Free. I'm not one. I'm not two. I'm free. And I want my daddy. I told you."

I sure did surprise them both, T.J. thought. *They didn't think I could talk. I'm not a baby. I won't say this out loud because they'll learn soon enough that I'm going to cry until my father comes home. I don't care how long it takes.*

But he could not put his plan into action. T.J. forgot to cry and fell asleep in his sister's arms.

30

Hope was the first one out of bed as the Honolulu sunshine warmed her face. Having slept only a few hours, she was too excited to stay in bed one minute longer even though she knew she would be tired before day's end.

Wanting to let her mother catch a bit more sleep, Hope quietly closed the bedroom door behind her. She could get T.J. up and dressed for the day and spend some one-on-one time with her little brother while she made coffee for her mom.

Hope knew it was always a good idea to make mom's coffee before she got up.

Pops made the coffee at home in the Cape, but Hope remembered how her mom liked it and had it brewing in no time at all. She loved to do little things for her mother, and since they both got to bed very late, her mom would need her coffee the minute her feet hit the floor.

She wondered if Pops would be making coffee for himself on this particular morning or would he head over to the Café for a bit of conversation. Without admitting it, he would be looking for Eugenie.

Hope knew Pops was in love! He often talked with her about Eugenie when they went down to the dock to sit in his boat. Some of their best conversations happened as they sat side by side, looking out at the ocean in all its glory. Mavillette Beach stretched as far as the eye could see, and then became one with the ocean. High tides and low tides brought new secrets ashore day after day.

There was a lot going on at home in Cape St Mary, and here she was hanging out in the condo she once shared with her dad. Just the two of them for so many years.

"Did you hear me say that, T.J.? Maybe I didn't say it out loud but the Cape is my home now and if you and I get together and carve out a plan I bet we can go there with our dad *and* my mom."

T.J. wasn't listening.

"How does that sound to you, T.J.?"

"T.J. want daddy."

"Yes. Yes. Yes. You said that last night. Stop repeating yourself," Hope said, smiling at him.

"Daddy."

"You stink, little man. Come with me."

Hope had T.J. cleaned up in no time. She was hoping he only wore diapers to sleep because she didn't want to be on diaper duty all day. For a little guy he sure could stink up a room.

She spoke softly as she took T.J.'s hand and walked him around and around the tiny condo. She figured he needed exercise, so why not start first thing in the morning? Plus it gave Hope the chance to remind herself where her dad and now her brother kept everything.

Thomas was a neat freak, as Paradise had once said, and nothing had changed. Everything was where it had been the day Hope had left.

T.J.'s bed was new, of course, and his bedroom was what had once been their dining room area. It was conveniently located near the kitchen. Probably when Thomas came home in the morning after his regular night shift at 2.0, he would sleep while the nanny looked after T.J. and kept the rest of the condo in order.

"T.J., what is this? You have your own blackboard on one entire wall? I love it. I love your artwork, too. Clearly this is your own personal workstation."

Up and out of T.J.'s reach in one corner of the blackboard Thomas had written, 'Just a reminder if anyone calls I'm off looking for Wikolia's family and might be gone for a few days. You know how to reach me.'

On the next line Thomas had written a few telephone numbers where he could be reached. This note must have been for the nanny, since Paradise and Hope's arrival had been top secret. Hope wasn't sure why.

She was grateful that Thomas had not given T.J. the tiny alcove she called her room. It was almost the same as she had left it. Her journal was still on her little desk, but so were lots of her dad's work papers. She was okay with that. In fact, Hope was happy to think of her dad working away in her space. She felt sad to think she had become so distant with her own father.

"Daddy, do you ever think of me?" Hope whispered. A tear escaped her eye. She brushed it away before T.J. could notice it.

31

Lenny went out of his way to disguise his appearance but not be too conspicuous about it. He made it to the departure gate at the Halifax International Airport without raising the suspicion of anyone, as far as he could tell. So far, so good.

His hair was chemically bleached to a very harsh blond. His fitted suit was clearly not fitted for his body because he was bulging out of it. Lenny felt like he might as well have taped a "running from something" sign to his back, even though nobody had given him a second look.

But then he clocked someone who did not fit.

The beautiful stranger seemed out of place and even a bit nervous. She approached Gate 23 for the flight to Toronto and seemed to know exactly where she was going to sit in the lounge. Lenny pretended to concentrate on his magazine; he was good at looking where he didn't seem to be looking.

He watched the woman touch her flowing red hair and tug on her silk blouse and jacket, like an actor off-stage waiting for the cue. Then she started to walk, seeming to look for something in the waiting area but moving ever closer to him.

Lenny resisted the urge to fiddle with his own hair, or to look up at her even when she stopped within a foot of his left leg. He could not avoid scanning the lower thigh, knee, calf and shapely ankle she had placed within touching distance.

"Is this seat taken, handsome?"

He turned a page in the magazine.

"I'm going to sit beside you on the flight, so why don't we start getting to know each other now?"

Lenny put a finger on the page as if not to lose his place in whatever article was in front of him and looked up. Her blouse was open two buttons too many and her face was as scannable as her leg, but he would bet fifty bucks that her hair colour was no more authentic than his own.

"I don't mean to be rude, madam—"

She feigned shock. "Did you just call me 'madam'?"

"—but there's tons of available seats. So, yeah, this seat is taken."

"For God's sake, I don't want you to father my firstborn. We're going to be seatmates, so I simply want to get to know you. I'm Bonde, by the way."

Lenny was oh, so tempted to take the bait and say, Bonde, Jane Bonde? but he held his tongue.

Undeterred, she slipped into the seat beside him and leaned into his personal space. "I didn't get your name."

"No, you didn't." Lenny returned to his magazine, bringing it close to his face as if he were nearsighted.

Out of the corner of his eye he saw Bonde dig into her designer purse and tensed fractionally until he saw her bring out her ticket, and not a pearl-handled automatic. He found himself wondering what else might be in that purse, and then forced himself to actually read the sentence he had been staring at.

Moments later something landed lightly in his lap. He looked down and saw it was her ticket, followed closely by her hand.

"Beg your pardon," Bonde whispered. "Butter fingers."

Her hand glided more slowly than it needed to across his thigh and down between his legs under the edge of the ticket. He was just deciding which of her fingers to break when she finally seized the ticket.

Not a muscle moved in Lenny's face, although he didn't know how long he could keep the rest of himself still.

Fortunately, she ended it, withdrawing the ticket before he had to do anything about it. "Well, fuck you and the horse you rode in on, you snobby son of a bitch," she whispered, her breath tickling his cheek. Then she rose and strode over to the counter to try her charms on the ticket agent.

Lenny stopped pretending not to watch. He was pretty sure now that she was not working with the people who had been following him. She was just a freelancer trying to make a playmate for the long plane ride, and maybe for more than that. But what was she up to now?

Bonde was leaning on the counter, deploying her cleavage as she tried to make some point with the ticket agent. She waved her ticket at him as she made her case. So she was trying to change her seat assignment...

But the ticket agent had seen hundreds of cleavages pleading for special treatment of one sort or another. He listened politely, waiting for her to be done, looking about as receptive as a hanging judge.

When Lenny saw him glance his way, he made a definite no sign with his hand. The clerk nodded slightly, then turned back to Bonde and interrupted her presentation. Whatever he said shut her up. She whipped her head around and glared at Lenny, but he was innocently reading again.

The harangue at the ticket counter went on for a bit and Lenny lost interest. In a different time, in a time before Paradise, he would have jumped at the chance to score such a seatmate. Now? She just looked like trouble.

And then there she was again, standing in front of him, looking not the least bit seductive. "Stop looking so smug, asshole. I wouldn't sit beside you now if you paid me."

"Enjoy the flight and I will do the same."

He kept an eye on her until she found a seat a dismissive distance away, then scanned the waiting area for any other wild cards. But nobody raised his hackles.

All Lenny wanted was to board the plane and quickly cross into American territory. He could smell freedom but knew it wasn't going to happen while he was in Canada. His flight would take him to Toronto with a too-long stop before he would board his direct flight to Honolulu.

No one was following Lenny; he was pretty sure of it now that Bonde was put in her place. Payback wasn't knocking on his door just yet, but he didn't want to take any chances. They had a better chance of sneaking up on him in Canada than they would back in Honolulu.

Why couldn't it have been Paradise? he asked himself, while wondering if he deserved to hold his head high. Canada and Paradise were to have been his 'happy ever after.' Was that too big a leap? Things had been working out well between Lenny and

Paradise and he was certain he had found the small village that could be his own paradise on earth.

Lenny had come to love Pops, Hope and Paradise. But that stranger in town asking about him showed he was putting his loved ones in danger. He had no choice but to leave and draw the stranger, whoever he/she was, out of town with him. Thank God he left when he did because it became all too apparent he was in a heap of trouble. His mind rolled back over his latest tight scrape, looking for ways he could have avoided it.

Shootouts were never fun, and in Lenny's past there had been many of them. Way too many. More than once he was used up and thrown out. This had been his first gunfight in Halifax, and he hoped there would not be another.

Medical help directly following the shootout had not been the kind you seek by going to the emergency department of your local hospital. It would be hard to stay under the radar by presenting with a bullet hole straight through his arm.

Lenny had been relatively sure the bullet had exited his body. He hoped he would need stitching up and nothing more. His shoulder, where the second bullet hit him, would require surgery. If that could not happen in his room, he would have to chug pain killers and take the bullet with him to Honolulu.

He knew someone who knew someone, so once he made it back to his room in a by-the-hour hotel on Lower Water Street Lenny made a phone call. Soon a doctor with a forgettable face and dirty fingernails was stitching him up.

Repairing the arm was not too bad. Lenny sat silently through it, though not exactly in comfort.

"That's the easy part," the doctor said.

"You've done enough."

"Not hardly, Superman. You won't get far unless I dig the slug out of your shoulder. Or I can drop you off at the emergency room."

Lenny hesitated, but only for a second or two. His hit of adrenaline had long since ebbed away, and he felt more like crap than he wanted to admit. "Do you think you can dig it out?"

"Shoulders are kid stuff," the doctor said, rummaging in his bag for some torture devices.

The next ten minutes held some of the worst pain he had lived through in his entire life. It was all he could do to keep still enough so the doctor could do his thing. He kept trying to call up Paradise's face, but he couldn't make it focus.

But then the work was done and the dressing was in place and Lenny felt both crappy and better for getting that slug out of his body.

"You're lucky they were shooting small calibre," the doctor said as he finished collecting his gear into one bag and bloody wads of stuff into another. "A forty-five would have taken your arm right off."

Lenny didn't know the man's name and hoped never to have to see him again. It was a cash transaction, and once the money changed hands the doctor was out the door and Lenny could indulge in a few moments of uncontrollable shuddering. Then he had had to ease himself into his shirt and jacket and call a cab for the airport.

With all that behind him, Lenny had not wanted to talk to anyone, not even the owner of a class-A cleavage. But he hadn't intended to be so harsh with Bonde. Perhaps he would send a drink to her once they were safely in the air.

But sleep came quickly for Lenny and before he knew it the plane was touching down in Toronto. Bonde had shimmied out of his mind. He had bigger problems to face.

32

"Mine."

"Okay, T.J., here you go." Hope picked up another toy to put it in the toy box.

Same chant, one more time. "Mine." It appeared no one was to touch anything that belonged to T.J. Hope was beginning to catch on, but she had to try one more time so she picked up a yellow school bus.

"Mine," came even louder this time and in addition to using his outside voice, T.J. took a swing at Hope.

And T.J. seemed to be used to getting what he wanted.

Hope got off the floor and moved to sit beside her mom on the comfortable but worn yellow and red sofa she had sat on as a very young child. It felt like a lifetime ago, she thought. "Mom, do you think T.J. is spoiled?"

"Hope, no parent appreciates you suggesting their child is spoiled. Be careful not to throw that word around when your dad gets home."

"But I could ask dad to his face if he thinks T.J. is spoiled couldn't I?"

"Be my guest, but be careful. It may seem our little man here is spoiled, but it's easy to see why. He's a darling, isn't he, and your dad has done a great job raising him. Let's not overstep when Thomas gets home."

Paradise picked T.J. up to give him a big hug and a kiss on the cheek. She wasn't sure he was ready for a smack on the lips. Not from her anyway.

"Remember, your dad works 12 hour shifts—and always the night shift. He took over my shift when you and I went to Canada. T.J. spends lots of time with the nanny, and when you have a one-on-one routine the child can often be spoiled. He receives all the attention, all the time. Does that make sense to you, Hope?"

Hope could see her mom falling in love with T.J., just as she was. He was a heart-breaker in more ways than they could count. He seemed comfortable with both of them, but with some reservations. They could tell.

"Sure. It makes sense. I know daddy works hard at being a good dad. He's always been good to me, too, hasn't he?"

It wasn't really a question, so Paradise reached over and simply hugged her daughter.

Paradise went on to explain that, since Wikolia first became ill, T.J. had lived with Thomas. The nanny had to ensure T.J. remained relatively quiet during the earlier part of the day so his daddy could get some sleep. Paradise imagined that Thomas didn't get much sleep at all. If only she had listened to Thomas when they spoke on the phone.

There were too many 'if only's to count.

"Honey, to be perfectly honest I feel some guilt for all your dad has been through, raising his son, working 12 hour shifts, and being at the hospital with Wikolia as often as he could."

"What does guilt feel like?"

"You'll know when you feel it, so come and talk to me then, okay?"

"Sure."

All three heard the key in the door, but T.J. saw her first. "Nanny. Nanny. Nanny. Pick T.J. up. Quick."

He made it sound as if his life was in danger. Nanny picked him up and swung him around. He loved it, but he had news.

"Look. Look," he shouted as he pointed first to Hope and then to Paradise. Clearly he felt these two women were intruders.

Paradise realized they had pretty much dismissed the nanny when they arrived late last evening. A bit of humble pie was in order. "My gosh, I don't even know your name." Paradise extended her hand.

"That's my mom, Paradise, and I'm Hope. Did daddy tell you about me? Daddy and T.J. both call you 'nanny' so we have been calling you that as well. How rude are we?"

Paradise stepped in to stop the onslaught of questions Hope was hurling. "We were a tad tired last night and didn't properly use our manners." Hope extended her hand as well.

"Please call me Mae, short for Dorothy Mae. Dorothy Mae Dodge. I wasn't born here in Hawaii but have lived here for many years. I have actually retired my 'nanny-hat' with the exception of this big boy in my arms. Isn't that right T.J? You are my only sunshine."

"My sunshine. My sunshine," shouted T.J.

"T.J. and I have a game we play when it's singing time. T.J. does love to sing." Hope decided to give it a try. "T.J. you are my sunshine, my only—" She was rewarded with a slap on her arm and a hard 'NO' from T.J.

The ladies tried very hard not to laugh but it truly was funny.

"You sing Nanny. You sing."

Mae started the song, and T.J. joined in. They sang the verse several times before T.J. was satisfied.

"Oh. My. God." Hope said.

"Language," Paradise said sharply, but with a smile. It was always their little song.

"You sing beautifully, Mae," Hope went on. "Are you a trained singer? It sure sounds like you're a professional."

"I have a background in music and have sung publicly all over Hawaii, but no further than that. T.J. is my only audience now."

Mae sat down and pulled T.J. onto her lap. He smiled up at her and kissed her arm. Paradise and Hope hid sudden tears as they observed the affection he was showing. Clearly she was far more than a nanny to him.

They talked whenever T.J. settled into an activity that did not involve singing, Paradise pitched in with lunch-making, letting T.J. direct her in the making of a sandwich with very unlikely ingredients.

When he went down for a nap, Paradise and Mae sat near an open window to enjoy the breeze. Hope insisted on hovering near T.J.'s bedroom door for a while 'just in case', but they finally persuaded her to come sit with them.

"I think," Mae said carefully, "it would be fine to leave T.J. in your care. You are family, and all. Although I will hear from Thomas with some pretty sharp words if I am wrong."

"You aren't wrong."

"Wikolia falling ill turned everything upside down, of course, and I think Thomas is more protective of T.J. than he needs to be. I keep telling him that his little boy is getting spoiled. Really, he does not understand the word 'no'."

"How did Thomas take that?"

Mae laughed. "He's not good with 'no', either. He said, 'I'm not spoiling my son and that's the end of it.'"

"I can hear his tone. Enough to lift bark off a branch."

Mae looked into her coffee cup. "I'm afraid I have spoken where it was not my business to do so. Thomas is my employer and I've been disrespectful. I'm sorry."

"Mae, this conversation will go nowhere, you have our word. Doesn't she, Hope?"

"Is that even a question? I don't want to be the one to bring up spoiling T.J., especially when we just got back here."

When T.J. got up from his nap and found the two new women still there, they could almost see the gears turning in his head: this is the new normal. He made much less of a fuss than Paradise had feared when it was time for Mae to go.

As he and Mae sunshined through one last round of their song, Paradise said quietly to Hope, "Let's not think of T.J. as being spoiled. That could get us into a heap of trouble with your dad. T.J. is part of our family. End of story."

"Roger that, Mom. Roger that."

33

"Home sweet home."

Thomas was happy to see his condo come into view. He put his left-turn signal on and manoeuvred the Waikiki traffic so he could make the turn and safely enter the underground parking garage. Thinking nanny might have taken T.J. to her home for a couple of days and nights Thomas was looking forward to a hot shower and a very long sleep. He could feel the comfort of his own bed.

His journey had not been a success. Wikolia's family seemed to have vanished. There were rumours, and Thomas chased every single one down with no resolution. He placed this trip under the failure column in his mind. He'd find her family another time and was able to rest somewhat easy with that thought.

Thomas wanted to speak with Wikolia's mother but couldn't imagine the words he would choose when that day came. Wikolia was not close to anyone in her family except, perhaps, for her mother. Every now and then she would say, "My Momma's gonna love her some T.J." Thomas had once commented that she should make the expression, "Your Nanna's gonna love her some T.J."

"Where did that memory come from?" Thomas decided hearing the sound of his own voice would help him stay awake. The quiet was lulling him to sleep with his hands firmly on the steering wheel and the car still rolling through the garage.

Thomas was certain her mother had not reached out to Wikolia for years, and while that spoke volumes about her it didn't look good on him, either. Thomas should have found her family when Wikolia was *first* hospitalized. Her mother might have wanted to come and help with the care for T.J. or even just spend time with him now and then. Life got in his way and he couldn't find the time to do everything. There were days when Thomas was totally overwhelmed and at day's end he felt like he had accomplished nothing. Not like him, and he knew that.

Thomas had truly missed his son. On the long drive home he decided he would take T.J. with him the next time he headed out on the road and they would make it a father and son adventure. He had hopes tucked away that T.J. would be by his side when they found his Nana. What a perfect memory that would be for T.J.

Mae, the nanny, had retired and Thomas knew that T.J. was the only remaining child she cared for. She had tried to convince Thomas that this was her choice because she loved T.J. so much, but Thomas knew better.

With Wikolia having recently passed away, Mae was feeling a bit sorry for T.J. and Thomas. She wasn't prepared to leave them just yet. When they were ready to be on their own she would leave, but not now.

Thomas had been reluctant to make this particular journey with T.J. because he knew if Wikolia's family wanted to fight over custody it could result in a knock-down-drag-'em-out fight right there on the spot, with no one winning the battle.

Some years earlier, Thomas witnessed a family fight when Wikolia took him to her hometown to meet her family. The entire family got into a brawl, with Wikolia and her mother being the last two standing! That didn't go over too well with any of Wikolia's brothers. Thomas had heard about family fights but he had never seen one like the one he had tucked away in his memory box.

As Thomas and Wikolia were leaving her family that day they didn't get to say goodbye to the boys because they were all engaged in a sidebar fist-fight. They were pissed off that their sister and their *mother* of all people had knocked them flat on their asses one at a time. They were already practising for the next round. At the time Thomas couldn't wait to get out of there but in the moment he wished he had found her brothers during this trip.

No one remembered what caused the fight, but, as Wikolia explained to Thomas, "It doesn't matter, my love. We have been fist-fighting for as long as I can remember. My brother broke my nose when I was only four years old during a game he called, 'Duck or I'll break your nose.' I didn't. He did."

Thomas was brought back to the present as he turned a corner in the garage and found a rental car in *his* parking spot.

"*Gentle Jesus.*" This was not how he had pictured his long day on the road would end.

It was the middle of the night, so Thomas took an empty spot and hoped he could get this resolved before someone got angry with him for parking in their spot. This happened often, but it was the first time it had happened to Thomas. He made a mental note to bring this up at the next condo meeting.

It was dark as Thomas entered his condo. Trying not to wake T.J. he didn't turn on the light just inside the foyer.

Then he heard his son's voice. "What the...?"

He tripped over unfamiliar backpacks in the foyer. Mae knew he hated clutter and in a small condo it was important to put everything in its place. Mae had his room while he was away, yet she left not one but two backpacks just inside the door? Yes, Thomas was definitely taking T.J. with him when he continued his search for T.J.'s grandmother and her family. And he would have a word with Mae about the state of his condo. It was true he was paying her only to care for T.J., but she had never before left a mess in the living room when she went to bed.

"Daddy!" T.J. untangled himself from his blanket and ran to his dad. "My son, I have missed you. What's going on here, buddy? Our home is a mess. Did you have anything to do with this?" Thomas said as he picked T.J. up. Then he turned as he heard his bedroom door open.

"Dad?"

Thomas shook his head to ensure he wasn't dreaming.

Hope walked over to him and put her arms out wide so she could hug her dad and her brother at the same time. T.J. tried to put some space between his dad and his sister.

"Jealous a bit, son?" Thomas said as he returned Hope's embrace.

"I didn't have any idea when you would be home, daddy. I wanted to surprise you and I'm so sorry about the mess."

"I am surprised."

"A good surprise, I hope?"

"T.J., let's you and daddy give Hope a really big hug like the one she gave us. What do you say?"

Thomas was proud of his son when he spread his arms welcoming Hope into the hug he was offering. His kids were getting along with each other and for some reason this made him very emotional.

"You're sharing the bedroom with Mae, I assume?"

Oh, Hope was loving this.

"Do you know if Mae has the rental car that's parked in my spot? Normally she doesn't drive over, especially when she's coming to stay with T.J. overnight, so I'm assuming it's not her car."

"Let me make fresh coffee, Dad. We have so much to talk about and I think you're going to need a pot and more."

"And maybe a glass of milk for this little guy while you're in the kitchen."

Hope knew her mom wouldn't stay hidden much longer. She had been sound asleep when Hope closed the bedroom door behind her, but T.J. wasn't using his inside voice. Within the next half hour, her mother would open that door and all would be revealed.

Thomas was going to have an even bigger surprise than coming home to find his daughter in the condo. This condo was about to be extremely crowded.

34

Paradise knew without a doubt her heart belonged to the man on the other side of the bedroom door. The daddy answering T.J.'s questions and asking Hope a million questions of his own was the man Paradise had loved for her entire life. That much was crystal clear.

Running a brush through her tangled hair, Paradise whispered, "I love you Thomas. I love you so much and I'm sorry..." No, she would apologize another time. Today was about love and connecting after so much time apart.

There would be time to reflect on why she had wasted even one day away from Thomas. Perhaps he always knew she would return to him.

Paradise decided she needed coffee and she needed to ensure Thomas knew how she felt about him and their life moving forward.

Thomas heard Paradise before he saw her. He sensed her in the room. "Hello, my love," she whispered.

Thomas was sitting cross-legged on the floor, watching T.J. play with the new car Daddy had brought for him. Hope was pouring her mom that all-important first cup of coffee. With a seven-hour time difference between Nova Scotia and Honolulu Hope was prepared to cut her mom some slack. Paradise had slept in and that was a first.

Hope was worried about how all this stuff between her parents would play out. If they wanted to be together as much as she wanted to have them under the same roof, this would be an incredibly good day.

When she saw her mom and her dad share their first glance after way too much time apart she relaxed. She offered a steaming cup. "Here's your coffee, mother, made just the way you like it."

Then Hope picked T.J. up and took him into the bedroom. Privacy was always a good thing, and if her parents ever needed privacy it was now. But she wondered how much alone time she should give them. Would they have to hide out here until the old folks came and released them?

"T.J., this is going to be a great day. So I am going to let you jump on the bed to celebrate. Would you like to jump right here in the middle of Daddy's bed?"

T.J. answered the question as fast as he could. He rolled over to the centre of the bed and extended his hands so Hope could help him stand up. He kept losing his balance. "Hope help?" he said with a laugh. Fun times ahead.

35

Paradise opened her arms as she approached Thomas. "I've missed you without realizing it until this very second."

"What about Len? I need to know where that stands."

Thomas didn't mean to sound harsh, but he had to get it out immediately. He was nervous and suspected Paradise might be as well. He was jealous of Len and he wasn't proud of it. He wasn't sure he would share that with Paradise.

"Paradise, this is important to me. So let's do this. I can't park this for later."

"Really, Thomas? Lenny is the first thing that comes to mind when you see me?" This conversation was not going well and certainly not the way Paradise thought it would, especially after so much time apart.

"Oh, I see. When did it change from Len to Lenny? Has that been during your long walks on the beach?" Thomas wanted to bite through his own tongue to make himself shut up. If he ruined this because of his stupid jealousy he knew there might not be another chance to make things right. He was running out of chances.

'Let's start again, my love. How does that sound? I won't go back into the bedroom and make another entrance, but if I thought it would help I would do that and more." Paradise thought she could make Thomas smile and ease the tension a bit. When that didn't work she was unsure what to say next. "You didn't answer my question. What about Lenny? This is exactly where I want to begin this conversation."

"Okay, I suppose I deserve this, so let me tell you that Lenny, as I know him, is not in my life anymore. In fact he left the Cape."

"When was this? Am I correct in assuming he is only out of your life because he left town?"

"I don't know the exact date, but apparently he left some time ago." Paradise took the time to refill her coffee up. She wondered if Thomas would interrupt her again, but he did not.

"Yes, we walked the beach every morning with our first cup of coffee and, yes, we talked about lots of things, but we did not cross the line, my love. It's you my heart belongs to. Not Lenny. Not anyone else. I really don't know what else I can say."

Clearly Thomas wasn't ready to resume their life together. Had it been a mistake for Paradise and Hope to arrive back in Honolulu without asking Thomas if he wanted them in his life? Was it possible he didn't love her any more? Hope had said she didn't think a surprise was the right way to go. Paradise wished she had listened to her daughter.

"I've needed you so many times. When Wikolia was dying I had no one. No one to talk to and no one to tell me I was doing the best I could. Where were you then?" Thomas knew his tone was harsh, but the torrent flowed out of him. "I guess I expected you to silently interpret what I was *not* saying, and that's all on me. I've been such a mess during all of this, and for me it began a lifetime ago when I dropped you and our girl off at the airport for a *brief* vacation in Nova Scotia."

Paradise sat as if lost in thought, paralyzed by what she was hearing.

"Did you know then that you weren't coming back anytime soon? Did you and Hope have a plan to leave me and have me go on with my life, assuming you would return before school began in the fall? Do you know how stupid that made me feel?" Thomas knew he was digging a hole for himself but he wasn't finished just yet.

"And my work. Christ, Paradise, imagine what I was going through at the warehouse. Word about your departure spread through the halls at 2.0 and I can imagine now the jokes they told behind my back when I asked others why Len had disappeared and had he in fact entered the Witness Protection Program as planned. Remember how you and I used to talk about how, in all our time in the PI business, we had never once encountered anyone in a WPP?"

Silence spread between them like something nasty leaking out on the floor. The events of the day were not shaping up to be a good reunion. Memorable, maybe, but not in a good way.

Paradise tried again. "Here's what I'm prepared to do. I'll go into the little kitchen over there and take my time while I make us a fresh pot of coffee. You can check on our children. See if there's some way Hope could entertain T.J. for a bit longer. Tell her we'll pay her. Money has become very important to our girl."

Seeing Thomas' puzzled look, she said, "Hope has her own little business and she desperately wants to earn money. I'll let her fill in the blanks another time. Thomas, you'll be so proud of how thoughtful and generous she has become."

Thomas lay back and closed his eyes. He had not slept in over forty-eight hours. He had been looking forward to some rest, not the surprises that awaited him when he came home in the middle of the night. If he could just rest for a moment, perhaps...

Paradise sat with Thomas for a few minutes, watching him sleep. Then she poured her coffee, found a few fruit drinks in the fridge for the kids, and silently walked into the bedroom to see if she could start her day over yet again.

"Mom, watch this! T.J. can hold tight to my arm while I raise him into the air. He's a very strong little boy. And, as you can see he's handsome." Hope was loving this, Paradise could tell.

Hope said with a smile, "T.J.'s smiling at you, mom, and he's acting like he knows exactly who you are."

"I believe that's because I'm holding a soda, isn't it, young man?"

"For me?"

"Yes, very soon. Let's get dressed and tiptoe outside and have our drinks there, so daddy can catch some sleep. Can you be as quiet as a mouse?"

They gathered up their coats and shoes without too much racket and tiptoed out of the condo. Thomas slept on like an enchanted prince in a fairy tale.

"Okay, kids, can you help me get reacquainted with the neighbourhood?"

As they strolled, T.J. diverting this way and that to explore a bug on the ground or watch a bird. Hope said, "Mom, I like it when you refer to both of us as your kids. Do you think one day T.J. will feel like your own little boy?"

"Honey, I hope you'll understand, but your question is a bit too heavy for me right now. Can we park it for a later discussion, please?"

Hope replied with a big hug and a pat on her mom's back.

36

Paradise knew she was carrying around a ton of change. She could feel the weight of it in her purse as she navigated the sidewalks and streets with Hope and T.J. Fortunately she had converted funds to US currency before leaving Canada. She knew they were heading for the mall and a plan was forming in her mind. Paradise always had a plan at least partially developed…

"Hope, where is the toddler play-station in this Mall? Do you remember? I thought it was right in front of us but I don't see it."

"I'm pretty sure we just missed the turn for the kid-friendly area," Hope offered. She turned T.J. around and pointed him in the right direction. "Back-track not too far and…it's right here."

"Push me, Hope. Push me on the car!" T.J. was comfortable using his outside voice and running as fast as he could to the toy cars. His daddy and his nanny both brought him here. Mostly it was nanny who brought him to the Mall in the morning when Thomas came home from the night shift and needed a bit of quiet time in the condo.

"Hey, kid, slow down. Judging by your yelling, this is your happy place. Clearly we came to the right spot, mom."

"Push me. Push me." T.J. stood tall and climbed into his favourite red car.

"You're repeating yourself again, kid."

Knowing that her brother Wilmot wanted to speak with her about something that seemed to be both urgent and important, Paradise remembered there was a row of pay phones directly in front of the play-station. She knew she could make a call to the Cape while watching both of her children. She wasn't sure it was something that could be resolved over the phone, but she needed to at least encourage her brother to share his worries with her. She had a nagging feeling that she knew what the urgency might be and talking with her brother would confirm her suspicions or, and this would be ideal, prove that she was wrong.

"Hope, I'll be watching you two while I'm on the phone, but from the second I hear a voice on the other end you're in charge. Just give me the high sign and I will drop the phone and come to you."

"We've got this, mom. Stop worrying about everything."

Paradise knew before they left the Cape that Wilmot wanted to speak with her, but there had been no time. She had asked Pops to explain the urgency of their trip and to let him know she would definitely be in touch from Honolulu.

"Hello?" Paradise heard nothing at the other end.

Knowing Marie was still uncomfortable speaking on the telephone, Paradise was giving her time to react. This was all part of Marie's recovery process and she really hadn't answered the phone more than a few times since she left the rehab centre.

"Is this Marie?"

"This is Marie speaking. Who's calling me? Who is this and what do you want?" It startled Paradise to hear the fright in Marie's voice. She could picture Marie trembling as she reached up to answer the phone, hanging a bit too high on the wall, in their tiny home overlooking Mavillette Beach.

"Marie, dear, it's me. It's Paradise."

Paradise heard Marie drop the receiver and shout for Wilmot to hurry and come to the phone. Paradise was glad she had called and at the same time felt guilty for not having made time for Wilmot and Marie before she left the Cape.

"Paradise, are you home? We'll come right over, if that's okay with you. When did you get back?" Wilmot was talking so fast Paradise could hardly keep up with his thoughts.

"Slow down, brother."

"Sorry, I just didn't expect you to be back so soon. Did Thomas come with you?"

"I'm calling from Hawaii."

"Oh My God, as your daughter would say. Is something wrong? Why on earth are you calling from Hawaii?"

"You and Marie were desperate to tell me something before I left town. Something about me being in trouble. Or was it you and

Marie who were in trouble or danger? I haven't been able to get it off my mind. Now, *what's wrong?*"

"Nothing that I'm going to share with you half a world away. Don't expect me to do that, please."

"Please, Wilmot, what is going on? Maybe I can fix it from here." She could hear Marie in the background saying, Tell her. Tell her now. "My God, Wilmot what is it? What has Marie in such a state?"

Wilmot took a few deep breaths and hearing him do that bothered Paradise.

"It's that bad?"

"It's about the man who beat Marie and left her for dead. It was the same night I was beaten nearly to death by Meat."

Paradise remembered the horrible scene, the shoot-out, and Meat sinking to the ground for the last time. "Get to the point, Wilmot."

"Marie and I believe the man who left her for dead is the same man we know here in the Cape as…Lenny Calhoun."

"Oh, no. No. No. No. God in Heaven, don't let this be true."

"I'm sorry, but once we figured it out we have been frantic with worry that you might be in danger being around him."

Paradise couldn't move and couldn't speak. It took her a few long and precious seconds to compose herself.

"Wilmot, I want you to leave this with me. I'll personally call the local police. I can trust my department with this. You know Sergeant Curtis, yes?"

"We figure the police might be in cahoots with him because, surely to God, they would have done some sort of a background check on Lenny when he moved to our Cape. What do you think, Paradise? Do you really trust Curtis?"

"I do trust Curtis, Wilmot. And you can, too."

"We sure are trying."

"I believe you also know Lenny has left the Cape. I'm not sure anyone knows exactly where he is but if anyone can investigate this and find him it will be Sergeant Curtis and his team. My next call will be to Curtis."

"God, I hate to leave this mess with you, especially since you are over there giving Thomas a hand."

"Listen to me, Wilmot. Can you and Marie leave this with me? Can you leave this burden with me and try to feel it lift from your shoulders. Can you?

Wilmot could only whisper, "Yes."

"Wilmot, I'm so sorry I called under these circumstances. We left the condo so Thomas could get a few hours' sleep. I can call you back from the house phone when I know something concrete. I think I need a few hours to process this though. To think Lenny could have actually beaten Marie up and left her for dead – I can hardly say the words."

"I'm sorry, too."

"I want you to tell Marie I believe her. Above all else she needs to know *I believe her*. Should I tell her myself, Wilmot?"

"I would like to tell her, Paradise, but I appreciate you making the offer. Thanks, sis."

37

Pops was busy in the kitchen. He was making a special supper for a special lady. And he was some excited.

Mrs. Foss, his neighbour and friend, had made a perfect casserole dish and had just delivered it to his kitchen, complete with instructions. Then she interrupted herself and fixed him with a schoolmarm stare.

"Put the kettle on, Pops. I can see how nervous you are and it can't be about my cooking, so spill. What's going on at 548 Cape St Mary Road later today?"

"Nervous? Honest to God, I am so nervous I could pass out right here on my kitchen floor."

"I can see your floor is spotless so getting any dirt on that lovely new shirt you're wearing won't be a problem if you do fall." Mrs Foss thought he would tell her what he was up to if she waited around long enough.

But he stayed silent long enough that she thought she might as well jog him. "I'm not leaving, Pops."

"You must have guessed this dinner and evening is for Eugenie. Finally we can have a quiet meal without interruptions, and I can tell her what's on my mind and in my tired old heart. It's a dinner for two, so I'll thank you not to stay once I see Eugenie coming down the street. I hope that doesn't seem rude to you."

"Not rude at all, but you better start talking while I pop this casserole into your oven to warm up. Lordy, Pops, you didn't even turn the oven on like I told you to. What am I going to do with you?" Mrs. Foss grabbed the dish towel and snapped it on his arm.

"I was pretty sure you would stay for a visit, which meant you would heat the casserole up for me while we talk," Pops said. "Some of this you already know. I have tried several times to talk to Eugenie about us but she always seems to have someone hanging around her. I hate that and I all but told her so the last time it happened."

Mrs. Foss checked that the oven was warm. She carefully put the casserole in the oven, closed the door gently then turned to give Pops a warm hug before sitting down at the kitchen table.

"You can do this, Pops. I know how much you care for Eugenie. I think it's wonderful to find love at your age and I mean that as a compliment not as a slag to your age compared to mine"

"Thanks for clearing that up. I wouldn't even have thought of you throwing out a slag, and that is a new word for me to look up in my dictionary." Pops was clearly deep in thought but Mrs. Foss sat quietly, knowing he wanted to say more.

"I don't know if this is a warning sign that I'm doing the wrong thing, because there are days when I feel like nothing more than a tired old and confirmed bachelor. Maybe that's where I should leave things. Am I making any sense at all?"

"Not yet, but keep talking."

"Let me just push this curtain back so I can see when Eugenie is on her way."

"I really don't know Eugenie at all. Is she aware of how you feel, or have you been bumbling along all this time?"

"I'll find out over dinner now, won't I!"

"Pops, you have clearly gone out of your way. Your table looks lovely and I can sense you really want to be with Eugenie. All you need now is one very special guest. Should I get out of your way?"

"I think we can finish our tea."

He gave one more glance out the window, then sat at the table. "Did I ever tell you about my bride back in Paradise, the one in Newfoundland? I didn't think I would ever love another woman after all these years gone by. The good Lord took my bride and she took part of my heart up to heaven. She was a jewel of a lady and I know she's lookin' down on me today. What I don't know is if she's agreein' with me."

"We've talked about this. Use your proper words rather than lookin' and agreein'. You've worked very hard to learn how to speak properly so don't give it up now. I bet that's one of the many things Eugenie loves about you."

In his heart, very deep in his heart, Pops knew Eugenie brought out the best in him. In his books, that was love. He hoped he wasn't just being an old fool, but had already decided Eugenie was worth making a fool of himself.

"She's some easy to talk to, Mrs. Foss, and she listens to me and seems to like hearing me talk about just about anything."

"Don't talk too much, though, Pops. Men, in my opinion, talk way too much. And some think they know everything too, though that's not you."

"Right after we first met I told Eugenie I had been married once at a young age to an even younger lady. When my bride died I moved here. She died in my arms. I guess that was too much information."

"Maybe keep the details about deaths for another time," Mrs Foss said with a smile. She wanted to turn the conversation back to Eugenie and the good days ahead for Pops and his lady.

But, Pops wasn't quite done with his sad, as he called it. "I asked the Lord to take her pain away and take her to heaven with him. She was in terrible pain for so long. The Lord heard my prayers."

"Like I said, Pops, this is a bit too heavy as a pre-dinner discussion. We need to lift your spirits before your gal knocks on the door."

"Eugenie has been married to the Lord for most of her life. I know she's not always comfortable around men, but I think she likes being with me. She's kind and she's gentle and she's caring."

She made him laugh. Pops hadn't really laughed in years.

Since his Cole.

~

While Pops prepared for his guest, Wilmot and Marie crossed paths with Eugenie on the other side of Cape St Mary Road.

"Look at you, all dressed up and walking with a bounce in your step. Where are you headed, Eugenie?" Marie was curious.

Eugenie liked the young couple very much and she loved their company. "Pops has invited me to his home for dinner. Where are the two of you going?"

"That's exactly where we're headed! We have some news for Pops so we'll walk with you and tell both of you our news at the same time. Is that okay?" Wilmot didn't catch on that this was dinner for two not four people.

"The more the merrier," Eugenie replied. "Walk with me. I'm sure Pops has lots of food prepared because, just between you two and me, Mrs. Foss made dinner and took it over to Pops. I think she has done that a few times since Paradise and Hope went off to Hawaii to be with Thomas. Terrible news about Wikolia's death. Such a young woman."

Eugenie knew Pops was making a fancy dinner for her and she suspected he had romance on his mind. She was some nervous and needed a distraction for at least the first few minutes that she was in Pops' home. After that she would probably be okay on her own with Pops.

She couldn't think straight. For the first time in her life that she could remember, Eugenie wished she looked better.

Only recently had Eugenie started to fuss over what to wear and who might see her if she wandered over to the local Frenchy's store to see what might look good on her. Everyone shopped at Frenchy's and it wasn't likely anyone would even notice her, but so far her nerves always got the best of her.

Today was different, though. Eugenie awoke in the morning thinking, 'I'm going to buy a new blouse at Frenchy's and no matter what I'm buying something new today!'

"I'm all dressed up, compliments of our local Frenchy's. My, but they have good clothing there and I'm just discovering the world of designers thanks to the many bins of clothes that fit me."

Eugenie didn't know the names of any designers, but one of the young girls who was on cash kept rhyming off their names as she encouraged Eugenie to pick a skirt that would go with her new sweater. She loved her outfit and, if the truth be known, she had a bit of lipstick on, too. That was definitely a first.

Even words could be romantic, and with Wilmot and Marie walking with her down Cape St Mary Road Eugenie knew she had a bit more time to think about this. What should she say, and would she and Pops be able to have a conversation all through their meal?

Over the past few months she had seen Pops soften a bit around her. As if that wasn't enough, he was now talking about emotions and feelings and stuff he had never spoken of before. Eugenie loved it.

But recently Pops got a bit too personal over a mid-morning coffee at the Cafe. That's how Eugenie figured out this dinner was about more than dinner. He had come right out and asked if Eugenie ever thought about being on her own as she grew old, and did she think she might like a companion. Imagine the nerve! She shut that talk down as fast as she could and high-tailed it out of the Café.

Having been married once, Eugenie was having less than agreeable thoughts about a second marriage. When your first marriage has been to The Lord...it's hard to put anything into words. Eugenie felt disloyal to her faith and she would have to deal with those feelings before facing another marriage. She knew, of course, that any mortal marriage could not compare to her first. That is, if marriage was even on Pops' mind.

Eugenie was very religious and faithful to her Catholic Church and she knew Pops hadn't been inside a church since his grandson's death. She had heard the story of Cole's life and death a few times, and she cried every time Pops spoke of his Cole. Pops cried, too.

~

The casserole was cooling on top of the stove, and to his own surprise Pops found himself lighting a candle and placing it on the table. He wasn't sure he had ever lit a dinner candle or even had the notion of doing so before today. There wasn't even a power outage. This wasn't Mrs.'s Foss idea, either. He thought of the candle all on his own.

He moved the kitchen curtains a bit so they would not catch fire from the candle, and spotted three people walking up his lane. Three people. Eugenie, of course. But Pops couldn't believe it when he saw her chatting away with Wilmot and Marie. He had not invited either of them to dinner.

What in God's name do I do now? Am I supposed to invite Marie and Wilmot to join us for supper?

Pops was certain Eugenie knew this was supposed to be a special dinner for two. They had talked about it several times and she bloody well knew he had put a lot of personal effort into this day.

Just like that – dinner for two became dinner for four. Pops tried without success to put a smile on his face as he opened the door to invite his guests in.

38

"Oh no, I fell asleep. Where is everyone?"

It took Thomas a couple of foggy moments to realize he was speaking to an empty condo. He moved muzzily from room to room to confirm he was the only one home, and started to check for signs that kidnappers had broken in before giving his head a shake. They were being kind to the old man.

He felt uneasy about his behaviour, both the fight he picked with Paradise and the way he had nodded off. It was no way to greet Paradise and Hope at the end of their long journey from Cape St Mary.

During their long time apart, Thomas had convinced himself that Lenny had found a place in the heart of the woman he loved. But interrogating Paradise had not been his finest hour. He still wanted to know about their relationship, but perhaps that could wait for another day. He wasn't even sure where his jealous streak was coming from. They had been through so much to find their way back to each other.

Thomas decided to make good use of his free time and be ready to greet his family long before he would hear the familiar chatter at the front door. After a quick shower, he cleaned the bathroom thoroughly. Four people would be using it going forward. "This is going to be one Hell of a squeeze," Thomas said to himself with a big smile in his heart.

He got the bedroom in order, as best he could with all the bags on the floor. He piled all the oversized purses and backpacks against the wall at the far side of the room, so at least getting from the door to the bed was not an obstacle course. Then he tackled the living room, getting everything back where it belonged so T.J. could put it all out of order again.

Sooner or later, Paradise and the kids would walk through the door and Thomas was hoping for a do-over with his lady.

He sat on the couch and thought back to a quieter time when he was raising Hope on his own. He heard himself saying, as he had more than once, "Sooner or later, Hope you're going to understand why there are rules." Her innocent reply got to him every time.

"Is it sooner now, daddy? And when does later come? Is it coming on the day or on the morrow? I don't really know when sooner comes."

Thomas couldn't remember how many times he had explained to his daughter that she should use "today" and "tomorrow", not "the-day" and "the-morrow". But when he called her on it, she would put her hands on her hips and say, as if explaining to a slow learner, "I *know*, daddy. That's what I *just said*."

Where had she picked up those phrases and that stance?

Thomas had a million memories tucked away already, and Hope was still so young. There would be many more and they would include T.J. That is, if everything works out, he thought not for the first time.

Hearing a bit of a commotion in the hallway, Thomas knew his quiet time was about to vanish. He wouldn't have it any other way.

His two children ran through the door as soon as it was open. They were using their outside-voice and laughing through their words. "Please, lower your voices, kids," Thomas said with a smile as they both literally jumped on top of him.

Paradise followed the kids through the door and laughed out-loud. Their eyes met, speaking volumes.

"Nicely done, sweetheart. The house doesn't look at all as we left it a few hours ago. How long have you been up?"

"Cleaning up a small place doesn't take long. Don't give me too much credit."

"Oh. My. God. Dad, you would not believe how long it takes to clean our home in the Cape." Hope didn't realize she was driving a stake through her dad's heart when she alluded to the Cape as home.

Watching Thomas flinch Paradise jumped in. "Hope, it looks like we're fortunate to have two homes at the moment. All four of us, right?"

Hope shrugged and gave her mother one of her 'sorry' looks. She had not missed the smiles her mom and dad had exchanged, but she had no idea what that was about. And she didn't have a room she could retreat to so she could puzzle it out, either.

Hope figured the only person in the room who didn't worry about having a bit of privacy was her brother. T.J. used every room and every person to his advantage. And he was cute enough to get away with it. For a little guy he sure could make a mess and he could do it in the blink of an eye.

Because she knew her dad was a neat-freak, Hope wondered if he ever tried teaching T.J. the ditty she had memorized.

Use the hangers and the hooks,
Pick up your clothes and your books,
Or watch for daddy's dirty looks.

Hope guessed T.J. might still be a bit young to memorize anything, so she would give him a bit of time before she passed the rhyme along to him.

"We've all had lunch, Thomas, so you don't have to feed us for a few hours anyway. Our children have been well fed. Please don't ask me if it was a 'healthy' lunch. I did try." Paradise shrugged her shoulders at Thomas and then went on. "I do think T.J. is tired and should go down for a nap." She realized too late that her words may have sounded harsh.

"Not sure we can expect T.J. to sleep during the day with three adults in the same room, but let's see how it goes." Thomas was in charge. "If he gets cranky, I'll deal with him then." Thomas hoped this would shut the conversation down but it did not.

Paradise had more to say. Knowing she had already upset Thomas she waited for a minute or two and tried to gather her thoughts. "What if I take him into the bedroom? I could lie down with him and see if he sleeps at all. He really is tired from his trip to the Mall."

"Paradise, I heard you the first time. I'll make the call on that but if he does have a nap it won't be in the bedroom. Mae has him well trained to sleep in his bed out here in the living area. With me working nights, it has been very important that T.J. know without question that the bedroom is off limits."

"Of course. I'm sorry if I said too much." Paradise hoped for a reply but none came. As it turned out, it was T.J. who came to her rescue.

"Outside? Outside daddy?" T.J. took his jacket off the hook and tried to open the door by hanging himself on the doorknob. Thomas knew what was coming and that it would prove him wrong about the nap.

"Son, you've been outside with Paradise and Hope so you are not going outside again today." With that Thomas picked him up and took him over to his bed in the alcove off the living room.

T.J. saw it coming and began to punch and kick his dad while yelling as loud as he could. "No. No. I said no daddy. I want nanny."

"You'll have to settle for your favourite teddy bear, my son, so here it is. Now lie back down." Thomas tried to finish with a more serious tone but he wasn't sure his words had gotten through.

He sat on the floor beside his son's bed and each time T.J. attempted to get up, daddy ensured that he did not. After twenty minutes of yelling that sounded all too much like a screaming fire alarm, T.J. dozed off. The only sound heard was the hiccups that almost lifted him off his bed. He was having a much needed sleep.

Moving over to be closer to the girls, Thomas quietly shared one of his greatest worries. "He pits me against his nanny when it suits him. Every time I discipline I hear screams for nanny."

"Can I say something? Please." Hope looked at both of her parents. She felt she had remained quiet long enough. "Dad, while we were at the Mall, T.J. wanted everything he saw and it didn't matter if it was me or Mom who said no, his answer was always the same. "I want nanny."

Looking at her mother she went on, "Didn't you notice that, mom?"

"Of course I did, Hope, but listening to your dad, it seems he knows about this. We don't need to rub salt in the wounds."

"Okay, that has to be an old person's saying right? Salt? Wounds?" Hope attempted to lighten the mood and it worked. Smiles all around.

"Ladies, if you'll excuse me I'll move all the way over to this corner and into my office."

Closing his invisible door, Thomas completed a bit of paper work while Paradise and Hope sat quietly reading their current books of choice. Hope was a reader just like Paradise. This alone brought a smile to her mother's face.

Several hours passed and Thomas wondered if Paradise had learned anything about cooking while living with Pops. "Is anyone hungry?" Don't worry about waking T.J. up. If he doesn't get up soon, we'll never get him to bed later."

Paradise and Hope spoke in unison. "What are you making, Dad?"

Thomas had his answer. He would be the one making supper and was happy to have something to keep him busy while he gathered his thoughts. Having someone there to watch his son while he made their meals was a great gift and he reminded himself not to take it for granted.

"Hope, why don't you help me by setting the table?

Paradise worried that Thomas was avoiding her, so she stepped in. "Hope, you keep an eye on your brother and I'll help you in the kitchen. I do know how to set the table, at least."

"Well, thank God for small miracles." Thomas dodged away as she aimed a mock punch at his shoulder. Then, lowering his voice, he added, "Thank you, my love, for referring to T.J. as Hope's brother earlier. That means the world to me."

"Easy to do. They are your children so they are my children, too."

Thomas knew he would need to change the subject or he would be in tears. "Cooking is still not so easy for you, I gather. Who does the cooking in the Cape? Or do I want to know?"

They reached for each other at the same moment and Paradise moved into his embrace as if they had never been apart.

Baby steps – again.

39

"Let's not make this awkward when it comes to bedtime, okay, T.J? Look at me, kid. I'm talkin' to you."

Hope was enjoying this. She was smiling as she continued to pretend she was speaking with T.J. In reality, she was speaking to her parents—to their parents—while looking at her brother. She would explain this moment to T.J. when he was older. "It's important to know when to make yourself scarce," she whispered to her little brother.

Hope wasn't fooling anyone and she knew it. She was totally okay with that because it meant her plan was working.

The adults in the room gave each other a virtual high-five. Hope would sleep on the sofa near T.J. rather than the girls in the bedroom and the boys in the living room. That was her plan but it might have been their plan, too. The bedroom on the other side of the closed bedroom door would belong to mom and dad.

Memories were made of this.

Hope had a lot on her mind. She was already thinking about their return to the Cape. Ideally, they would be a family of four departing Hawaii this time. They sure did have enough room in their Cape home, but Hope knew that wouldn't be the only consideration.

Did Thomas want to travel to the Cape and did her mom even want him to make the trip with them? She hoped so, but wasn't convinced just yet.

Was it just in her head, or was Hope seeing little to no romance between her parents? Deciding to go for it and make a joke or two before she and T.J. pretended they were tired so their parents could go to the bedroom, she jumped in. "So you two, I expected to see all that kissing and hugging and feeling each other's bodies like I used to see before we moved to the Cape. What? You didn't think I was watching you, mom? You're the one who taught me to use the eyes in the back of my head. Do you remember that conversation? So funny."

She could see this was all falling flat and she was trying to recover before she got reprimanded. But, sure enough...

"Our business is our business, young lady," Thomas said in a firm tone. "I would suggest you stay out of what doesn't concern you."

What the hell. She was in trouble anyway, so Hope continued. "But it is my business, because your life together affects my life and I want my life to include parents who love each other and can't keep their hands off each other like I see on the cover of those magazines I'm not allowed to buy." And that was about as deep as Hope was willing to dig her own grave for now.

"Hope, I'm disappointed in you," Paradise said. "But this is a conversation for another day. Grab your pjs and meet me in the bathroom."

"Oh, great, here comes the girls' time and the girl talk, meaning you will be talking to me not with me. I hate that, mother."

"Hope. *Now*. In the bathroom and not another word."

Hope retreated to the bathroom, thinking she might have taken everything just a tad too far.

40

The plane arced and hit turbulent weather.

Lenny awoke with every bone in his body screaming from too many hours in a seat not meant for sleeping in even if you were a regular-sized man. For a man his size it should have been impossible, even leaving aside the bullet wounds. Because he had slept so soundly Lenny was paying the price.

Stiff limbs wouldn't kill him, so Lenny tried to dismiss the discomfort. He had bigger issues to face, beginning with placing a call to Lieutenant Commander Jalen Lexis, the head honcho of Hawaii 2.0, to beg for his job back. His job and a place in the witness protection program, if he hadn't burnt that particular bridge.

He knew it was a long shot that anyone would even talk to him. A number of people had worked long and hard to help him enter the WPP, and he had walked away to follow the visions of Paradise in his head.

Having no idea how long he had slept, Lenny wondered how much think-time he had before the plane landed in Honolulu. He had made it this far without that beautiful stranger, Bonde, invading his space, and he was mildly amused. He would have bet money she would be in his face the minute they were airborne. And why was she in his head in the first place?

Never was a ladies' man, Lenny thought to himself. He had always kept his life free from commitment—until Paradise entered his world. Then he wanted to commit to her so badly he followed her all the way to the Cape. He hoped details of his journey hadn't gotten into the gossip mill within the walks of 2.0. He knew he wasn't in a position to ask for any help, but he had to try.

The landing was smooth. Since he had not much more than a backpack, Lenny was off the plane quickly and with ease. He was ready for the authorities to get in his face and arrest him between the plane and the terminal, but nobody spared him more than a passing glance.

Luck was on his side, just as it had been that day in Point Pleasant Park. Against the odds, Lenny had walked out of the park. He was the only one.

Shaking that memory off for a moment, Lenny stopped at the first payphone that came into sight. He quickly dialed the one number he had committed to memory in case, just in case, he needed a favour. The phone rang once and was answered immediately.

"You have reached 2.0 and this is Lieutenant Commander Jalen Lexis speaking. Please identify yourself."

Lenny was shocked to hear the commander answer the phone himself. Something out of the ordinary must be going on inside the huge warehouse he had once called home. The warehouse had been his life twenty-four hours a day. Not once, not for a second, did he venture outside.

Back then, the plan had been to quietly slip into the Witness Protection Program, and that meant following the rules to the letter until everything was signed sealed and Lenny was delivered to his new life. Didn't happen.

"Identify yourself," Jalen repeated. Lenny was embarrassed to have called without having thought out just how he would make 'the ask.'

"Commander, this is Len. I need my job back." That was more blunt than he had wanted it to be, but too late now.

"Identify yourself with your password. Be advised that we are tracing this call."

"Menlove. That's my password, sir. I apologize for calling out of the blue."

The commander's tone changed from suspicious to something with a little warmth in it. "What in God's name happened to you, son? I leave the warehouse with you waiting for the handlers who would deliver you to WPP. I return not even an hour later, and you're gone but not into WPP. Something about a woman? Is that true?"

This was not going as Lenny would have hoped. If only he had thought it through. "Sir, I made my decision at the last minute, and only after my handlers arrived. I was all ready to follow the WPP plan when we shook hands. After all you did for me, I figured you'd be glad to see the back of me. I didn't want to burden you with any more shit than I had already asked you to take on. I don't know what else I can tell you."

"So, was it a woman? Is it a woman?"

"It was, sir. I didn't handle that well, either."

"Stop calling me Commander or Sir, and let's sort this out. Start with why you need your job back."

Lenny glanced around: passengers coming and going, but nobody lurking within earshot. He wasn't sure if Jalen knew he was calling from the airport. Before he had a chance to explain further, the commander continued.

"One rumour floating around had you chasing Paradise to some place at the butt end of a dirt road on the other side of the world. If that's true, Thomas might shoot you himself if you walk back into the warehouse. Have you thought this through? Is Paradise with you now? What a mess you have landed in."

"God, no. She was never interested in me." Lenny had to struggle to keep his voice level, to act like there was nothing in such a rumour. In his head voices argued with each other about whether he was lying and, if it was true, how he could say it without sobbing. "I had to learn that the hard way but, believe me, lesson learned. Paradise was never with me."

"So you were on a fool's errand."

"I guess I still haven't thought it through, sir, I mean Jalen. But I'm also worried that I'm still being hunted."

"Len, you know we don't discuss certain things over the phone. If your life is in danger, do not tell me where you are calling from. Present yourself to the protected site where we first spoke with you. Can I trust you to do that?"

"Roger that, sir. On my way, and thank you."

"Don't thank me yet. Keep your head down and move. I'll meet you personally and will expect all details before making any further decisions. Is that clear?"

"Yes."
Instantly the line went dead.

41

Bonde observed him en route to Honolulu. She had never seen Len Calhoon in person and this handsome man did not match her mental image of him. She snapped a full-frontal picture of him as he returned to his seat from the airplane-head area. He was in disguise and suspected nothing, she would bet her paycheck on it.

From a safe distance, Bonde watched the suspect stop at a bank of pay-phones. She turned and walked in the opposite direction to ensure privacy for her own call.

Her orders were to make contact immediately upon landing. Bonde pulled out the codes she would need the minute someone answered the phone.

"You've reached 5.0."

Bonde knew nothing else would be said so she immediately input her code, all seventeen numbers in it. They don't make calling 5.0 easy, she thought.

"Employee investigations. Input your code."

This time her code had only eleven numbers.

"Bonde, talk to us. Did you get eyes on our man?"

Realizing she was talking to more than one person, Bonde was selective in her response. "I have a photo and will drop my camera off to you following protocol. I believe the man is Len Calhoon. He did not suspect I was anyone other than a dumb blond. I play that part well, by the way." Silence at the other end suggested these people don't do small talk. "He has definitely been shot or at the least sliced up a bit on the left side. My guess would be that he has at least one wound and has been poorly stitched up."

"No guessing, please. Continue."

"You boys need to get out more often, for Christ's sake. I'm just doing the job I have been hired to do."

"You are a contract employee, Bonde. We don't know you well enough to 'chat', so let's continue."

"Suspect made a phone call at the first bank of phones in the terminal He is walking with a limp and favouring his left shoulder."

"Do you still have eyes on him?"

"No."

"Explain."

"My contract was to find the suspect. I was given his flight detail to Toronto and on to Honolulu, although I was told if he flew anywhere it would likely be to Toronto for medical attention. Seems I'm not the only one who did a bit of guessing."

"How did you lose the suspect?"

"I did not lose him, boys. My contract says very clearly that if the suspect returns to Honolulu I am to follow and not lose sight of him until his plane touches down and he hails a cab. Once he is in the cab I am to contact you. So here we are."

"This concludes our call."

"No no no. I wanted to ask if you have another job for me."

But she was talking to a dead line. Bonde made a nice chunk of change from finding and following the suspect and she could use another assignment. But she knew the drill.

"If 5.0 has work for me in the future, they'll find me," she said to herself while raising her arm to hail her own cab.

42

Lieutenant Commander Jalen Lexis ran a tight ship in his massive Hawaii 2.0 warehouse. He put up such a fierce, no-nonsense front that few suspected that Jalen had a soft spot for ex-cons trying to rehabilitate themselves and return to society.

He was not always successful with his choice of the cons he would personally mentor, but there was no question that Len was one of his favourites if not the most favourite of all those Jalen had seen walk through the 2.0 doors.

Jalen had completed considerable research on Len's life history before accepting him on his payroll the first time, some years ago. The 'early-years' level of detail in Len's file struck Jalen at his core. None of it was stuff Len would want shared with anyone. He did not deserve the headache or heartache life had served up for him.

As a young man, a boy really, Len had watched his father, Big Len, shoot and kill his mother and sister. Putting his gun on the chair between them, Big Len said, "You're a coward. I'm ashamed to have you as my son. You don't have the balls to go for that gun even to save your own life." Len knew his father wouldn't hesitate to kill him. He was the only witness to what had happened in the sadness of the shack they called home. He was nowhere as big as his dad, and Big Len evidently wanted to get a bit of fun out of Len's death.

Len took a slow step to the left and his father mirrored it, as if they were jockeying for the last seat in Musical Chairs. They took another step. Soon the back of the chair would start to block Len's path to the gun.

He started to take the next step, then let his eyes flick to the right, as if he was seeing something in the doorway behind his father. Big Len half-turned, then realized it was a fake out.

But by then Len had the gun. He didn't hesitate to use it.

Jalen knew this story, and more. How Len, with virtually no education and blood on his hands, had drifted into the world of pimps, drug dealers, murderers-for-hire. He did what they told him to do and asked no questions. He could shoot and use his fists or a knife, but he could barely read even his own name.

The commander had never discussed with anyone how vulnerable he felt Len must be out in what they knew as 'the real world.' The inside of the 2.0 warehouse was anything but the real world.

Len arrived at the agreed location first and that had been his plan. He didn't want the commander to see or hear the next bit. He remembered at the last second that he had no money to hire a cab but Commander Lexis had already hung up so he wasn't even able to ask him for a loan of his cab fare.

He got out of the cab and leaned in the driver's side window. "I can't pay you, buddy."

"The hell?"

"But I wrote down your cab number. You'll get your full fare with a nice tip. You have my word."

"I can't buy gas with promises."

Len let his tough face show. "And you can't buy gas if you're dead. You don't want to hang around for what's about to happen here."

The driver still hesitated, so Len moved his hand toward his jacket pocket. It held a notebook, not a gun, but the cabbie wouldn't know that.

The little charade did the trick. The guy roared off as if his life was in danger. Len hated lying to anyone and he really would pay the fare, but he could not afford witnesses for the meeting. He wasn't yet sure he had the support of the commander but he was sure the he wouldn't want anyone but Len there when he arrived.

Even that effort took more out of him than he had thought it would, though. Len twitched this way and that, but his body was just not comfortable.

He thought he could find a hiding place and just sit down and try to catch up with himself until Jalen showed up, but here came the car. He nodded as it came to a stop about twenty feet away. He knew he was being sized up from the other side of the tinted windshield.

Jalen got out of his car and crossed the gap between them. For a huge man he moved with lightning speed, and Len had to work hard to avoid flinching.

"Commander, sir, thank you for meeting me. I—"

"Shut up, son. Don't make me remind you of the rules, starting with calling me Jalen. That's the last damn time I'll remind you of that simple rule. I'm serious."

Jalen looked him up and down. "You're standing funny."

"I might have got shot here and there."

Jalen nodded and started back toward the car. Len hurried to catch up with him. "I've had friends down at 5.0 headquarters check out your 'I'm being hunted' story. Murder is never a good thing, Len, but I tend to agree with what I'm sure was your logic at the time. Kill or be killed." A small smile crossed the commander's face. "You've been spending time at a shooting range."

Len knew better than to comment until his boss was finished.

"You and I better get our stories straight before Thomas runs into you at the warehouse."

"I understand."

"First things first, then. Is Paradise truly why you left your job with us?"

"Yes."

"So why did you dump her after working so hard to track her down?"

"Strangers were asking about me in Cape St Mary. It's just a little town, so if a stranger starts asking questions you gotta get out or get found. The guy looking for me used to work for Meat Cove. Meat was the king of crime—"

"—in Toronto. Yes, I know."

"So you probably know I once worked for him, too. And that he tried to kill me."

"Get to the point, Len. I'm a busy man."

"So I left town, went to ground in Halifax, and set a little trap for the guy. When I thought I had drawn him out I went deep into Point Pleasant Park and waited. He wasn't alone."

"But you're standing here alone, more or less in one piece. So that man and his pals are dead and there's nobody on your track. Is this correct, Len?"

Len suddenly thought of Bonde making a bee-line for him at the airport. "Nobody I know of."

"These people had no chance to report back." Jalen nodded. "But they tagged you. Who patched you up, and how did you manage to avoid a trail that would lead right to our door at 2.0?"

"No hospital, no clinic. Doctor, or whatever he was, came to me, never heard my name, and did what he did for cash."

"Or whatever he was?"

"He did enough to get me this far, and I can show you the stitches later. But to tell you the truth, I'm not feeling the way I would want to."

"Are you in pain?"

"I've been in worse," Len lied.

"Get in the car, and then let's get you back to 2.0. I'm going to give you a couple weeks to get yourself healthy, and will assign a doctor to your file as soon as we arrive. Then you will return to your twelve-hour shifts and your personal residence. Enough?"

"More than enough, sir, I mean Jalen. I appreciate you and I won't let you down. I'll be healthy in no time."

The two men remained silent until they pulled into the commander's private parking spot at 2.0. Jalen turned off the engine but made no move to get out of the car, so Len sat tight.

"Now hear me out," Jalen said. "You disappointed me once when you shook my hand and then built up a bunch of plans behind my back. You walked away from 2.0 and from the witness protection program. I swear to God, if you repay me that way again you will live to regret it. Do you understand me?"

"Roger that." Len knew better than to try to explain anything or ask any questions at this moment in time. He reached for the door handle. He was getting antsy and needed to stretch his legs.

"Not so fast, son. There is one more thing. Do not – do not – approach Thomas until you know I have spoken with him on your behalf. I don't want you to even say hello to the man until you hear from me. Stay out of his way completely. I don't want to lose our contract with Thomas, and I fear if he sees you he'll quit on the spot. Now we're done."

The commander opened his door and got out of the car with his normal speed and grace. It was all Len could do to avoid crying out as he got to his feet and followed Jalen toward the solid doors of 2.0. Both men, each for his own reasons, hoped that Thomas would not be inside waiting for them.

43

Word of Len's return spread like wildfire, and his peers were relentless.

"Hey, lover boy, did you get the girl?"

"Your departure let us fantasize about Paradise out loud. We should compare notes."

Commander Lexis wanted to act swiftly to alert Thomas. Len was the butt of many jokes his so-called friends at 2.0 threw into his face. But that was nothing to what Thomas might do. Jalen knew there would be a lot more of this when Len started back on his twelve-hour shifts. He would be constantly out on the warehouse floor and, with a male-only crew at the moment, comments would not be kind. Jalen wondered if Len would be able to take the slagging without lashing out.

"I didn't think there would be so much interest in your love life," he said to Len as they ran into each other in the medical corner of the warehouse less than twenty-four hours after Len had returned.

"I'm afraid I did," replied Len. "You would not believe how many on the team are convinced they are absolutely in love with Paradise and that, if they only got the chance, Paradise would welcome them with open...everything. They've always talked about her body, her smile, her mind, her walk, the gap between her legs and oh those long legs. I was right there in the thick of it until I realized I was truly in love with her."

"You're the exception that proves the rule?"

Len's face got red. "Yeah. Yeah, I am. And now that talk makes me sick. I want to protect her."

"Paradise isn't the only woman they've been talking about recently," Jalen said. "Thomas's friend Wikolia? Don't know if you heard she died."

"I didn't, no. Accident?"

"Not at all. The rough end to a sad story. Shocked everybody here. Thomas took some time off to care for her, and then to mourn her, and at the same time he's been learning to be a single parent."

"T.J.?"

"You'll have seen him, I think. Thomas brought him to work more than a few times."

Len wasn't much for noticing kids, but he tried to nod sympathetically. He had a vague memory of a little squirt tailing Thomas around the warehouse now and then. "What will happen to him now?"

"Thomas isn't giving the boy up, if that's what you mean." The commander stared hard at Len. "Thomas is a good father, and he loves his son. You may not believe that's possible, but he is."

"I wasn't saying anything bad about him."

"Make sure you don't. And make sure you stay out of his way until I can sort the situation out with Thomas." As soon as a staffer had taken Len to his living quarters, Jalen sat down to call Thomas. He hoped the kid was having a nap so they could talk.

"Hello?"

Jalen knew the voice didn't belong to Thomas, and he knew exactly who had picked up the phone. "Paradise, is that you? Good Lord. I didn't know you were back in town."

"Surprise, Commander, and good ear. You haven't heard my voice for years and yet you identified me in one word."

"It's good you're in town, Paradise. That man of yours has been to Hell and back, as I'm sure you already know."

"I know. I wish I could have been here while it was happening, but I didn't find out till after Wikolia was gone.

"Are you here for good, or just passing through?"

There was a pause. Jalen knew that he had moved from chat to interrogation far too soon. "Sorry, Paradise. That was pretty blunt even for me." He tried to move back to conversation mode.

"Actually, sir, both Thomas and I would like to speak with you about a number of things and—"

Okay, forget conversation mode. "What is it, and why does it take two of you to tell me? Why do I feel I'm about to hear some news I won't like?"

There was another pause at Paradise's end. Jalen pushed ahead "I think I should sit down with you and Thomas. A phone call won't do. How does your schedule look over the next week or two, Paradise?"

"Thomas isn't here so I should confirm with him, but why don't we plan to meet with you this coming Friday? It would give me a chance to say hi to everyone."

"You're always welcome here. However, for this meeting I'll come to you. Name the place, but just not here at the warehouse. I'll explain when I see you." God knows the last thing Jalen needed was a surprise visit from these two.

"I really would rather come to you, sir."

"No. Not going to happen."

"Roger that. I will speak with Thomas later today and have him contact you soon." Jalen could tell she was writing in her journal.

"Oh and I do look forward to seeing you sir. In many ways I miss the simplicity of my job at 2.0"

"Not sure that's a compliment but I too look forward to seeing you and Thomas very soon. It's important."

44

"Thomas, there are some things I haven't told you."

"Are you kidding me?" Thomas was on instant alert. "Not again, Paradise. Something else you haven't told me?" Paradise knew she would have to share this detail carefully. It was still all very new to her and she wasn't sure how to unwrap it.

What Paradise was about to share would cause Thomas to doubt everything he had heard about quaint and quiet Cape St Mary. He would be concerned for both Wilmot and Marie, but most of all Thomas would have serious concerns about her ability to judge the honesty of others.

Part of their Private Investigator's training had covered the need for a PI to read people instantly so they could spot a 'problem' lightning fast to ensure their own safety and the safety of others. If she had missed *this*, what else had she missed, in the Cape and elsewhere?

Hope was earning her first pay cheque since arriving back in Hawaii. She was staying home with her brother while their parents went out for a bit of quiet time. She didn't want to call it babysitting since T.J. was her brother, but she was not above being paid.

Business was business after all, she had explained it to her mother. "I'm no different than anyone else, mother. I need money. I need to be able to earn money."

Paradise had tried not to laugh when Hope made her case, and had mostly succeeded.

She had packed a lunch and then she and Thomas drove to the North Shore. The day felt easy, but not so the conversation they had to have. As they sat side by side on a blanket, food ready to hand, she braced herself for whatever his reaction would be. "Okay Paradise. You've set the stage. What is your news about this time?"

She noted the way he was pressing his lips together, as if to keep words from spilling out. She had to speak before her hesitation became a statement in itself.

"I want to tell you everything important from the time we have been apart. And I want to hear everything important that happened to you. My turn right now, so I'm going to ask you to listen. Just listen without interruption, please. Can you do that?"

"If I say yes, will you yell at me for interrupting your narrative again?"

Paradise reached over and gave her guy a kiss, then pulled him into her arms. She figured if she didn't look into his eyes she wouldn't have to see the disappointment on his face.

"Here it is in a nutshell," she said past his ear. "I'm laying myself out before you, and I will be totally brutal about every mistake I've made. It relates to Len."

She felt his muscles tense, then relax. When she was sure he was able to listen, she went on. "You know that Len and I met on the night shift at 2.0. I knew only what he wanted me to know. It was clear to me he had the full and total support of the commander, and if you have that no one asks questions about your history. You know that, Thomas, correct?"

Thomas simply nodded.

"We developed both a working relationship and a working friendship, if that makes sense. Len opened up with me, mostly over coffee before we began our shift. He shared that his skin had not felt the outside air in over a year. I was fascinated with the whole Witness Protection Program he outlined, and I wanted to learn more about him and the WPP before he disappeared 'into the night' as he put it."

She remembered Lenny saying, "Paradise, there is no one on earth who would miss me because no one knows I'm alive." Haunting.

She was ready to look directly at him as her story continued. "Apparently, if anybody asked about Len, the line was that he was no longer among the living. The program wanted to discourage anyone to keep looking for him, as much for their own protection as for his. He didn't even seem sad when he told me that."

Although her voice was steady, Paradise realized that a tear was trickling down her cheek. She brushed it away quickly.

"Thomas, I admit I was fascinated by all of this and I allowed it to cloud my judgment. But, on my life, I swear to you it was not personal to the point of even hugging. Professional to the core, I promise you."

She sat back so they could look at each other. "I know you want to hear everything, but how am I doing so far?"

"Carry on, please."

She could see he wanted to press her to fast forward to wherever the story was going. She loved him for keeping himself in check.

"You know that taking Hope to Toronto and on to the Cape was a bit of a snap decision. You and I discussed it, but I didn't share this with Len or any of the others at 2.0."

She remembered how Thomas had been so ready and willing to handle things with the commander so Paradise could concentrate on Hope and what Hope called "their summer adventure."

"As God is my witness, I didn't even recognize Len the first day I saw him at the Cape."

Thomas shifted position as if something was hurting him deep inside. He motioned for Paradise to continue.

"He was just there at that 'welcome home' party Pops arranged. I looked at him then right past him in the blink of an eye, thinking he looked like someone I knew, but in the moment I didn't give him another thought. It came to me later who he looked like, so I asked about him. People knew him as Lenny. It seemed like too much of a coincidence to ignore."

She left a pause, partly caught in memory and partly giving Thomas a chance to interrupt if he had had enough. Continued silence from Thomas.

"A few days later Lenny knocked on our door, and I almost fainted. I was alone in the house and I didn't want to let him in, so I agreed to meet him at the Café. It was him, but him being Lenny, not Len, and being out of the warehouse made things...different."

She stared at the sea, at the flying birds, and the grass moving gently in the breeze. Nothing was going to give her a welcome reason to stop the story. "That's how the friendship began. We met for coffee. We talked. After a while we started meeting in the very early morning to walk along the beach before the Cape woke up. I started looking forward to those walks. Lenny brought coffee and I brought stories about Hope and Pops."

Thomas remained silent, but she could see he was getting restless. 'This is where the tough part comes Thomas so should I stop here?"

"No." Thomas was no longer looking at Paradise.

"One day Lenny wanted to hold my hand. I spent my hand-holding years in the convent, studying to become a Nun, so this was not something I was looking for. Your hand will forever be the only hand I have ever really wanted to hold other than the Lord's. Lenny didn't push and I appreciated that."

Paradise wasn't sure there would ever be the 'right' time to share her full connection with Lenny. She hadn't yet mentioned Marie's connection, either, but she was beginning to feel that this story was already more than Thomas had wanted to hear.

"Lenny and I went on having those morning walks, and one chilly day we did start holding hands. It felt good. You and I were so distant and you seemed to be moving forward with Wikolia and I didn't think we were going to—"

"*Don't you dare,* Paradise." He pushed himself to his feet and looked like he was barely restraining himself from walking away. "Don't you dare bring Wikolia into this. She was in a mental health hospital and I was a single parent to T.J. How is that 'moving ahead'?"

"Thomas, it seemed to me that during our phone calls we only talked about Wikolia and T.J. You stopped asking about Hope and you stopped asking about my life altogether. Pops seemed to be a distant memory to you. I'm not trying to lay blame here, my love, but please help me understand where I'm wrong in thinking all of these things."

"I'll save my comments for after you finish, so keep talking."

Paradise got up and stood facing him. He was staring out over the water, not looking at her. "I still don't know if you really want a future with me, but understand this: there is no Lenny-and-me. We had a friendship; that's it. Then some stranger turned up and started asking about a Len or Lenny in our little village. Pops was frantic about it and he told Lenny exactly how he felt at the Cafe. Everyone heard Pops shouting."

"Enough about Pops, please."

"I'm trying to share something you must be able to understand. After that confrontation at the Cafe, Lenny left, with no goodbyes. His departure was a total shock to me."

Thomas nodded to encourage her to go on.

"Curtis at the Cape police station seems to think Lenny has left not only the Cape but possibly the province. I was going to try to figure out where he went and why, but because it was a mystery and I'm supposed to be a detective, not for any other reason.

But then the news came about Wikolia. And here we are" Paradise stopped abruptly as if she was surprised to have finished her story.

After a time, Thomas turned to face her. "Are you done?"

"I think so."

"In my gut I feel there is more to this story. But you may be right: maybe there's no point in spending any more time on someone who is, hopefully, out of our lives forever."

After another achingly-long pause, he gathered Paradise in his arms."I'll promise you this: I will try every day of our lives to rid myself of any jealousy towards Lenny or anyone else. As your God is my witness, I will try. I was afraid for a very long time that I might have lost you. This notion that absence makes the heart grow fonder is bullshit."

"Language," came with a smile from Paradise.

She leaned into him, grateful that now he knew that much of the story, at least. Wilmot and Marie's revelation about Lenny being the hit man who came after Marie all those years ago still lay ahead, but today was not the day for it.

Paradise felt like this had been the most exhausting picnic in her life, but at least it had had a better ending than she had dreaded. They packed up slowly and headed home to their kids.

45

Pops didn't need to be hit on the head with a two by four. He got it. He finally understood. He didn't like it very much, though.

"Oh I understand all right," he yelled at the stars as he sat on the wharf near his beloved boat.

Eugenie was never going to let Pops 'pop the question.' She wouldn't even entertain the possibility of talking about it. Those weren't her exact words but they sure were her actions. Pops was heartbroken, but he tried to keep that to himself.

The second love of his life was either surrounded by people, all of her own doing, or she would suggest she was too tired to talk. Pops had been tempted to say he had never met a woman who was too tired to talk, but he figured she wouldn't see the humour. He decided to tuck that comment away, though, because it was a good one, and if...no, *when*...they finally got together he would find a way to include his joke in a conversation.

Eugenie didn't mind having coffee with Pops but that was it, or at least that's how she made him feel. She had even suggested she was too old for romance. Pops assumed she was kidding, since she gave a bit of a laugh when she said it. It could have been a nervous laugh, though.

"Pops, romance isn't only about sex. We've had this conversation and I'm not sure we need to repeat it."

Pops later wished he had explored Eugenie's thinking a bit further. He figured they had both danced around the topic of sex long enough.

He held on to every word Eugenie had spoken to him from word one. His memory was good for an old goat like him. When they were just getting to know each other and there were no strings attached, or whatever it was she called it, Eugenie seemed more open to talking.

Eugenie shared with Pops what life had been like in the convent and how safe and loved she felt, being married to God from her teenage years until a few years ago. When she moved home to the Cape, she had been stunned to see men working shirtless on the roof of homes or in their gardens. "I don't care if you take me seriously or not, but I had never seen a man shirtless. Shameful is what it is."

Pops got to thinking about that, and he wondered if her hesitation was more related to seeing him stark naked than anything else. He figured she likely couldn't imagine any of that.

"I'm not sure I blame you there," he said as he slowly stood up on the wharf to head home. The stoop was not that comfortable but it had been his wharf-chair for as long as he could remember.

He thought back to the very first day Eugenie had walked into Café Central with knees shaking and couldn't find an empty table. She later told him, "I asked to share your table because you have a good reputation and I thought I would be safe. And I was right. You have a way of settling my nerves."

He never forgot how that made him feel – some good.

Before she even realized it Eugenie was actually comfortable talking with Pops. "You seem to be genuine," she had said.

Those were the early days. Pops wished Eugenie could be as open about her feelings now as she had been back then.

He thought about how weird it was that someone would consider herself married to God. And what a rival God was. When the boys were building his new home Pops always loved the humour in Aurel's "Hey, I'm not God" comment whenever anyone challenged his work or suggested a better way to do it. Pops wasn't God, that was for damn sure. Eugenie better not make that comparison and if she did he didn't want to know.

Pops had found himself going into the Café more often, primarily to see if Eugenie was there. If she wasn't, he often left hastily, hoping no one caught on to the fact that he was canvasing the joint for her. He didn't want anyone thinking he was just an old fool stalking the former nun who had recently broken up with God.

The reality of it, though, was that Pops didn't much care what his friends or anyone else thought. He was interested in the woman and he would bloody well have coffee with her any time he could.

Recently, though, Pops had begun dreaming of making coffee for Eugenie in their home, not paying for her coffee at the Café. He wanted more than anything else in the world to at least have a real conversation with the woman so he could explain how he felt about her. Pops wanted to make sure Eugenie knew he would like to be with her day and night.

He was beginning to have the unsettling thought that perhaps Eugenie was not attracted to him. He decided she was going to have to say that to his face before he believed it. He was damn well going to find out what was going on in that woman's head. If she liked some other man, leaving God out of it as a rival for now, he wanted to know so he could step aside.

46

Thomas and Paradise decided to continue their conversation later that evening when the kids were sleeping. With the bedroom door firmly closed, they lay naked in bed and ready to continue a conversation that would hopefully end at the conclusion of airing any and all facts tonight. It wasn't so much a conversation as it was Paradise baring her soul and Thomas trying hard to not show any reaction that would throw her off her story as she spoke.

"I'm not sure what else I can tell you, Thomas. I've shared everything I'm feeling. Surely you can see that?"

"What if I'm seeing only what you want me to see? What if there's more you aren't saying?" Thomas knew he was wading into dangerous territory, but he had to press on. "You've been gone for so long and it turns out you've been holding hands with Len, or *Lenny*, and I'm supposed to brush that off as nothing? How do I know you didn't share this beautiful body with that man?"

Thomas ran his fingers lightly along her hip, and then inward. He stopped just below her navel, letting his fingers ride the movement of her body as she breathed. Despite himself, he felt his passion building.

"That's not fair, my love, and you know it. Lenny was a friend when I needed one. There is not one person in all of Cape St Mary who would think even for one minute that anything illicit was going on between us. My friends there know everything about me, about us, Thomas, and not for one second did I worry about gossip behind my back."

She pressed his hand down against her belly and held it there. "Isn't it time we talk about us? About now? About our future together with our two beautiful children sleeping just one room away? Can we leave the past in the past and agree to move forward without reservation? And, forgive me, my love, but I have to say this: can we stop with the jealousy, too, please?"

She kissed Thomas as she wrapped her arms around him. She tried without success to coax a smile from that beautiful face she loved so much.

"I love you so much, woman. I didn't think you would ever stop talking, so while I have the courage please let me talk. No interruptions. Your turn again once I'm done. Agreed?"

"Roger that. Talk away and I'll lie right here beside you with my mouth firmly closed. You have my word."

"Paradise d'Entremont Rhodes, or Paradise d'Entremont minus the Rhodes—any way you say it—I want you to marry me and be my partner in every way. Parenting our children, working side by side at our PI business, and everything in between. I want you beside me for the rest of my life. Whatever life throws at us, I want to stand up to it with you. Only you. Will you Paradise? Will you marry me?"

Her eyes widened. Her heart pounded. She opened her mouth but before she could speak he was miming falling off the bed. She could hear him thumping around on the floor and could not suppress a snort of laughter.

Then Thomas got up on one knee. He was holding what looked like a ring box. "I hope you will make an honest man of me, Paradise. I'm asking you to marry me."

He extended his hand slowly, offering her the box, aching for "Yes" to escape her moist lips.

After a stunned moment, Paradise grabbed his wrist with both hands and pulled him onto the bed, as if she was hauling a drowning man onto a boat. She fell on top of Thomas' hot, sexy and clearly aroused body.

For what seemed like the very first time Paradise and Thomas made love. It was slow and intense and passionate and deep and wild and fast all at once. And quiet, very quiet to avoid any interruptions from their two housemates one thin wall away.

When they were done, and floating on the calm that follows passion, Thomas said,"Was that a yes?"

She lay her head on his chest and hugged him, but what sort of answer was that? "At least tell me you're anxious to see what's in the ring box."

Paradise gave him a mock punch and sat up. He could barely hear her because of her naked beauty. "You know how much you mean to me. I have loved you forever. And I am both wiser and more confident now than I was on my 16th birthday, the first time you proposed."

"When you said no." Thomas slowly sat up and put the ring box on the bedside table. He didn't know if he could survive being turned down a second time, if that's what she was getting ready to do. He had said his piece and popped the question and she had said—nothing.

But perhaps there was still a chance. Thomas put his dreams on hold and waited for Paradise to continue.

"I didn't realize you would propose to me so soon, my love. Have we talked about all that concerns you? Have we talked about all that concerns me?"

Thomas moved away so his body wasn't touching hers. This didn't sound good.

"Please let me tell you why I don't have an answer for you at this very moment. It has nothing to do with having made a decision to marry you or not to marry you, Thomas. I like to think my love for you is evident in every move I make. I now see it's more about what I don't say."

"That's the problem. You're saying nothing at all, Paradise. For certain you're not saying why you won't become my wife. What about our children? Hope and now T.J. deserve both parents living under the same roof. Don't you feel any obligation to our children?"

Paradise didn't give Thomas the opportunity to dig a hole any deeper for himself. "Let's use our words carefully. I'm feeling blindsided by your proposal and I don't think I deserve the words you have thrown at me."

She was feeling overwhelmed with heartache. Thomas had turned on her and she wasn't sure someone who loves you should be like that. Especially moments after making love.

"You have said all these things because I didn't answer right away. I'm almost afraid to reply to your proposal, but I need to speak my truth."

Thomas waited, almost afraid to breathe. "When I turned down your first proposal I was just a girl. I tried to explain that while I loved you my heart was full of love for God. That day I chose my words carefully, and yet what did you do? You got up and you ran away from me, Thomas, and you know it. You bolted. How do you think that made me feel?"

"Not my finest hour, Paradise. I've apologized a million times for that."

He reached out for the hand planted firmly in her lap, but she pulled it away.

"I would never say 'too little too late', because I know how sincere your apology is. No need to apologize again. We were both young, so let's leave that story where it belongs – in the past."

She waited until Thomas gave a nod in agreement.

"My early days at the convent were filled with learning the rigid rules relating to that life, my devotion, and my shock to learn I was pregnant. I was carrying your child. The baby we conceived the very first time we made love. I know you remember that day as well as I do."

Again, a slight nod.

"After the birth, I put all of my heart and soul into determining if life as a nun was to be my life's work. For five years on the inside, as some of us called it, I tried every hour to make God's work my life's work. I failed, as you know. That doesn't mean I love my God any less. My decision needed to be and still needs to be, after being married to my God could I now marry you and live my fullest life, or would that diminish my love for God? I could never let that happen. I don't know if I'm even explaining it correctly."

Paradise stopped to wipe the tears from her face. Clearly Thomas wasn't going to touch her given that he had rolled over to 'his' side of the bed.

"That's just one issue to contend with, Thomas. What about our home? Is it here in Honolulu or is it in Cape St Mary with Pops and the life Hope and I have built there? We can't count your surprise trip to the Cape as your first visit, so let's erase feelings on both sides from that. Your first visit there lies ahead."

Thomas waited, took a breath, raised his eyebrows significantly.

"Oh, yes: I've stopped," Paradise said with a small smile. "Your turn."

"I gave this a lot of thought while you and Hope were in Nova Scotia. Once we find Wikolia's family and establish a connection for T.J., if that is possible, I think we could either rent out or sell this condo and move our little family to the Cape."

"Really?"

"If that's what you want. I know Pops has been very generous with his offer of having me move in 'any time at all' as he put it."

"Pops likes you a lot."

"But what do you say? Is this a plan you could work with? Would you be willing to try?"

Thomas knew he didn't have much left in his arsenal. The next move would belong to Paradise. He would go to the end of the earth for this woman, but only if she believed he could love the Cape as much as she and Hope did.

He gathered Paradise in his arms, held her close, and waited for her next words.

And right on cue they heard T.J. cry out for Daddy.

After a few seconds of comedy pantomime as he wrestled some clothes on, Thomas was out the door. He blew a kiss at Paradise and closed the door, hoping against hope she might be able to get a bit more sleep. They had talked and made love almost the entire night. Talked more than they touched, and he wasn't sure that was a win, but...

Mercifully he found T.J. had fallen back to sleep on the tiny bed, with Hope right beside him. At some point during the night his son had abandoned his crib to be with his sister. Seeing his two children at peace, and at peace with each other, made his heart sing.

Thomas quietly moved to the kitchen to make stealth coffee, keeping one ear open to hear if the children stirred.

Memories are made of this.

47

Lieutenant Commander Jalen Lexis stood uncomfortably in the lobby of Honolulu's Sheridan Hotel on the Waikiki strip. The sun was shining and the lobby restaurant was filling up. After confirming his reservation for a table off to the side to allow a bit of privacy, Jalen returned to the lobby and found a comfortable chair facing a rather large sofa with a coffee table between the two.

Jalen knew a man like Lenny would have no connection to the swanky hotel or the area and that's exactly why he selected the location for his meeting with Thomas and Paradise. "Who am I kidding?" he said under his breath. He had no connections to the hotel either.

He could only hope Thomas and Paradise had not yet heard of Lenny's return to Hawaii 2.0. He was cutting it close by having put off meeting with them until today. Jalen knew Lenny had ventured out of the warehouse a few times and each time he had wondered if Lenny went out in search of Paradise. God, he should have followed Lenny himself.

Paradise arrived first. If possible she was more stunning than ever and she had been a stunner back when she had worked the night shift with Lenny.

That had been about two years ago, or could it have been longer? Jalen wasn't sure of the particular timeline, but he would be sure to ask. Timelines were his specialty and somehow he couldn't put this one together.

"Hello, beautiful PI lady."

"Commander, I was thrilled when Thomas shared your kind invitation with me. Dinner at a posh hotel like this is a rare occasion for me. If I forget to tell you later, I had a wonderful time." Paradise laughed at her own joke.

"Thomas is parking the car?" Lexis didn't want to say much until Thomas joined them. Even small talk was off the table until then.

"Yes, he should be right along. In the meantime, tell me all the news at 2.0. Do you miss me?"

"More than you know. Let's wait for Thomas before we delve into all that. Is that okay with you?"

"Okay with me, Commander, but what's a gal got to do to get a drink around here?"

Paradise waved her hands around as if to attract someone's attention. She was in such a good mood and Jalen hoped his news wouldn't ruin it.

And then Thomas was with them. "Sorry, Jalen, traffic is busy along the strip today. I had to duck into an alley and circle around a second and third time. Found a spot just out front, though, so I'm not complaining."

Thomas took a seat beside Paradise, facing the commander.

"Thomas, right up front I want to say I wasn't in the office when the call came in about Wikolia's death. Please know how very sorry we all are for your loss. I know you were dealing with a lot at the end of her life and I know you were doing everything on your own, too."

Women have been doing it all forever, thought Paradise. Although she was smart enough to keep that thought to herself, her face must have shown something.

Jalen reached out and touched her shoulder gently. "Bad choice of words, Paradise. When my wife was alive she and our five daughters would have hung me up by the balls if I dared to even whisper something like that at home. I'll just apologize and then keep my mouth shut for at least the next sixty seconds. Bail me out here, Thomas. I'm begging you." Jalen pretended to get down on one knee.

"Not much more needs to be said on that subject. Paradise has heard it all, haven't, you my love?"

Jalen caught the waiter's eye. "Let's order a drink here before we move into the restaurant." He knew he was stalling but he was having trouble finding his way into what had to be said. Over drinks, and then burgers and more booze, Jalen caught the others up on the news, rumours, and tall stories at 2.0. He made sure to name no names to avoid leaking info to some nearby diner.

Finally, as he pushed himself back from the table and the last of the fries, Jalen knew it was time to get down to business. He decided to dive in and take his chances.

"I didn't get to the one reason in particular I wanted to see you today. Please hear me out before jumping down my throat." Jalen took a gulp of his coffee and signalled the waiter for more before continuing.

"He's back and I wanted you to hear the details directly from me."

Jalen took the time to look both Paradise and Thomas in the eye before going on. Thomas looked blank; Paradise had the beginning of a frown as if she, at least, suspected who 'he' might be.

"Len is back with us at 2.0. He's on his original shift of 7 pm to 7 am. I thought both of you would want to know. I suspect Len will finally go into WPP. The Witness Protection Program is where he was headed before he...took a little break. I knew Len had gotten close to you, Paradise, during the long shift schedule, but he more than shocked me when he told me he followed you to Canada."

Paradise reached out to touch Thomas. She wanted to calm him before he said a single word. She was too late.

"Jesus Christ Almighty. When were you going to tell us? What if I had walked into the warehouse to see you and ran into that fucking bastard? I might have killed him." Thomas looked like he was about to have a stroke.

"Easy, boy." This was a side of Thomas that Jalen had not seen. "I'm telling you now, and I'll thank you to never speak to me in that manner or ever use that tone with me again. Never. Do you understand me?"

Paradise didn't know if she could make either of these two men settle down but she knew she had to try. "Enough with the tough-guy talk, Thomas."

Both men were now standing. Paradise did the same and had a pair of her red killer high-heeled shoes on so she would match Thomas in height. Jalen not so much, since he stood well above pretty much everyone. "Will the two of you just shut up already and sit the hell down so we can carry on a civilized conversation?"

"Language." Thomas tried to lighten the moment but he would have to try harder if he wanted to help Paradise calm down.

Jalen said, "Just to be sure I understand what is going on here: I invite you both to lunch. My treat. Over coffee following said lovely lunch, I share 2.0 news that I feel you should know before one or both of you show up at the warehouse. And this is how you repay me? What am I missing?"

"It's a long story," said Paradise.

"That's putting it mildly," Thomas added.

"If either of you wants to say what in God's name is going on, speak up now. Or I'll pay the check and leave you to work out whatever brought this 'mood' on."

"Wait," Paradise said. "Let's just all sit down. Hear us out for a couple of minutes and then you can decide if you want to walk away.

After a long moment, Jalen took his seat again. Paradise sat quickly and Thomas, realizing how silly he looked looming over the other two, sat down last.

"I have to say, I'm disappointed in you," the commander said.

"I'll go first," Thomas said, "and then you can tell me what you think."

"No," Paradise said. "The bulk of this sad story is on me and I'll own it. I'll share details with you, Jalen, despite the embarrassment I feel even before I begin to tell you what you deserve to know."

"Kids, I have absolutely no idea where this is going but I do not need so much detail that anyone would be embarrassed. Use that as your jumping off point, please."

48

"Lenny and I working together on the night shift at 2.0 is a good place to start."

Paradise took a deep breath before she continued. She could make this very simple and simple might serve her best.

"Over time, and especially during breaks and meal time, and, to be honest, during those late hours on shift just before saying good night and going to our separate quarters, Lenny often told me about his life. He shared enough to help me understand why WPP was best for him. He felt strongly there was a bounty on his head and that if he left the building he didn't think he would even make it to his car. In fact he wasn't sure his car was still there." Paradise silently chastised herself for being so detailed.

"I left to go to Cape St Mary with my daughter. I thought it might be a bit of a 'country coming out party' for Hope, who is, or was, not very worldly. I was shocked to learn Lenny had followed me. Totally shocked. He claimed to be in love with me. I felt badly but I had to tell him my heart belonged to Thomas. No one else. Only Thomas. I do admit to early morning walks along Mavillette beach but nothing happened between us and it's—"

"This is what I mean about wanting only the facts, Paradise. I don't need a visual of you beach walking with my employee. In the name of God, give me facts only."

"Paradise, maybe you've said enough." Thomas stood and walked to her.

"No, Thomas. When I sit down you will know I'm done." She wasn't happy with the way Thomas made his last comment. She felt it was a bit condescending and would park that for a later discussion.

Paradise waited until Thomas retreated to his seat before continuing. "Lenny became a friend. Just a friend. Recently, though, Lenny disappeared from the Cape. My friends with the local police force said they had no idea where he had gone. Or why he had felt the need to leave. Lenny had made many friends at the Cape and he had earned the respect of the locals. He surprised almost everyone there when he left, when he snuck away, to be honest."

Paradise took a sip of her wine. Mainly so she could gather her thoughts. "Only a couple of days ago I learned from my brother, Wilmot, that his wife, Marie, realized Lenny was a man who had worked for a mob boss. Late one evening, with Wilmot not at home, a monster broke Marie's door down. He beat her nearly to death. She remembered the kicks, the nasty things he said, and the blood. She only began to get her memory of that horrible evening back recently. Wilmot called me to discuss this breakthrough in Marie's treatment and memory, but also to warn me about Lenny. And that's the story so far."

She started to sit, but then stood up again before Thomas could take the floor. "I turned this information over to the Cape police force, at least I had one phone conversation with lots to be discussed in person when I return. I understand they were going to turn the file over to the RCMP. And that's a wrap for me, gentlemen."

She sat with a thump. The commander and Thomas eyed each other, then Jalen spoke. "Your input has filled in a couple of blanks for me, Paradise and I thank you for that." He reached over and shook her hand.

"You are one tough act to follow," Thomas said as he got to his feet. "I'll be brief. Lenny came into my view just before he left 2.0. He worked the opposite shift to me and wasn't on my PI team, so our paths didn't really cross that much. He disappeared overnight and the gossip was that he was in the witness protection program, never to be heard from again. I had no reason to doubt this story until many months later, when I arrived in the Cape to surprise my girls. Neither Paradise nor Hope knew I was coming. And I found Lenny there. *With my girls*. He and I didn't have words, but I swear I wanted to kill the son of a bitch for following my family to Nova Scotia."

"I get the picture, Thomas, so sit down." Lexis was back in charge. "I have all the intel I need from both of you. I'm wondering if working with Lenny is going to be a problem for either of you, because he is on the job as we speak. And I'm not going to throw this man to the wolves. You don't know Len's history. I do."

Thomas turned to speak directly to Paradise. "You asked me about moving to the Cape, and I said I needed time to think about it. I've thought about it. Let's move Private Investigator's Unstructured and our family to the Cape. My answer is yes."

Paradise jumped to her feet, causing both men to flinch in surprise. "Thomas, you asked if I would marry you and I said I needed time to think about it. I've thought about it. My answer is yes. I will marry you."

They stepped toward each other, started to embrace, then turned with embarrassment toward Jalen, who stood up.

"And that's my cue to say congratulations to the happy couple. I will need a bit of time to work out the details of your resignation, Thomas. You will hear from me."

He gave a final nod, turned, and left the couple to complete their kiss.

49

"The kids are going out this afternoon with Mae so they won't be home for a few more hours. Let's not say a word until we drive to the ocean. This all happened too fast, and I want to relive every second with you—alone with you. Okay with you, honey?"

"Roger that." Paradise offered Thomas a peck on the cheek with her reply. "I need time to process what has happened over the past few hours myself. I need us to have a bit of quiet time."

She leaned back in her seat and closed her eyes. "I don't have to tell you that I have made many decisions during my life, and I have made more than a few of them during what I call 'windshield' time."

"I'll lead the way to the ocean and we can collect our thoughts and memories en route," Thomas replied.

Paradise opened her left eye just enough to see his lovely smile. She wanted to be in his arms so badly she ached. She knew he felt the same.

Earlier that morning, Mae had been happy to hear from Thomas and even happier to learn he and Paradise would like to have her come to their condo for the day while they were out. Mae missed T.J. and was excited to be spending time with him and his big sister.

Since Paradise and Hope had joined Thomas and T.J. in Hawaii Mae had not heard a word from Thomas, and that saddened her. However, Mae did acknowledge she was now able to feel fully retired and, given her recent cancer diagnosis, she was thankful to have all of her time to concentrate on all of her worries. And there were many. There was no history of breast cancer in her family and Mae was in the throes of researching different types of breast cancer and their treatment protocols.

Mae would tuck away her memories of her days with T.J. for the dark days she feared were ahead. Thinking of T.J. would help her to remain positive. She wasn't the first woman to be diagnosed with breast cancer and she wouldn't be the last.

"Today it's all about the two of you. Let's make some memories for you to pack up and take to Nova Scotia." Mae was so happy to be comfortably crushed between T.J. and his sister. Kisses and hugs all around.

"Your parents said they might go out for dinner, so let's see what's in the kitchen that we can turn into a meal for the three of us."

"I want hot dogs," T.J. said. "Two hot dogs. No bun. Nothing on them. Just two hot dogs. on my plate. I have my own plate."

"Mae, could we go out for supper? There are so many restaurants here and I would love to try a new one. Perhaps a fancy new one?" Hope crossed her fingers. "Honest to God, Mae, in the Cape we have one Cafe and that's it. I *never* get to go out."

"If one of us is eating hot dogs. and nothing else we are not going to a restaurant and paying for them. I'm sorry, Hope. Why don't you come to the kitchen with me and help me find something you might like. You could help me put supper together."

"Sure."

Before she knew it, the day had passed in a blur. Both T.J. and Hope were in bed and asleep. Mae sat down with a hot cup of tea to relax while she waited for Thomas and Paradise to come home.

50

"Our love will last a lifetime," whispered Thomas with his hands on either side of his beloved's face. "I could look at this face all day long."

Both love and passion were evident as they shared their words and bodies in a quiet, secluded corner of the wild and sometimes-gentle beach along the North Shore. Today was a gentle day all around.

Both Paradise and Thomas were finally certain of their love for each other. Next would be planning their wedding.

"Hope can be your 'best man,' Thomas, and T.J. can stand with me as my 'maid of honour!' How does that sound?" Thomas replied with a smile and a nod.

"I've carried this ring in my pocket, my love, since the day I went down on one knee and proposed to you. I'm hoping you will agree that this is the right time to slip it on your finger." Thomas spoke through his tears.

"Yes." No other words necessary.

"T.J. might not stand *still*, but that's what little kids are all about."

With a beautiful diamond now on her finger, Paradise was perhaps like many brides. She wanted to make a list and make it happen.

"I'll ask Pops to walk me down the aisle. He'll probably shed as many tears as I will." Tears formed in her eyes even as she spoke.

"You couldn't make a better choice," Thomas said.

A few days later, Thomas and Paradise gave Hope the news. They were excited, but Hope, not so much.

"Yes, I saw the ring on your finger, mother. I was waiting for anybody to clue me in. As usual, I never get the news from either of you in real time."

"Really, Hope," Thomas said sharply, "are you saying you should have been with us on the North Shore when I proposed to your mother? Apologize to her."

"Enough for now," responded Paradise. "I'm excited, Hope, and I was hoping you would be excited with me and for me."

"I can be excited about things if you tell me news when it's still news."

Paradise suggested they 'park' all wedding plans until they sold their little condo in Hawaii, packed everything up and made it to Cape St Mary without a negative word from anyone. Suddenly everyone was on edge. Especially Hope.

This was a big deal for her. *A very big deal.* She had spent most of her life in Honolulu, apart from her trip to Nova Scotia with her mother. That was meant to be a vacation and not a permanent move, so she couldn't wait to get to the airport back then.

"So, this was your plan all along, right, mother? I knew it. I knew you would force us to live in the Cape. Sure I love it, but permanently? I don't think so. Not a chance. I've lived in this condo most of my life. My home is here."

"My beautiful daughter, this is happening so, as you love to say, deal with it." Paradise knew Hope required a bit of tough love.

"You don't get it. I am *trying* to deal with it." Hope took a couple of breaths to keep from crying. "Like, first you tell me this is going to happen, and now you tell me it's going to happen right now. When am I going to get to see all my friends, even just to say goodbye to them?"

"I think you will have time for that," Paradise said. "The condo won't sell in a second."

"But it might! And you'll want me to pack not just my own stuff but help with yours and T.J.'s. You'll want me to help get ready to do a thing I don't want to do."

"If you just do a bit each day, as your father and I are doing—"

"No!" Part of Hope knew she ought to try. A bigger part knew she had never totally left any of her friends forever. This felt like what she thought death might feel like, and it scared her. She found herself yelling. "*I am not packing a single thing today, mother.* Deal with it!"

"It will just leave more to pack tomorrow."

"What happens if I refuse to go to the airport and to what I heard you telling Mae would be 'our fresh new life'?"

"Hope, what do you think will happen? You'll still end up going."

They stared at each other. Paradise's heart was aching for her girl, and Hope was trying to figure out an apology she could manage to share without choking. Finally she turned and stomped off to her room.

At least she closed the door without slamming it.

Later, but before Hope had worked through her sorrow, there was a knock on her door.

"We're closed."

"Then I'll talk from here," Paradise said. "Your father and I were talking about how tough this must be for you. How about we help you throw a small party this weekend? You could have all of your friends over so they can wish you well on your way."

Hope knew her parents were trying to do a good thing, but she was too sad and mad to respond as she knew she should. All she could manage, after a long pause, was, "I'll think about it."

After a longer pause, she heard steps move away from the door; two people. So her father had been there, too.

Hope passed a long night. First, before she managed to fall asleep, she squeezed every drop of righteous indignation she could out of this mess. How could they think of moving her right out of her life in Hawaii? How dare they state that exile in the Cape would be a 'fresh, new life' for her? What would she do, out in the middle of nowhere with nothing but a beach to explore?

In the middle of the night, she had a terrifying dream that the move was done, but that they had forgotten one box. And in that box was her name. Nobody in the Cape knew what to call her, so they just did not talk to her. Hope was lost.

Then the morning was bright and innocent, and for no reason she could put her finger on, Hope found that her despair and panic had moved away. All that was left was figuring out what to say to her parents.

They were at the breakfast table when Hope poked her head into the room. She had made sure to wash her face and brush her hair and put on the shirt she kept for occasions when she wanted to get something out of them.

"Mom and daddy, I'm so sorry for the way I have acted about your engagement and about moving all of us to the Cape. Today's a new day and I hope you'll forgive me—maybe without punishment, please, please?"

"No punishment required, Hope."

"Ditto from me," said a very happy dad.

Every morning from that day Paradise had a list ready to review with Thomas and every morning Thomas said he didn't need a list. "I'm getting rid of most of the condo contents, honey. We'll pack up clothes and toys, lots of toys, but not much more. But, if you need a list, my love, then you go for it. I know what I have to do."

51

"Hello. Private Investigators Unstructured, Canada. This is Clint speaking."

"Hello, yourself. PIU USA coming to you from Honolulu. This is Thomas speaking."

"Hey, Jim, where are you?" Clint called to his partner. "Get on the extension, quick. Thomas has resurfaced." He knew Jim wouldn't want to miss this conversation. It had been a long time coming and they had been worried about Thomas. The last they had heard, he was struggling a bit as a single father while Wikolia was in hospital.

Jim got on the extension. "You been in the slammer, Thomas, or just hiding under a rock?"

"First things first: what kind of business do we have in Canada these days? Still just the two of you in our little offices in Port Hope?"

Jim and Clint glanced at each other. Sounded a bit like Thomas was thinking they might have grown the operation and not kept him in the loop.

"The first thing before that first thing," Clint said, "is for you to catch us up. How come we haven't heard a word from you for so long? We've been worried, buddy."

Thomas sighed. "Where do I start? Settle in and let me try to tell you the short form of a long story. You know that Paradise and I signed a lucrative contract with Hawaii 5.0 and have been working exclusively in their 2.0 division." Something was 'off' with Thomas and Jim tried to lighten it up a bit. "We don't give a rat's ass about PIU right now. We want to know how you are doing. We'll even listen to you go on and on about that kid of yours."

There was silence from the other end of the phone. Clint motioned for Jim to shut up and leave it to Thomas to talk when he was ready. Jim nodded and 'zipped his lips.'

Finally Thomas broke the silence. "Okay, then. My son's mother, Wikolia, is dead. You've heard me speak of her being in hospital for some time. And now she's gone. Paradise and Hope came to help me a bit and we're now talking about moving to Nova Scotia. Do you know Cape St. Mary?"

"Thomas, first let me say we are so sorry to hear about your friend. Details please, or is that appropriate to ask?" Clint's booming voice filled the airways. He didn't have a 'quiet' voice filter.

"Guys, I don't have the energy to get into that right now. Sorry. I'll share everything when I can and that has to be okay for now."

Jim said, "Of course," quickly before Clint could put his foot in it again."

"Paradise is out with Hope and T.J. so I wanted to call you while the condo is quiet. I wanted to tell you that while I'm not moving to Toronto, I am moving to Canada. Have either of you ever been to Nova Scotia?"

"We have not taken one vacation day since PIU opened," Jim said. "So, you get yourself moved and settled and then we will take a road trip to visit with you and Paradise and the children."

"That sounds very good."

Clint was waving his left hand at Jim, pointing at his ring finger.

"Clint just reminded me that we too have some big news to share. I'm not sure if this will come as a surprise to you, Thomas, but we got married."

"Both of you?"

"Ah, yes," Clint said. "That would be both of us." Clint was enjoying this. "You mean you didn't figure me out when we were in RCMP boot camp together in Regina? You had to have known."

There was another pause. Then Thomas said, "I feel like I've walked into a different story. What are you telling me without telling me?"

Jim said through laughter, "And you call yourself a detective."

Thomas listened to the two men, tough, manly men, laughing at him down the phone line. "God help me if I've got this wrong, but I'll dive in anyway. You didn't get married to two women. Or even to the same woman."

"God, no!" Jim and Clint said at the same time.

"So somehow...you got married to each other?"

"Give the man a gold star!" Clint shouted. "Your PI partners are gay, and married *to each other*!"

"Congratulations to you both. I'll worry about you, though. Gay marriage is not legal, as far as I know. I doubt it will ever be legalized. You're smart men and I know you would have thought this through but—"

"But what, Thomas? What are you saying? You have something against us being gay and married?"

"Not fair, Clint. Not fair at all. You throw this at me after I tell you Wikolia is dead and we might be moving to Nova Scotia and my emotions are all over the place. This is information about two of my dearest friends and I'm just hearing it now, so cut me some slack. You both know I have absolutely nothing against the gay community." With that Thomas was tapped out and his partners could sense it.

Jim spoke up. "Thomas, we really weren't planning to tell you this way. We have tried to connect with you a few times and one of those times was on our wedding day. Nothing is legal, of course, but it's a marriage to us. We aren't going to advertise it either, so other than Paradise we would rather you not tell people."

"Thanks for letting me off the hook with my reaction! I am truly happy for you both. Looks like we all got our forever-afters."

52

Coffee for two and warm muffins were barely on the table before Pops started talking and making no sense at all. He was a nervous wreck. He was going to get to the bottom of this today and if Eugenie didn't want to be with him he would bloody-well shut up about marrying her. He might even stop meeting her at Cafe Central and that would really piss her off.

Pops knew he should have thought this through before sitting down. Too late…"Listen, I know you don't want to marry me but I don't know why. I'm not bringing it up again."

"First of all, don't you *dare* 'listen' me again. How rude of you, Pops. What's gotten into you this morning? What are you talking about?"

Eugenie knew exactly what he was talking about, but she was not going to take any guff. "What makes you so sure I don't want to marry you, anyway?" She reached over to the plate and snagged a muffin. She needed to keep her hands busy for a second so she could settle down.

"I don't know. Maybe heaven has something to do with it, so you tell me when you're darn good an' ready."

"Pops, when have you specifically asked me to marry you? You dance around the topic like a fool but you never come right out and ask. And that's a fact, so don't even think of arguing with me."

"Eat your muffin instead of picking it to death. I paid good money for that breakfast, I'll have you know." Pops knew he was burying himself.

Eugenie opened her hands and brushed the disassembled muffin onto her plate. "For now, Pops, I think I should leave you with your coffee and bad attitude. I will see you another time. Some other time when you're not so ornery, perhaps? You have no right to assume anything about me."

She stood and opened her purse. "And here's for my muffin and coffee. I wouldn't want you to spend your good money on me."

"Ornery? I sure as hell am not ornery. And I'll thank you to take that back before you go off all in a huff."

"No need to shout, Pops. I believe everyone in the Café is hearing you quite clearly. It got very quiet in here some time ago, but you might have been too ornery to notice."

Eugenie couldn't help but smile to herself. She knew everyone in the Cafe was hearing every word and, for once, she wasn't sorry about speaking up for herself. She didn't care who heard her.

"Oh, please," Pops said. "Let's not end our conversation this way. My intention when I saw you sitting here was to buy you a coffee and a muffin, nothing more. If I'm being ornery and you're in a huff we should talk more, shouldn't we?"

He was some embarrassed and she needed to know that. "I'm talking to you, woman!" Pops wasn't sure where that came from but he knew it didn't help his case.

He was talking to the back of Eugenie's head as she left the Café in what he was positive was a huff.

53

Thomas and family finalized plans for a road trip, maybe their last Hawaii road trip for a long, long time.

"T.J., we are going to find your mom's family if they're living anywhere in Honolulu." Having looked already, Thomas wasn't sure he would be successful this time either. But he wanted T.J. to meet his mom's side of the family, if only once before they moved to Cape St Mary.

"I don't know when we'll be back in Hawaii, my son, so we need to do this now." Thomas hoped he could make it happen and felt strongly he owed this to Wikolia.

Everyone was excited.

T.J. didn't understand what the excitement was about but he was happy to play along. There had been some discussion about leaving T.J. behind with Mae, but if they were successful in finding Wikolia's family, Thomas wanted to introduce T.J. to his relatives right away.

It was Hope who sealed the deal. She let T.J. fill his little backpack and get ready for his first real adventure. Each time he turned away to find another essential toy, she snuck in socks or underwear or some other essential.

"Mom and dad, I was just thinking about how much money you will have to pay Mae if we leave T.J. behind."

"Not your concern, Hope, but what are you suggesting?"

Hope knew she had their attention. "I'll look after my brother and I'll cut Mae's figure in half. What do you say? T.J. could join me in the back seat and it will be an adventure for him. I promise I'll do all the 'heavy lifting' to keep him happy."

Thomas thought it was a good idea. Paradise thought it was a great idea.

It was all systems go early one morning as they filled their bellies and then collectively filled the car. T.J. was ready to meet his mom's family, he just didn't know it yet.

As Hope helped T.J. settle in beside her in the back seat of the car with some of his toys and his favourite stuffed animal right beside him, she was beaming with pride. "We just finagled ourselves a road trip, little buddy. You're welcome."

Keeping the conversation going, and in a whispered voice, Hope shared a secret with her brother. "Mom and Dad have all the hard work to do. I know it's hard work because I saw Dad pack his .45 calibre Remington pistol. Don't tell him I shared this little tidbit with you, though. Dad once told me he knew my mom and me both love guns and everything there is to know about guns. But he also said I shouldn't be too proud of this particular interest. Researching guns I mean."

For whatever reason, T.J. wasn't totally interested in whatever it was his sister was talking about. His mind was on deciding what toy to play with first.

"I have never shot a gun and if mom and dad have their way I will never shoot one. I will say, T.J., that this particular .45 pistol of dad's is a real beauty. Not all .45s look this good. Can you whisper .45 for me?"

"Whore-five Daddy. Whore-five."

"You're killing me here, T.J. It's a .45. Can you say that for me please?" Hope knew this was getting her in trouble but she couldn't help laughing. Clearly T.J. was listening to her after all.

"Whore-five."

T.J. was definitely not using his inside voice, and while Hope's friends would have found this funny, the look her dad gave her as he caught her eye in the mirror suggested he was not at all amused. Hope couldn't believe her bad luck. Tell a secret to a kid and he blabs it only seconds later.

"I object to any punishment during this trip, Daddy. You can't send me to my room, after all." "Technically, you're correct, young lady. But I sure as Hell can reduce your final pay cheque if I decide it's warranted." One quick look at Paradise's face and Thomas knew he had some explaining to do but not in front of the kids.

"Not fair. Not one bit fair. We agreed on that amount." Hope knew she was fighting a losing battle.

T.J. reached out to take Hope's hand and seemed to understand he might have said the wrong thing. "Whore-five," he whispered.

"Do you understand how much trouble you have gotten me in? It's a .45—is that so hard to say? .45. Do not say it again. Please."

"Whore-five. Whore-five."

"Hope, I guess you saw the gun I packed. Were you rummaging through my things?"

"I most certainly was not. I saw you take the gun from under your bed and slip it into one of your socks. At lightning speed you tucked the sock into your suitcase. By the way, 'lightning speed' is a joke, dad. You were taking your good old time."

Turning to Paradise, Thomas tried to hide his smile. "Where did we get this smart ass sitter and what have you done with Hope?"

"Whore-five, Daddy. Whore-five." At least T.J. was happy.

54

Having had enough peer-shaming at work, Len desperately wanted to speak with everyone on his shift and shut the gossip down regarding him and Paradise. He was sick of all the comments. If Thomas ever heard any of them, Len would be a dead man. Maybe even literally.

It wouldn't be easy to spill his guts, but if he spoke from his heart his peers at 2.0 might actually listen. Some had suggested in the past that he didn't have a heart at all, so maybe they would learn something. And, sure enough, Len proved them all wrong at his own expense.

Both day and night crews assembled in the lounge area of 2.0 for a rare meeting with Lieutenant Commander Jalen Lexis. Or, so they thought.

The commander had suggested to Len that he could manage to be a few minutes late if Len really wanted to speak to the full team privately. Lexis was never late so this would very quickly be seen as a set up. Nevertheless, Len liked the idea. He appreciated that he could bare his soul without the boss being in the room, even though Len was sure he would be close by, listening to every word.

Len looked around and saw that everyone was present and accounted for with the exception of Thomas and Paradise. No time like the present, he figured so he stood up. "I don't really want to talk about this, but I'll feel better after I do. I hope."

Before he could continue, the guys started to make their own comments. He knew this would happen. Christ on a stick, what now? He knew the commander would not come to his rescue. This was his shit-show.

"Hey, Romeo, did you bring the little lady back with you? We haven't seen her yet. And we sure would like to."

"Len, my man, you've got standing room only here, so what's up? Were you really chasing our own Paradise? And you thought you had a chance with her? I figure even you couldn't be that stupid."

"You do know Thomas will kill you with his bare hands, right?"

Len couldn't see who made that comment. The faces all sort of blurred together into one gawping mouth under mocking eyes.

"Tell us the secret about her long legs, Len. We all know how they lead down to her feet and into those killer high-heeled shoes. Now tell us what's at the top of those legs, Len."

The laughter was like a tide that would drown him. He had to speak.

"Shut up. Just shut the fuck up, every one of you. This is not easy for me. But how many of you have never made a single mistake along the way?"

This was not the Len his peers were used to. The room fell quiet.

"I asked the commander to give me a few minutes at the beginning of his meeting with all of us. Even asking wasn't easy, so please in the name of God let me say what I need to say."

Len's hands were sweating so he took a second and wiped them on his jeans. "It's true. I left my job here to chase after Paradise. I went all the way to some little village half a world away, and guess what? Paradise had no romantic interest in me at all. The joke was on me. Nothing you could say can hurt me more than that."

He paced a few steps as if trying to find his next words somewhere on the floor.

"Then I had to take off. The people I came to 2.0 to escape were on me again. I could have easily avoided them if I had followed the plan and gone into witness protection."

They were following him closely now, visualizing an escape, a manhunt, all the twists and turns he didn't have to spell out for them.

"You can make fun of me all you want, but please leave Paradise out of this. She doesn't deserve any crap from you guys because of me. I'm the gangster. The loser. The bum. The murderer. You should run the other way just seeing my face. But she's none of those things. Take me on if you want, but leave her out of it."

The commander walked to the centre of the warehouse and took over just by his stance. He didn't have to say a word. As the team would soon find out he had plenty to say.

"Stop selling yourself short, young man. You did what you had to in self-defence."

Attention shifted to Commander Lexis. Len noticed men shifting in their seats to seem more attentive, more respectful.

But Jalen had more words just for Len.

"I would wager my pay cheque that no one in this room suffered the childhood you faced. You did what you had to do to survive. I know there are sins you would like to address sometime, but you don't need to take that up with any of us. I commend you for wanting to try. In some aspects you're a stronger man than I."

The commander stepped over to Len and offered a full-on bear hug. Then he turned to his full team.

"Stop the gossip and cat calls. Not just about Paradise; about anyone. You are all better than that. If I hear even one more slam at Len you'll be answering to me. Is that clear?"

"Yes sir" came the reply from a score of voices.

"Len, you're safe with us. We will protect you on the inside and down the road we will reassess your WPP request. No more comments about your personal life as it relates to Paradise."

Len was stunned by the show of respect. In his whole life no one had ever spoken to him this way. No one had ever had his back.

Jalen addressed the whole group again. "I have met with Paradise and Thomas. She flew in to be with Thomas as he grieves the death of his friend, Wikolia." Silence.

"I shared Len's news with them. Paradise wishes you well and Thomas seems to want to rip your eyes out and your head off."

A quiet chuckle came from a few of the men. "There is more to share, so don't walk off just yet. Both Paradise and Thomas have given me their resignations. They are moving back to her little village in Canada."

All eyes turned to Len who was clearly hearing this for the first time. After a moment, he lowered his gaze to the ground.

"Are there any questions? Not about Paradise and Thomas, of course, but about your work. We don't often meet like this, so take advantage of the offer."

"Will we have a chance to say goodbye to Paradise and Thomas?" one of the men asked. "Possibly, but we will have to wait and see. They have a bootload to do before they take off."

As the meeting broke up, a few men came toward Len. He couldn't help tensing, but relaxed as the first man to reach him stuck out his hand for a handshake. Others patted him on the back.

Nobody said much, certainly nothing in the way of apologies. They weren't that kind of guys. But it was enough.

Len had a few hours before his next shift. He went to his room and collapsed on the bed. He was tired but sleep wouldn't come.

He was crestfallen to hear that Paradise was leaving for good this time. And leaving with Thomas. That really hurt, and he had nobody to talk to about it.

Len was pissed at Lexis. He could have given him a heads-up that Paradise had resigned and would be leaving with Thomas. Surely the commander knew this news would be gutting for him.

However, he did give Len his job back, and the prospect of a new life under witness protection.

Unsettled but exhausted, he fell asleep with thoughts of Paradise running through his head.

55

Eugenie walked down Cape St Mary Road to number 548 with more determination than she realized she had. She was clearly on a mission on a cold and windy morning. When the wind blew off the ocean, as it did that morning, it felt like knives on your skin.

On this particular day Eugenie didn't care how bad the weather was, she was going to see Pops.

"*These Boots are Made For Walkin'* isn't the right song for how I feel this morning, but, by golly, the title fits me to a T," she said to the air. Then she glanced around to make sure no one else was walking along the road behind her. Anyone listening to her talking to herself would really have something to gossip about, and she didn't need that.

"No time like the present," she said under her breath as she knocked on the door of Pops' beautiful new home. With the girls off to Hawaii she was relatively sure she would catch Pops alone, and that's what she wanted.

"This is a surprise, Eugenie. What can I do for you?"

No invitation to come inside, so Eugenie took charge earlier than she thought she would have to.

"Invite me in, for gosh sake, Pops. Where are your manners?"

"Oh, of course! Please do come on in at this early hour."

"I wanted to catch you before you headed over to the Cafe for your coffee, Pops. Don't you think we should talk?"

"*Talk*? About what?"

"Well I never. You're going to make me spell it out? Pour me a cup of coffee and come and sit down beside me. If this has to happen in the kitchen that's okay by me."

Pops heart was beginning to soften. "You're right, Eugenie. Let's have coffee in my front room so we can look out at the ocean. It's a real pretty place to sit. I'll even let you have the window seat." Pops picked up their coffee and lead the way.

Wasting no time once she was seated, Eugenie got down to business. She was afraid if she didn't speak up she might lose her nerve, like Pops had done a few times. She wouldn't bring that up, of course.

"Pops, please let me say what I have to say and then you can tell me how you are feeling about the two of us, okay?

Thinking of the one word answers he had heard Hope use on occasion, Pops didn't want to get this wrong, so he didn't want to say much. He was eager to say something and he hoped he could break the ice. Or at least crack it a bit.

"Sure."

It worked! Eugenie offered the first smile since she had walked through the door, so Pops figured he said the right thing.

"Pops, it is, of course, not right for a lady to ask a man to marry her. We both know that. If that's what you've been failing to say, you might be pleasantly surprised by my answer."

"What I know is that you avoid being around me any time it looks like it's going to be just the two of us."

Eugenie sat back. "That's not what I expected you to say. I made myself pretty clear, didn't I?"

"Ah what the hell."

Pops put his coffee cup down and moved over to sit beside her on the window seat. He took her coffee cup and sat it down beside his so he could hold her hands.

"I'd get down on one knee, Eugenie, but you'd have to help me get up and believe me that wouldn't be pretty."

"I see. And you have a question for me?" Eugenie was baiting him now and they were both enjoying it.

Pops took a deep breath, let half of it out, and then met her steady look. "Eugenie, will you marry me and agree that we will spend the rest of our lives together?"

"Yes!"

"You will?"

"Yes! I will marry you and I would be honoured to spend the rest of my life in wedded harmony with you."

She gave Pops a small hug that turned into a bigger hug than she was quite ready for. When she could catch her breath, she said, "Now, that wasn't so hard, was it?"

"I love you," declared Pops. "Let's move you in here with me. Let's move you in today. What do you say?"

"In the name of the Lord, you think we should live together before marriage? Pops, I'm surprised at you."

Now it was his turn to sit back. He frowned, calculating. "So, how fast can we get married? I'm not getting any younger."

Eugenie knew she would have a nervous breakdown if they didn't discuss 'certain' things right away, so she dove in. "Pops, I have only been married to my Lord and that means in this world I'm a virgin."

He tried to keep a straight face, "Many women are virgins when they marry, if I'm not mistaken. I don't see a problem here."

"Nor do I, except I'm a little nervous about it."

There was a silence, and suddenly Eugenie felt even more nervous. Would he now think less of her because she brought up the topic of sex? Would he think she was just after him for his body? There was a little smile on his face; was he laughing at her wanting to start getting physical at her age?

"Pops you got all quiet there. Tell me what you were thinking. Don't hold back."

She saw a blush spread right up to his eyes. "Eugenie, I'm eager to lay naked with you and make love just by touching each other. Intercourse isn't something that has to happen. To be honest, and I hope this doesn't make you change your mind, I'm not sure I can still perform as I used to."

"In the name of the Lord, I will thank you to keep your PJ's on at all times in the bedroom. There will be no naked, is that understood?" Eugenie was stunned with how easily Pops spoke of sex.

"No naked of any kind? How will you ever take a bath?"

She burst out laughing. "Pops, when we marry, and we will, we will make love to and with each other by a simple touch, by proudly holding hands in public, the way we look at each other across a room. I'll tell you truly, the idea of pure intercourse scares me."

"It scares everyone."

She looked hard at him. "Really."

"Everyone, not just the ladies. Every bold fella is scared to death inside when the first time draws close. So you are not alone."

She pondered for a moment. "I never considered it that way." Then she took his hand in both of hers. "If pure intercourse has to happen, maybe we can just let it surprise us instead of running at it."

"Sure." Pops thought he might be the happiest man on earth as he took Eugenie in his arms again.

56

"Thanks for seeing me, Wilmot. And you as well, Marie. I love your little home here in the Cape and we all hope you never leave us."

Sergeant Curtis was still standing outside Wilmot and Marie's cottage and could see pretty much the entire living area just over Marie's shoulder. It looked small but very much a home.

Wilmot had done a lot of work on the outside of the house and that's how Curtis had come to meet them. He stopped by one day to confirm he was looking into Lenny's past as well as his current location and had promised to knock on their door the day he could offer up real facts.

"What are the chances of being invited inside? You know why I'm here, I'm sure." Keeping it light, he hoped, would encourage them to open the door, which at the moment was firmly in the half-opened position.

"Of course," Marie said. "Where are our manners? Please come in, Sergeant."

Living in a small community, with a new circle of friends, was helping Marie find her voice more often. She knew Wilmot had doubts about Sergeant Curtis, but she felt they ought to be civil. Wilmot had expressed his concern that the Sergeant and this criminal, Lenny, seemed to know each other extremely well and might be 'in this together', whatever 'this' was. Wilmot had never confronted Sergeant Curtis with this and Marie hoped today wouldn't be the day.

After a few long and uncomfortable seconds, Wilmot stepped aside and motioned for the Sergeant to come in. Marie could see he thought this was a mistake. This day could change everything if what they suspected was true.

"Can I get you something?" she asked nervously. "Coffee or tea or a cold drink?"

"No, thanks, Marie. What I'm hoping you might give me when I explain what I now know is a simple thank you. That's all I need."

They sat in the tiny front room, knees almost touching. Sergeant Curtis shifted his equipment belt, hoping none of his gear would snag on the fabric of the chair they had pointed him to. It looked like somebody's great-grandmother had hooked the seat cushion, which had endless little loops like a trap for the unwary.

"This information will be hard to digest, hard to accept and hard to hear," he said, "but I know you want to know everything, so here we go." He pulled his notebook out of his chest pocket and flipped to the right page.

"I also know you don't have any sympathy for this man, but you may find this background of interest. As a child, Lenny—"

"I don't give a rats ass about this criminal's childhood," Wilmot said, "so cut the crap."

Marie could see the 'don't do this' look on her husband's face, but she had to say something. "Wilmot, I thought we both wanted to know everything. I would like to hear details dating back to this monster's childhood, if that will help me understand and ultimately forgive."

She knew her voice was breaking up, but she continued, "I know you're not the forgiving type, but I need this to be able to move forward. Please let the Sergeant give us the entire story before we spew our venom for Lenny."

"Carry on," Wilmot said stiffly. "But this better have the ending I want or, so help me God—"

"Wilmot, this affects me a lot more than it affects you, so I say let's be quiet for a few minutes. Force yourself to sit still, darling, for me."

With an obvious effort, Wilmot stifled himself. Sergeant Curtis took that as his cue to continue.

He took them through the bare outline of the horrid events when Big Len murdered his mother and siblings, and Lenny had to kill his own father. He could see both Wilmot and Marie were interested despite themselves.

"Len dropped out of school and began his life on the run. My notes don't tell me what schooling he had completed, but he had not gotten far. He stole food and he stole money. He broke into private homes and cottages when he needed a roof over his head. He had seen much more than any child—anyone!—should. His mental health had to be pretty screwed up and fragile." He laughed slightly. "You can understand he probably never found himself in a position to seek mental-health counselling."

Marie reached out to fill his now empty glass of water and he took a drink before continuing.

"One extremely dark day, Len met a gang leader by the name of Meat Cove."

"Like the town?" Wilmot asked in disbelief.

"Nothing like the town. This Meat Cove was a monster. He took control of Len and groomed him. He became Cove's main hit man. It would have been Cove who ordered Lenny to kill you, Marie."

Marie was sobbing with Wilmot's arm around her, and Sergeant Curtis stopped for a minute to ensure she was hanging in there.

"The fact that you both survived is a testament to your resolve to live, to find each other and to build together the life you had planned. I hope you're writing a book! You have a compelling story even if you never share it." He could see Wilmot knew he was stalling. He needed to plow ahead.

"Len assaulted and killed people for a living until one day, it seems, he had had enough. He walked into a police station and confessed to every bad thing he had done, starting with murdering his own father."

Sergeant Curtis looked from one to the other. Still, silence. "We still have questions about all this. I can tell you that Len got into some very big, very dark stuff."

"Darker than killing his own father?"

"Spy-novel stuff, on behalf of our own government and for other countries. They used him and used him until his tank was empty. He then became a candidate for the witness protection program and started a job in Hawaii in the arms division of something called Hawaii 2.0."

Sergeant Curtis checked his notes again." It seems Len came to the job with such a deep history of every gun imaginable he was an excellent fit for 2.0. This is likely why they hired him."

"This, Wilmot, is where Len met your sister. Paradise and Thomas were on a contract with 2.0. Paradise and Len became friends."

"Okay," Wilmot said. "But how does this get the bastard from Hawaii to Cape St Mary and our little world?"

57

Curtis could see that Wilmot was torn. He obviously wanted to end the conversation, but knew that Marie would not rest until she knew every possible detail about Len. The silence dragged on, and the sergeant thought of the work piling up on his desk at the station. He tried to keep a smooth, attentive expression, and got ready to sit there with them into the evening, if that's what it took.

Finally Wilmot brought Marie's hand to his lips for a quick kiss, then nodded to the sergeant to continue.

"Thanks, Wilmot. Believe me, I know how hard this is for both of you." He glanced at his notes. "While Len was with 2.0 he saw a therapist every day – seven days a week. At first he didn't see the therapist willingly, but his boss told me he 'came around' to it. This helped Len take responsibility for his past and focus on building a future. He knew he was heading for the WPP and a new identity. He had accepted both. Before he met Paradise, he had no one in his old life so he didn't care."

"Until he did," Wilmot said.

"Yes. As hard as it may be to accept, this monster-turned-model employee fell in love with Paradise. Should I continue?"

"Stop asking for permission and tell us what we need to hear so we can sleep at night. I can't take much more of this."

"Please continue," Marie said quietly.

"When Paradise left 2.0, I guess she didn't say much about why she went, Len no longer wanted to go into the witness protection program. He wanted to find Paradise and tell her how he felt. He assumed she had broken up with Thomas."

Marie's facial expression was haunting.

"Wilmot, your sister is probably the first and only person Len has ever loved. The fact that she didn't love him in return did not come into the equation for him."

Wilmot was on his feet. "You're selling sympathy for this monster? This crazy-ass monster?"

"I'm just giving you all the information I have, as you asked." Curtis bit off several comments about rudeness and tried to remember his training about talking with people in crisis. "When you know as much as I know, we can determine what we need next."

Wilmot stepped over to the window and stared out at the world. Curtis turned to Marie. "If I could have another glass of water, that would be great. I'm close to the ending of the story as I know it."

Marie provided the glass of water and a smile. "You're doing a great job filling us in, so please continue."

Wilmot heaved a sigh at the world and then returned to his seat.

"You know how Paradise shares things. She talked a lot about the Cape, about her favourite corner of the world. Len listened to every word. When she took off, I guess he figured out where she would be going. It didn't take him long to find her."

Wilmot whispered, "*Stalker.*"

"I gather from Pops that some strangers appeared here in the Cape not all that long ago. They were asking questions about Len. Where had he come from? What did Pops know about him? Was he living with Paradise?"

Wilmot turned to Marie. "How much more are we going to listen to? I can't think, let alone listen right now. Can we finish this another day?"

"We've come this far, Wilmot." She put a hand on his shoulder. "We're almost done."

"Pops is sure Len left town to protect Paradise and to draw the strangers away from everyone here in the Cape."

"How very noble," Wilmot said.

The sergeant shifted in his seat and resisted the temptation to glance around to see if anyone else was listening. "I should not be sharing the next bit. I have to count on you two not to talk about it with anyone, if you please." He waited until they both nodded.

"Sometime after Len left us, there was a gun fight up in Halifax. Do you know Point Pleasant Park?"

"I heard of it," Wilmot said. "Never been."

"It was part of the city's defences in the old day, but now it's just a nice place to go walk your dog. Anyhow, there were gunshots. It was all over by the time the police showed up, but they found three bodies. None of them was Len, and there was a blood trail that went out to the parking lot. Clearly the fourth man was wounded and left in a car. The three dead men had weapons and had used them."

Marie was pale as a sheet. "This is like something out of a movie."

"It is. Only a trained sharpshooter could have killed three men who were shooting at him."

"So where is he," Wilmot asked. He seemed interested despite himself.

"He disappeared. He didn't show up at a hospital, so we really don't know what happened. But he seems to have got himself patched up."

He flipped his notebook closed. "Paradise called last night, and, among her other news, she told me Len is back there in Hawaii, back at 2.0."

"Back with Paradise?" Marie asked.

"Let's remember he was never with Paradise, except in his imagination."

Wilmot said, "So now they put him in jail for murder."

Curtis spread his hands. "I put this story together for you out of bits of solid information, and piles of guess-work. There are no witnesses to what happened in Halifax. We have no way to link Len to those shootings except by coincidence."

"That just seems wrong."

"The point I am trying to make is, whatever happens to him, he is out of your lives. He is in the hands of very competent people. And, to draw a line under it all, his former boss, Meat Cove, is dead as well."

"We know that," Wilmot said.

"All right, then. Paradise knows the whole story, and probably many things I have missed. But I promise you I am not withholding anything. Wilmot, maybe you should give your sister a call."

Sergeant Curtis stood up and put his notebook in his pocket. "It is a miserable world at times. But misery does not go on forever.

These folks are out of your lives and you don't have to worry they will show up at the door again."

Marie looked down at her hands, then over at Wilmot. Finally she stood and faced the sergeant. "I hardly know what to make of it all."

"Will you be able to sleep any better now?"

"I don't know. Maybe after I talk to Paradise."

Sergeant Curtis nodded. "I know she'll be happy to talk with you. Oh, but remember not to tell anyone else but her anything I told you today. It would be worth my job if people found out I'd been spinning you such a story."

58

"Are you having a good time, Hope?"

Paradise and Thomas tried to ensure the scouring trip through the many miles that make up Honolulu would be a bit of a vacation for Hope. She continued to struggle with the impending permanent move to the Cape.

"I'm trying, mom." Hope reached out to the front seat and took her mother's hand.

Hope knew this road trip was all about looking for Wikolia's family and she appreciated that her parents were thinking about her and wanted to create a few memories for her to keep in her heart. None of it felt like a real vacation.

"We've been on the road now for eleven days. Eleven days straight and nothing at all. We are no closer to finding Wikolia's family than we were on day one." Thomas was discouraged and didn't try to hide it.

Not even a hint of where Wikolia's family might be living. They had done their best without a single lead and it was beyond frustrating. It felt like they had packed and unpacked their suitcases in every motel on the island. Everyone was tired of the trip but T.J., of course. He slept soundly whenever and wherever he wanted.

They had come up against many 'I think we're getting close to finding at least someone who knows the family' moments that ended in disappointment for everyone but T.J. He was living his best life in the back seat of the car with his sister, who did her best to respond to every question and comment he offered from his perch.

"I did not know that 'Lee' is Wikolia's last name. Did you guys know that?" Once again Hope wondered if she was the last to know.

Lee is one of the most common last names in all of Hawaii, so they met a lot of shrugs. Everyone knew a 'Lee,' but none of them were connected to Wikolia.

Thinking back, Hope chastised herself for the many times she said she was going to sit down and write Wikolia a letter. She didn't know her surname so obviously she didn't write a letter. Not one! Hope called that pathetic.

When Wikolia took Thomas to meet her family, she had told him her surname was 'Sky'. But that was her middle name. He had never thought to cross-check what she told him by grilling her family. Wikolia had run away from home, and somewhere along the line she had documents made that showed her full name as Wikolia Sky. Why would she hide that from the man she loved?

This proved to be a bit of a nightmare when Thomas began adoption proceedings to make T.J. his son. He could find nothing with the surname Sky, and it took help from a government employee to learn the truth. Thomas had hoped to discuss this with Wikolia, but he had put that conversation off until she could get better...and then she died.

This was only one of the many regrets Thomas had about his relationship with T.J.'s mom. He wished wholeheartedly that he had gotten to know her better. Not just her favourite movies, her favourite subjects in school, but basic things like her name! This would haunt Thomas for some time.

Before Paradise came back into their lives Wikolia was the only female figure Hope was truly comfortable with. Life was more exciting with Wikolia around. For a few hours a week they were a family of three. She loved their Saturday morning trips to the local mall.

Hope would never forget Wikolia and was profoundly sad the day they agreed over one more complimentary motel breakfast, that they were not going to find her family.

Paradise had her elbows on the table and her chin in her hands. "Fine detectives we turn out to be. I should hand my badge in and become a beachcomber."

"She spent years making sure her family couldn't find her," Thomas said. "Got pretty good at it, I guess."

"Elbows off table, mommy," T.J. said delightedly. He repeated it several times even after she had complied.

"Hope, what do you think?" Paradise asked. "Do we keep on searching or do we make another try sometime in the future."

"We'll go on, or quit, depending on what I say?"

"You're smart and you can see we're at a dead end. But maybe you see a path around it."

Hope felt a little shiver of delight that they were treating her as an adult. She focused on the question, crossing her eyes slightly. Thomas had to turn a laugh into a cough.

"Well...I know it means a lot to you, daddy, and to all of us. But it would still mean a lot if we tried again another time. Maybe we can come up with some better clues before then."

Thomas nodded, "Yeah. Maybe."

"So," Hope continued thoughtfully, "if I'm doing the planning now..."

"Yes?" Paradise said after Hope's dramatic pause.

Hope looked at T.J., who was trying to get his elbows on the table. She looked at her parents with the most grown-up face she could muster. "If that's true...do I get a raise?"

She had to move fast to avoid a barrage of breakfast rolls.

Thomas took the shortest route back to the condo, instead of the looping path they had followed through small settlements and past odd bars and restaurants at the start of the trip. Hope had her hands full keeping T.J. from jumping on the back seat, and she was grateful that this part of the trip would be short. She didn't want to lose her pay raise as soon as she had won it.

She barely noticed Paradise and Thomas murmuring in the front seat, but she did look up when the car made a turn onto a smaller road. "What's up?"

"What we need," Paradise said, "is a bit of fun. T.J. needs to be able to jump around and, to tell the truth, so do I. Your dad saw this sign and, well, here we are."

Hope stared out the window at the entrance of a small town fair, with the arc of a Ferris wheel behind it. A big sign said 'The Fun Fair.'

"Jeepers! Where is this?"

"Does it matter?" Thomas said. He swung open his door and got out of the car. "But you have another big decision to make, Hope."

She stopped part-way through getting T.J.'s shoes on him. "Oh no. What?"

"Rides first, or cotton candy?"

59

Wilmot and Marie were bursting to share their exciting news.

When they couldn't find Pops at Café Central for his early morning coffee and chat with the locals, they were off to his home to see if he was there. They hadn't been invited but that was not a problem. They had an open invitation to arrive anytime, day or night. Pops treated Marie and Wilmot like family because *they were his family now*. That's what he always said.

Nothing could dampen their spirits this morning and nothing would keep them from sharing their news with a loved one. Pops was their intended target. Wilmot knew even if Pops were busy he would welcome both Wilmot and Marie and their exciting news.

"Give me a hug, sweetheart. Then let's do this."

"We even look happy, Wilmot. No doubt about it."

They knocked perhaps a bit too loudly at the oceanside front door (this was the kind of news that deserved a front door entrance) of the home Pops shared with Paradise and Hope. Then they realized that Pops was not alone. He was speaking over his shoulder to someone as he opened the door.

Wilmot and Marie looked at each other. Run away? But it was too late! He grabbed her hand as if they were teenagers about to enter the haunted mansion.

Pops' voice trailed off. He stared at them a bit blankly, as if his mind were on something much more interesting, so Wilmot jumped in. "At this early hour it seems we're not your only guests, Pops."

There was a long pause. Pops filled the doorway, so they couldn't see beyond him, and that made them really want to know. Then Pops shook his head. "Where's my manners? Come on in." He stood aside to welcome his guests into his home.

Marie was shocked to see Eugenie sitting in the window seat, looking all comfortable with her coffee in hand. It was undeniable she had a housecoat on. What in God's name was going on between these two? She wasn't sure Wilmot had caught the housecoat yet.

Marie knew they had interrupted something, but Wilmot was on a mission. He was already talking and his feet were dancing.

"We had to come to you, Pops, and when we couldn't find you at the Café we came straight here. We have big news. Exciting news. Even shocking news, maybe." Marie put her hand gently on his back. "Wilmot, I'm worried that we have interrupted Pops and Eugenie."

"What? Pops and Eugenie?"

Wilmot scanned the room, found Eugenie, registered the housecoat, added two plus two and flushed beet red. "Oh. Oh my."

"Perhaps we should come back another time."

"Oh, no you don't," Pops said, so forcefully that at first Marie thought he was angry. "You kids don't get to barge into my home and trump my good news with your good news."

"You have good news, too?" Wilmot said.

Turning to Eugenie, Pops continued. "Do you want to share our news, my love, or should I do the honours?"

She didn't need to be prompted at all. "Pops and I are married!"

"What?"

"When?"

"From here on out," Pops said smugly.

"The bigger news," Eugenie continues, "is that Pops is moving into my home with me. We're just staying here while the kids are in Hawaii. We've been taking some of Pops' things over to my house every day."

Everyone except Marie was blushing now. A voice inside her head said, Of course: how lovely.

Eugenie put her hand over her mouth. "Pops, did I say too much?"

"Well, it's all out there now."

"It just feels some good to say it out loud. 'Some good' is the right phrase, Pops?"

Pops surveyed Wilmot and Marie. "You two are awful silent. I guess you don't agree—"

"No," Wilmot said quickly. "God, no, Pops, not at all. Of course we're thrilled for you. It's just that we have good news, too."

Turning to Marie, Wilmot said, "Do you want to share, my love, or should I do the honours?"

"We're getting married," Marie said happily. "We're getting married, too."

"I'll be damned," Pops said. "I'm proud to say at my advanced age I kind of got down on one knee, young man. I hope you did the same when you proposed to this beautiful lady."

"Yes, I did, Pops. And given the damage my poor legs took in my past life, it was no easy task for me either. But I damn well did it."

They were all laughing now. Through it, Marie had to raise her voice to beg for a cup of coffee. This was lovely, but so was that first cup of coffee in the morning. She didn't know how much longer she could be civil. "*I need coffee.*"

Pops was on his feet."How about I make a fresh pot? Then let's sit down and call our Paradise and share the news with her and the gang in Hawaii. I bet she will be as excited as the four of us are at this very moment."

Eugenie, the former nun, had the last laugh. "Wilmot, If you want to avoid trouble with Paradise you damn well better stop saying damn."

Pops called from the kitchen. "Conversations with Paradise tend to fall flat if she doesn't get a chance to say, 'Language.' every minute or two."

Eugenie went on with an afterthought. "For some reason men in general like to 'damn' this and 'damn' that in their daily conversations. Women know better, I suggest. We know to hold back until the damn situation damn well requires it!"

60

With second cups of coffee all around, including a second shot of Bailey's, attention turned to Eugenie and Pops.

"Tell us all about your wedding day and everything leading up to it," Marie said. This is very exciting."

She turned to the men, "Wilmot, you might learn something, so listen up. And, Pops, feel free to add to your bride's account."

"I wouldn't dare," Pops said with a smile. "Seriously, our wedding day was everything that we wanted it to be. It was important to me that the centre of attention would be my wife. I was pleased with every aspect of the day. I wouldn't have changed a thing."

Eugenie took a sip of her fortified coffee before she began. "First of all, I'm so happy to have shared the news with you. We have been married for almost two weeks now, so it's good to talk about it." Looking at Pops, she continued, "I'm sure I've driven you nuts with all my chatter about how happy I am and how my wedding was actually more than I could have ever imagined."

She paused to wipe her eyes. They were happy tears.

"My wedding suit was brand new and it was a lovely shade of grey. I know grey might be a strange colour for a bride, but remember I wore a grey habit while in the convent, and when I moved home I shopped only at Frenchy's. Mrs. Foss insisted I should have a new suit and she drove me to Digby where we picked it out. I'll show it to you before you leave."

Wilmot resisted rolling his eyes, sure that Marie was checking.

"Mrs. Foss did so many things to make our day special," Pops said. "We can hardly believe how generous she was with her time."

"I really wanted to be married at Saint Mary's Basilica in Halifax," Eugenie said, "and our parish priest here didn't know who to contact. Mrs. Foss not only got names for us, but she made it all happen. She knew we wanted to be married right away—"

"Not getting any younger," Pops said.

"—and she knew we wanted to make it a day trip because I... well...I wanted our first night together to be here, not in some hotel in the city. It may surprise you to know to this day I have never been in a hotel!"

"But in a hotel you get room service," Wilmot said. Nobody heard him.

"Mrs Foss contacted the mother house and sent word to all the Nuns I worked with, and you'll never believe what happened."

"Yes," Pops jumped in with a chuckle. "Imagine me walking into Saint Mary's and seeing it damn near full of nuns." Eugenie playfully slapped his wrist.

"It was so wonderful to see so many of my friends from 'the inside', as we call it amongst ourselves. I didn't want to leave them after the ceremony."

"I had booked a meal in Kentville for us on the way home," Pops said, "but those nuns had cooked up a storm for Eugenie and me. So I called and cancelled the restaurant."

"We had a feast at the mother house. I was so delighted. I was in heaven with a husband on earth. Who would ever have imagined?"

"Heavenly, indeed," Marie added.

"I forgot to mention that Mrs. Foss insisted on buying the most beautiful pink blouse for me. We were walking back to her car with my new grey suit and I stopped and commented on the lovely blouse in the store window. The next thing I knew I was trying it on. It fit perfectly and you'll never guess what Mrs. Foss did. While I was still in the changing room she paid for the blouse. And she added a pair of grey gloves and—"

"*Oh, no,*" Pops said, putting his hand over his eyes in mock shame.

"—and she somehow had enough time to pick out a beautiful nightdress for me. I even felt beautiful when we went to bed." Eugenie blushed, not for the first time.

Marie decided perhaps the Bailey's was behind the nightdress comment so she interrupted without apology. "May I officially say congratulations on your marriage. It sounds like the reception was perfect. We hope you will have another party with us after we are married. We thought we would invite a few friends back after the ceremony."

"Nonsense," Pops said. "You will have your reception right here in our huge home. And, if Paradise is back by then, I know she would want that, too."

Wilmot stood to shake Pops' hand while Marie and Eugenie shared a long embrace. They had just bonded over wedding and engagement news. This would be hard to beat in terms of excitement.

As the bride and groom snuggled later that night in their bed, Eugenie whispered, "I forgot to tell Wilmot and Marie about the rose petals Mrs. Foss arranged to have sprinkled all over our bedroom, *and* the bed. She thought of everything!"

"Wait a minute. What makes you think the rose petals were Mrs. Foss's idea and not mine?"

61

Thomas held T.J. in his arms until the darkness and the sandman took over.

He knew his son was too young to understand everything they had just experienced, but he didn't want to lose the moment. Thomas cradled T.J. until he was ready to share his feelings and when he did, he spoke in a whisper.

"I owe you an apology, my boy. I promised we would not end this road trip until we found your mommy's family. You've been a real trooper, T.J. sitting in the back seat day after day. Don't feel sorry for your sister, who had to entertain you, because she was earning money every mile we covered. We all know it wasn't really work for her, though, my son. Hope loves you so much. We can see it when we watch the two of you together. And of course Paradise loves you too. You have to get to know her first but once you do I know you will love Paradise as much as I do."

T.J. was restless, probably from all the nights in hotels. And the cotton candy, too.

"I'm so sorry we failed you, my son, but I promise you we aren't through yet. Your daddy knows people who can keep looking for your mother's family." Thomas made a mental note to make a few calls.

"We'll find your mommy's family. And when you're a bit older I will bring you back here to meet all of them. I promise you."

Paradise and Hope, even though they were as far away as the condo would permit, could hear Thomas weeping as he pulled the covers over his son, who was finally sleeping soundly.

Hope was sure she had the perfect topic for discussion to take her mom and dad's mind off their failed trip. As she made a fresh pot of coffee for her parents, Hope began her quest for a name. Not just any name but the proper name for her brother. She knew the 'J' in T.J. stood for Junior and that was not a real name. Hope had only just learned that Lee was Wikolia's last name.

When Thomas joined them, and with T.J. sleeping, Hope was ready.

"So, Mom and Dad, I've been thinking. Years from now, when we share the details of this expedition with T.J., I think we need a better ending to the story. We can't just say, 'We didn't find your mom so we moved away.'"

Paradise said, "Honey I haven't a clue what you're talking about."

Thomas followed. "Hope, we are all so tired. I think this can wait until the morning. Why don't you crawl into bed."

"No. Please at least listen to my idea. Then if you want we can go to bed without discussing it, but I want you to hear me okay?"

After a shrug from each of her parents Hope continued, "Thomas Junior will soon be old enough to understand his name. 'Junior' is not his middle name. Dad, when you adopted him what name did you put on the adoption papers?"

"Middle name is just an initial, 'J.' with no questions asked. So his full name is Thomas J Adams, and what's wrong with that?"

"I think there is something wrong, dad. When T.J. is older I want him to know we didn't let this go without lots of thought about taking him away from the only place he has ever known. Let's not give up just because we want to get on with our lives."

Hope immediately held her hands up in the 'stop' position because she knew she had gone over the line and what she was suggesting simply wasn't true. Her parents' hearts were as heavy as hers at the moment and she should have been more careful not to hurt them.

"Oh. My. God. I did not mean that and I know we're tired and all that but I'm almost at the punch line so stay with me."

"We have nowhere else to go, honey, so keep talking."

"We know Wikolia used 'Sky' when she left her family. She didn't want to be found. Wikolia Sky Lee would have been easy to find, so she dropped 'Lee'.

"And?" Thomas said as patiently as he could.

"Why don't we drop the 'J' and give him Wikolia's last name? How does Thomas Lee Adams sound? I want my brother to know that on this very day we gave him a piece of his mother's name as a reminder that she will always be with him and with all of us."

Hope paused with her fingers crossed. Paradise and Thomas held a silent conversation involving raised eyebrows, then turned to face her.

"I'm in," Paradise said.

"Wonderful tribute, honey. I'm in, too."

"Well, that was easy." Hope threw herself at both of her parents.

After a bit, Thomas sat Hope up. "Tomorrow we begin to pack, and your mother and I will wind down our business with Hawaii 2.0. We don't want to leave any loose ends behind. So, please, in the name of your mother's God, can we go to bed?"

"Let's start calling our boy Lee right away, so he can get used to it while we're still here."

"Hope, I need to sleep."

"We could tell him we refused to leave Hawaii until he knows his name is Lee."

"Hope, shut that brain of yours down for the night. There is no need to add to the story: it's brilliant." Thomas struggled to his feet. "Now please leave it at that."

"Sure."

"Good night, my intelligent beautiful daughter."

"But can I say one more thing mom?"

"Good night, Hope."

"Okay, okay, good night."

Hope turned so her parents wouldn't see her big smile and bounced out of the room. "Well, colour me happy," she whispered to herself.

62

Jalen Lexis was the first to greet Paradise and Thomas as they entered the warehouse to gather their personal belongings and say goodbye. He had a personal message for their ears only.

"No need to worry about running into Len today. I've arranged for him to be off shift while you're here. I decided that might be best all around."

Both Thomas and Paradise stiffened, as if they had forgotten the possibility that Len might be there. The commander pushed on. "You can both consider Len locked up until you drive away."

This came with a laugh. A large, booming belly laugh from Lexis. Without looking at Paradise, Thomas chuckled as well.

Only the boys were laughing.

Paradise didn't see the humour in the comment. "Commander, I'm not sure about Thomas, but I honestly need to have—"

Thomas jumped in and shut her down, leaving Paradise fuming. "Thanks for thinking of that. I wasn't looking forward to ever seeing him again."

"I wasn't looking forward to administering last rites to one or both of you after such a meeting," Jalen said. Thomas gave his head a shake. "Just one of us."

Paradise could see his fists were bunched, and decided to take herself away from this display of testosterone. "Will you excuse me for a second, gentlemen? I believe I remember where the ladies' washroom is."

She turned and marched away. She did not look back to see if they even noticed that she had left.

It was not lost on her that Thomas had instantly thanked the commander for 'making plans for Len to be off shift.' What was that all about? Did Lexis tip Thomas off in advance while saying absolutely nothing to her? Was the old boys' network doing its thing again?

"What do I do? What do I do? What do I do?" she asked her reflection in the many mirrors that lined the walls in the ladies' washroom. As far as she knew, she was the only female to work at 2.0. So there was nobody to give advice except her reflection.

The washroom was about the size of the condo they had just sold. Paradise allowed herself a chuckle of her own. They sure had been cramped in that tiny space.

She pulled a small notebook and a pen from her bag. She would need to make a list. Sadly, her list would be loaded with emotion, but it couldn't wait. "I can bloody well do this," Paradise said and began to write.

1. I need to speak with Lenny. I have questions and some unresolved feelings. I'm certain he does too. I will insist Lexis allow me private time with Lenny before we leave.
2. Lexis and Thomas blindsided me. My Thomas! I think they were in this together. Thomas will have to come clean the second we drive away.
3. Lexis should have told me about his decision before we arrived to say goodbye. Lenny followed me all the way to Nova Scotia. So there is more in play than just a work friendship. Need to discuss with Jalen while he's taking me to Lenny.

She tapped the pen on the pad, then spoke to the mirror again. "I don't give a rat's ass how anyone else feels. This is about me. My dreams, my hopes and fears, my trust issues, and my lack of self confidence. But if I say that to any of these idiot guys they will just pity me for being a girl with emotions. I am a girl with emotions, but I don't need anybody's pity for it."

Having observed how poorly the commander handled 'matters of the heart,' Paradise sort of understood his reasons for keeping Len out of the way. Jalen didn't like emotional confrontations, so he took the easy way out if he could, by getting rid of the problem.

"Give me a break," Paradise said to no one. It was not lost on her that she was using words and expressions she admonished Hope for using. She would analyze that later, but Hope would never know...

Maybe Len wanted to stay in his quarters and not face me? That stung a bit, but Paradise didn't really believe that was the case. In her heart, she could not think negatively about Lenny and his feelings for her.

And, just like that, Paradise began to lose her confidence. She seemed helpless in the moment and couldn't get out of her own way.

Again she looked at her reflection in the mirrors. Did Thomas know in advance that Len would be locked up? He did seem awfully quick with his 'Thanks for that' bullshit. Paradise would get answers, now or later. With luck, now, because later her confidence might be in shreds.

She suddenly remembered talking with her friend Elise over glasses of wine. She had been fuming over the way male cops treated her when they worked together on a case. "If we took a washroom break, the men came back to the meeting having made some big decisions on their own while in the bloody toilet."

"What did you say to them?" Elise had asked.

"What can you say to a bunch of guys who are sure only guys can be cops?"

Elise had nodded. "Cocks at work."

They had laughed so hard that people at other tables had turned to stare.

Her mind was spinning, and Paradise knew she needed to just stop, breathe and remind herself why she and Thomas were at the warehouse today. And where they were going in less than twenty-four hours. And that Thomas loved her with his whole heart. She was 100% sure of that.

For now, she had to suck it up, get out of the toilet and enjoy the reception being put on in their honour.

"I have bigger fish to fry," Paradise whispered to the mirror. Then she left the loo in pursuit of her future.

The goodbye party was in full swing. There were big circles around Thomas and the commander, but that left half the crowd for Paradise to harvest. She dove in with her emotions fully evident. She was crying before the first of her former peers opened his arms wide and gave her the warmest hug.

Paradise wasn't sure she could call 50% of the team by their first names, and she felt bad about it. Her brain reminded her that she had worked one shift, and most of the time with only one man —Lenny.

But it didn't seem to matter. Man after man came up to give her a hug or shake her hand and wish her well. The reception really was lovely. Paradise was overwhelmed and emotional.

As she worked the room, though, she edged closer and closer to the commander. She had to talk with him and it needed to be very soon. And then Thomas was beside her. "The boss wants us together, sweetheart. I'll join you here if that's okay." He extended his hand to the man who had just given Paradise a full on bear hug.

Speech time. Fortunately, people kept them short. The big surprise was when the commander presented their last pay cheque and they saw he had added an extra zero to the amount.

More tears of thanks.

Jalen spoke last. "We have enjoyed having you as part of the elite 2.0 team and you will be missed. You both managed to fit in on day one, and every day after that. I would like to think there will be projects we can join forces to work on in the future, so let's end on that note and promise to keep in touch."

Applause started up, but the commander stifled it with a raised hand. He wasn't quite done. "You will always be welcome at 2.0. Don't be surprised if you answer the phone one day to hear me asking for your help."

Now the applause rolled around the room. When it subsided, Lexis made a different hand gesture: Party over. "That's it, folks. We have work to do and these two have to catch a plane."

Everyone clapped, hooted and hollered until Paradise and Thomas disappeared from view.

The commander ushered Thomas and Paradise out of the warehouse. Not a word was spoken.

Until the last second, Paradise held out hope that Len would appear and apologize to her at least. She had so many questions. He was taking up too much space in her head and she knew it.

One final handshake all around. Silence. Paradise knew if she didn't speak up in the moment she might never have another chance

Silence.

Paradise was profoundly disappointed in herself.

63

Packing up their Honolulu lives, giving away what they weren't taking with them and selling their little condo had not been easy on the heart. Some family members had more difficulty accepting their life altering change than others.

One family member in particular was fighting a major hormonal battle and she was not quiet about it.

Too many times, Hope faltered and wanted to stay in the only home she had ever known. She knew it wasn't possible but she put up a good fight. Time and time again she had a meltdown.

Paradise and Thomas tried their best to remind Hope how happy her life was in the Cape. Hope didn't disagree and she didn't argue about her love of the Cape, but that was not the point, as she saw it.

"Oh. My. God. I. Am. *Not*. Moving." Hope was yelling and she knew trouble would find her if she didn't settle down. She just couldn't, that's all.

"Why doesn't anyone believe me? Tanya's mother said I can live with them for one year and that's what I'm doing. I'm taking my stuff to their house today. She's really excited to have me move in, cross my heart and hope to die."

"No, Hope, you are not doing that," Thomas said. "We didn't get the family together just to break it apart again." He finished closing a suitcase and stood up to ease his back. "How many more friends are you going to threaten to move in with? This has to end and you know it."

"Can't I stay here for one more year? And maybe all of you will want to move back here by then. It could happen!"

"Hope, this is wearing on my nerves," Paradise said. "We are moving to the Cape as a family. You love it there and you know it. Pops is there and you love Pops. You speak about Pops all the time. Since the day you first saw Mavillette beach you have called it home. Should I go on?"

"I do not want to move. Why the hell can't you hear that?"

Thomas let her language go unchallenged. He couldn't win 'em all. "I know you don't Hope. And you are repeating yourself. Your mother and I both know how sad and how angry you are. And we feel terrible about that. However, we are catching our plane in the morning. Get some sleep."

"You can't make me move," she said, but under her breath. Her parents pretended not to hear and went on with the endless final tasks.

"I'm not moving," Hope said, mostly to herself. She hated losing, but she was beginning to understand this was a fight she would not win.

~

Paradise was leaving Hawaii without discussing her feelings with anyone, not even Thomas. When they arrived home after their send-off at 2.0, there was another surprise. Mae had made a special goodbye meal for everyone. It was festive and Mae made it easy to be happy at least during their meal.

Hope and Paradise were sharing the bedroom for this last night because of Hope's poor attitude, so 'the talk' between Paradise and Thomas was off the table. It wouldn't happen now. But it would have to happen soon.

Morning came early. Not much sleep for anyone, so Paradise and Thomas hoped both children might sleep on the long flight to Toronto.

They ate a quick breakfast in silence. Even Lee seemed to understand what was going on. Then they loaded backpacks and suitcases into Mae's car for the run to the airport.

"Hope," Mae said over her shoulder as she drove, "please keep in touch. I need you to let me know how your brother is doing."

Hope was opting for sulky, so Thomas said, "We will definitely keep in touch, and you are always welcome to visit with us in beautiful Cape St Mary." He found himself a bit choked up. "You were right beside Lee and me during his very young days and you stepped in when it seemed I was running on empty. I will never forget what a friend you have been to me. To us."

"You always treated me as a friend. Thank you, for that, Thomas. Especially for that."

As they boarded the plane, everyone was lost in his or her memories of Hawaii. Everyone except Lee. He had a sucker in his mouth and all was right in his world. He offered a lick of his sucker to anyone who looked his way.

Just over three short months after Paradise and Hope had arrived in Hawaii to help Thomas as he grieved the loss of Wikolia, they were all on their way to Toronto and then the Cape. "Feels a bit too permanent to me," Hope whispered to Lee. He didn't look up from his sucker, now broken in two and sticking to both his hands.

"Listen to me, kid. You know I was pissed off for a few days, okay a few weeks, and I'm trying to get over all of that before the trip is over. So, do not piss me off again by touching me or getting that sucker on my nice new dress."

Hope knew he heard her but wasn't listening. She closed her eyes for a few minutes, wondering if Lee got that trait from her. For the last few days she had heard a million things but she definitely had not listened.

When she stood up and moved into the aisle to speak with her father, Lee didn't even notice. His sucker was 'some good.'

"Hey, dad, Lee wants you to sit with him for a while, so switch with me and I'll sit with mom."

"Is Lee getting fussy?" Paradise asked as Hope sat down beside her. Hope loved how her mother seemed to accept Lee as her son so easily. She wanted to tell her that but she hadn't been speaking with either of her parents, so even the positive things she would normally have said had been lost.

"Truth, mom?" Hope was smiling and got a tentative smile in return from Paradise.

"Truth."

"Lee is one sticky mess and I didn't want him to touch my new dress."

Paradise nodded solemnly. "Good plan to put your dad in harm's way."

"Mom, I need you to help me with something. Can you do me favour and tell dad about Francis-with-an-i? I talked to Pops last night and he said some girl is calling all the time. Pops said, 'She's hunting you down, young lady, and when you get back here I want you to tell me what's happening.' I told him you already know about Francis-with-an-i and you were going to hunt her down. Is it okay that I said that?"

"What's changed, honey? We've gone from inviting Francis-with-an-i to our home and now you want me to hunt her down. Then what? Is she not your friend any longer? When did that happen? And what do you want me to say to her?"

"I guess I haven't thought it through. I just don't want to see her any more and I'm afraid if I tell her that she might get all crazy with me. I already told you she's old but she's also tough and I'm sorry I even went to her place."

"I will definitely tell your dad about Francis-with-an-i as you have asked me to do, and I promise you this: your father will do the hunting and when he finds Francis-with-an-i he will have a very long conversation with her. She won't bother you after his visit, I promise you."

While listening to her mother, Hope was admiring her pretty dress. "Thanks, mom. I knew you would know how to help me."

She suddenly felt the need to change the subject. "And also, I'm sorry I haven't thanked you for buying this dress for me. I love it, and I know you went out of your way to take me shopping when your to-do list was a mile long. It will always make me think of the Waikiki dress shop where we saw it in the window. Thanks a lot. But just for the record, I do want to go back there soon."

Hope reached out and hugged her mom, who was breathing a sigh of relief. Everything would be okay.

In Toronto, Hope and Lee were spoiled, catered to, loved and introduced to what seemed like way too many adults. There was no shortage of invitations to return to Toronto soon.

Both Thomas and Paradise reminded the grandparents that they were all invited to visit the Cape. Always welcome!

Carol Ann Cole

64

When the time was right the family of four flew from Toronto to Halifax. They stretched their legs, had a snack and picked up their rental car. They were off to Cape St Mary and home.

"Kids, listen up: We've decided to take three days to get home. Our motels have pools so we will stop mid afternoon today and tomorrow and we can swim for hours. On the third day we will drive to the Cape. How does that sound?"

"Sure!" Hope spoke for her brother and herself.

Thomas and Paradise had made the decision to stop early each day to ensure the kids were well rested when they arrived home. A bit of a party had been planned. They didn't have details, but Wilmot had called them in Toronto and tipped them off.

"Just a word to the wise, Paradise. Your house will be full of family and friends when you get here, so don't show up looking all bedraggled and weary. In particular you have to look your very best, Paradise."

"Thanks a lot, brother dear."

Day one and two were uneventful. They drove, swam, stopped for meals and settled into their motel room. Within seconds of their arrival each day the kids were in the pool. They both loved to swim and, while Lee wasn't very good at it, he seemed to have no fear of the water.

The ocean would be a new experience for Lee and Paradise and Thomas talked about how careful they would need to be when Lee was on the beach. Hope would have to be reminded of the rules while at the ocean. In fact they could ask Hope to introduce her brother to both the beach and the beach rules. Both parents would be with them at all times. They could relax the rules at some point, but they needed to be vigilant initially.

The kids were all Thomas and Paradise talked about, which meant the ache Paradise felt over not having been given time to speak with Lenny was still there. She had said goodbye to everyone. Everyone except Lenny—the only person she had really looked forward to seeing one more time.

As the family edged closer to the Cape she tried to focus and stay in the moment. She didn't want to miss anything that could become a memory to cherish.

On the third day, early in the afternoon, it was Hope who first spotted what they were all looking for. "There it is, dad. Right up ahead. Oh. My. God. We are at Mavillette beach in beautiful Nova Scotia." Hope threw her hands in the air. "Mom do you remember when I was a kid and I called it Marvellous Beach?"

Hope's *happy* was back. Finally.

"It's actually 'Marvellous Mavillette.' See where you turn right on to Cape St Mary Road, daddy? This is exciting, isn't it, Lee?"

No answer but at least he wasn't sticky. Lee had been sleeping in her arms but she laid him down on his own side of the back seat so she could just look out the window. Lee remained fast asleep and had been for the last few hours. Even his sister's outside-voice didn't awaken him.

Pops had gone all out for their homecoming. He had personally written the invitation on nice paper and stuck copies to the Café walls. He wrote every single word himself. That took lots of time but he didn't mind. Anything for his family.

Pops had come a long way during the past few years, and Paradise congratulated him when they talked on the phone each evening. He was emotional when Paradise called at the end of day two of their family adventure.

"Can't wait to see you, Paradise. I'll be the first in line to welcome you home. I'm some proud of you. Did I say that right?"

"You said it perfectly, Pops. I'm some proud of you, too. We'll see you on the morrow, and, for the record, I can't wait."

The morrow stood directly in front of them as they turned their over-packed rental car into the driveway of their home.

'Memories are made of this,' thought Paradise amid the commotion about to erupt. It seemed they would not unpack or rest or reflect for a few hours at the very least. She was glad Wilmot had warned them.

"Hope, do you want to carry Lee?" They were speaking to the back of her head. Hope left her brother behind in all the excitement and was out of the car the second it came to a stop. She had people to see!

Thomas looked at Lee, still in the back seat. His heart skipped a beat as Paradise whispered, "I'll get Lee, honey. I would love to be the one to introduce our son to everyone."

"Perfect. Absolutely perfect." Thomas was about to get emotional and he wasn't out of the damn car yet.

It seemed everyone wanted to talk at once, but Pops had the floor.

"Hang on, everyone. I want to make a presentation, as the business folks like to say." Standing on a bench to make sure everyone could see and hear him, Pops addressed his audience while looking directly at Paradise.

"Paradise, there has been a wedding down at our town hall and the bride and groom have moved into the bride's home. Eugenie and I are married and as a result I officially give this home to you and your family."

There were cheers. Paradise opened her mouth, but Pops raised his hand to signify he had more to say.

"Hope, honey, I'm thinking you just might be the new occupant of my former room—the room with the direct ocean view. Marvellous Mavillette Beach and all its glory right there in front of you from your bedroom windows. You owe me one, kid."

Pops opened his arms and Hope ran to him and landed softly in his arms. Then he extended his hand to Eugenie, who joined them on the bench. It was a bit crowded up there but clearly they had practised for this moment.

"Hope, we figure your little brother might want to be closer to his parents as he gets used to all of this, so we moved you out of the room upstairs and we put a smaller bed in that room for T.J."

"Lee," Eugenie and Hope said at the same time.

Pops looked from one to the other. "Lee? I've missed something along the way but I think that story is for another day."

Eugenie was still quite shy and Pops was proud of his bride as he gave her a kiss in front of everyone. He had been waiting to do that. The world should know Pops and Eugenie had gotten hitched.

Paradise could see their guests wouldn't be leaving anytime soon so she decided it was her turn. "Thomas and I can't thank everyone enough for being here and for making this day so special for our children. Cape St Mary and Mavillette are so important to us and so are you. Pops and Eugenie, congratulations again to you both"

Then she saw her brother. "Wilmot and Marie, I hear there is a second wedding to happen in our little family. I hope you didn't go to the town hall to get married, too!"

Wilmot shook his head no.

"We were waiting for you to come home," Marie said.

Paradise had a sudden thought: they should let the spotlight fall on Wilmot and Marie, and hold off on their own wedding announcement until later.

She turned to find Thomas...too late.

There he was, down on one knee beside her. "There will be another wedding in the Cape, folks." "Who said that?" someone called from the back of the crowd.

"Me, down here!" Thomas said, waving his hand to get everyone's attention.

Amid the laughter he turned to Paradise and became serious. "Sweetheart, I know we talked about this and you've already said yes, but right here and right now seems the perfect place and time to make it official in front of your Cape family."

The crowd held its collective breath. "What do you say, Paradise? Will you marry me? Right here in the Cape perhaps in our home?"

Thomas recognized the silence.

Finally Paradise took his hand. It was not lost on Thomas that she made a point of not offering her left hand. It seemed to be permanently inside her jeans pocket.

He waited. Paradise said nothing.

Finally he whispered, "Paradise, you haven't changed your mind about marrying me, have you?"

"It's not you, Thomas. It's not that I don't want to marry you."

"Then what is going on here?" Thomas was standing now, and they both were very aware of the crowd around them drinking in the unexpected drama.

Thomas had grown to hate the sound of silence.

Carol Ann Cole

About the author

Carol Ann Cole is a best-selling author, a professional speaker and founder of a national fund-raiser. To date, her Comfort Heart Initiative has raised over $1.5 million for cancer research with the Canadian Cancer Society.

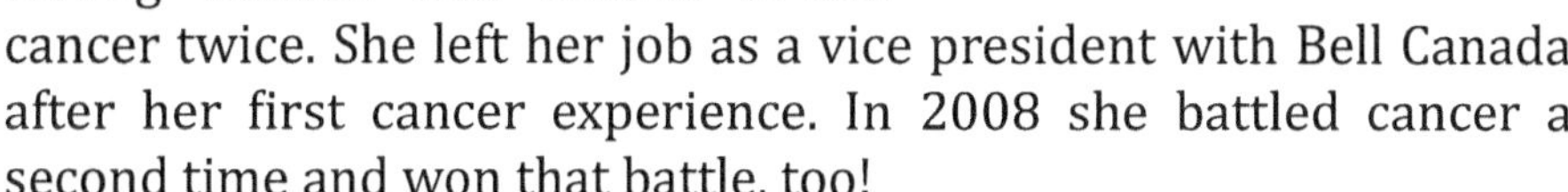
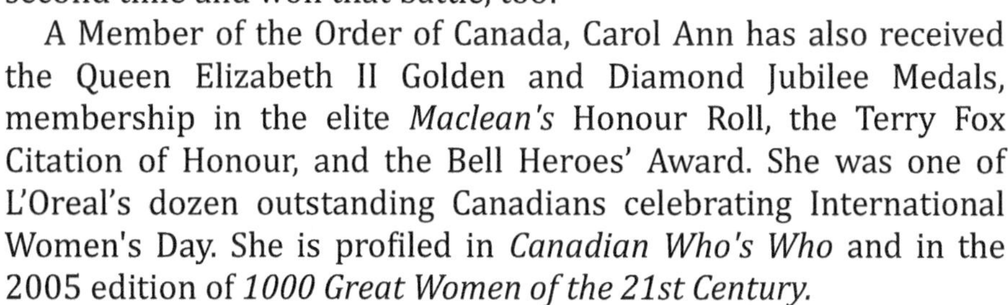

The author of four non-fiction books and three novels (so far) in the Paradise series, she is currently working on the fourth instalment, *Paradise Private Investigator*.

Carol Ann is a cancer survivor, having battled and beaten breast cancer twice. She left her job as a vice president with Bell Canada after her first cancer experience. In 2008 she battled cancer a second time and won that battle, too!

A Member of the Order of Canada, Carol Ann has also received the Queen Elizabeth II Golden and Diamond Jubilee Medals, membership in the elite *Maclean's* Honour Roll, the Terry Fox Citation of Honour, and the Bell Heroes' Award. She was one of L'Oreal's dozen outstanding Canadians celebrating International Women's Day. She is profiled in *Canadian Who's Who* and in the 2005 edition of *1000 Great Women of the 21st Century*.

www.carolanncole.com